Also by Libby Fischer Hellmann

The Georgia Davis Series

"There's a new no-nonsense female private detective in town: Georgia Davis, a former cop who is tough and smart enough to give even the legendary V.I. Warshawski a run for her money."
—*Chicago Tribune*

"Georgia Davis works the affluent suburbs north of Chicago, fertile territory for crime that's lain fallow far too long. Davis' arrival on the mean streets is long overdue."
—Sara Paretsky, author of the V.I. Warshawski Mysteries

"Hellmann writes in many genres, but her Georgia Davis series may just be one of the best crime thriller series being written today."
—*The Dirty Lowdown*

The Ellie Foreman Series

"A powerful tale... Foreman's pluck and grit married to Hellmann's solid storytelling should win a growing audience..."
—*Publishers Weekly*

"Libby Fischer Hellmann has already joined an elite club: Chicago mystery writers who not only inhabit the environment but also give it a unique flavor."
—*Chicago Tribune*

"A traditional mystery with a modern edge... the author's confidence shows from beginning to end... refreshing as soft serve ice cream on a hot summer night."
—*Crimespree Magazine*

Praise for Libby Fischer Hellmann

War, Spies, and Bobby Sox

"Libby Hellmann's prose is powerful. Every part of her WW II era yarns are methodically researched, taut, twist-filled and colorful with well developed supporting characters. A gripping performance."
—Charles J. Masters, author of *Gliderman of Neptune, The American D-Day Glider Attack*

"Libby Fischer Hellman powerfully illustrates what individuals could have faced while living in such perilous times. This is an engaging read with much food for thought."
—*BookReporter*

Havana Lost

"A riveting historical thriller... This multigenerational page-turner is packed with intrigue and shocking plot twists."
—*Booklist*

"Hellmann's writing has matured considerably since her early novels. Her plotting has become more solid and assured, her characters more realistic, her settings wonderfully described. This is a fine, extremely well told novel."
—*Deadly Pleasures*

A Bitter Veil

"The Iranian revolution provides the backdrop for this meticulously researched, fast-paced stand-alone... A significant departure from the author's Chicago-based Ellie Foreman and Georgia Davis mystery series, this political thriller will please established fans and newcomers alike."
—*Publishers Weekly*

"Hellmann crafts a tragically beautiful story... both subtle and vibrant... never sacrificing the quality of her storytelling. Instead, the message drives the psychological and emotional conflict painting a bleak and heart wrenching tale that will stick with the reader long after they finish the book."
—*Crimespree Magazine*

Set the Night on Fire

"A top-rate standalone thriller that taps into the antiwar protests of the 1960s and 70s."
—*Publishers Weekly*

"Superior standalone novel... Hellmann creates a fully-realized world...complete with everyday details, passions and enthusiasms on how they yearned for connection, debated about ideology and came to belief in taking risks to stand up for what they believed."
—*Chicago Tribune*

"Haunting...Rarely have history, mystery, and political philosophy blended so beautifully... could easily end up on the required reading list in college-level American History classes."
—*Mystery Scene Magazine*

High Crimes

HIGH CRIMES

Libby Fischer Hellmann

The Red Herrings Press
Chicago

This is a work of fiction. Names, characters, businesses, places, events, locales, and incidents are either the products of the author's imagination or used in a fictitious manner. Any resemblance to actual persons, living or dead, or actual events is purely coincidental.

Names: Hellmann, Libby Fischer
Title: HIGH CRIMES / Libby Fischer Hellmann
Description: Chicago, IL; The Red Herrings Press, 2018
Identifiers: LCCN 2018955074 | ISBN 978-1-938733-95-6 (Pbk.); 978-1-938733-52-9 (Ebook); 978-1-938733-53-6 (Audiobook)
Subjects: Davis, Georgia (Fictitious character)—Fiction. Murder—Fiction. | Politics—Fiction. | Chicago Metropolitan Area (Ill.)—Fiction. | Mystery Fiction. | Suspense Fiction.
Classification: Pending

To Suzy Fischer, who for the past two years has provided a beacon lighting the way through the dark

Chapter One

"Where is she, Curt? Dena's never late." The ten minutes of generally accepted grace time had passed, but Dena was nowhere in sight. Ruth had texted and called every two minutes, but her messages went unanswered.

Curt, a bear of a man with shaggy brown hair, beard, and puppy-dog eyes, shrugged. "She's probably stuck in traffic." He gestured to the crowd from the wings of the stage. "Look at these folks! Did you ever imagine . . . all this?"

Ruth dared to look out at the masses. Her breath caught. Thousands of people were streaming into Grant Park, three hundred sprawling acres in the middle of downtown Chicago. They were heading to the bandstand shell and stage at the southern end of the park. Ruth remembered the last time she'd been here, an unusually balmy November night in 2008. Obama had just won the election. It was a miracle that the entire world had shared.

Now, though, icy puffs of air aided by a stiff January wind frosted her cheeks and seeped through her coat. The crowd size wasn't nearly as large as Obama's, but people seemed buoyed by the cold, cheering and waving signs that proclaimed, "We Are the Resistance," "Never Give Up," and other political bromides. Some wore the knitted kitten hats that had become popular after the election. Most were grinning and joking as if the occasion were a rock concert or football game rather than a demonstration.

Curt peered up at the sky. "I hope there's a drone up there filming this. Maybe we could get the footage to use on social media."

Ruth glanced up, twisting the shoulder strap of her bag. "Yeah, good idea. But where is Dena?"

Another man, lean and lanky, the Jeff to Curt's Mutt, fiddled with a microphone stand on the center of the stage. He looked over at Ruth. "Chill. Traffic is shitty."

Ruth shook her head and waved her cell in the air. "She always picks up. But it's going to voice mail."

"Probably on the el." DJ ran a hand through his long blond ponytail. "But you're right. We can't wait forever. What do you want to do?"

"Give her another minute. Dena would never blow this off, DJ," Curt said. "Not after all her work."

A flood of memories washed over Ruth. The two of them in Dena's condo, full of plans and purpose. Working twenty-four-hour days, planning, eating junk food in the omnipresent blue-white light of their laptops. Hard to believe it had been more than a year.

"This is just the beginning!" DJ grinned. "After today, we'll have a real shot at accomplishing something."

But what if something happened? Dena had been getting those creepy calls. Ruth pushed the thought away. Lots of prominent people got crank calls, Dena had said dismissively. And she—*they*, Dena made sure to say—were famous. "Almost." They would laugh.

Some people in the crowd, clearly impatient, started to clap rhythmically. A signal for the show to begin. Others joined in. Ruth, DJ, and Curt exchanged glances. A wave of nausea climbed up Ruth's throat.

"Okay," Curt said. "Color me officially worried."

"Relax, people," DJ said. "Nothing bad's happened to Dena. She's indestructible."

"She was fine yesterday," Ruth said. "She was pumped."

"Did she go over what she was going to say?" DJ asked.

"Of course. She practiced—you know—rehearsed it with me. And Curt." She nodded at him.

"Well, you're *número dos*," Curt said. Was there a hint of resentment in his voice? Ruth wondered. "If she doesn't get here soon, you're on deck."

Ruth let out a tiny cry of terror. "I can't!"

"Why not?"

"There are thousands of people out there. They—they're expecting Dena."

DJ slipped his hands in his pockets. "The show must go on."

"There are way too many people. I'd rather die!"

"You have to try. Look, at least start. You're the only other person who knows what to say. You've been with Dena from the beginning."

"What do they say?" DJ added. "Pretend all the people in the crowd are naked?"

Curt waved a hand. "No. Just focus on what they need to hear. And feel. And do. That's what Dena would say."

"Yeah, but she's experienced at—at public speaking," Ruth said. "I've never done this before. I'm the backstage person."

DJ said, "Look, we'll help you out. And Dena will probably get here while you're talking. As soon as she does, you're off the hook."

Ruth's eyes raked the crowd. "Oh my God. I really have to do this."

A whispery whine made them gaze upward. Curt grinned. "I knew it. Thar she blows!"

Ruth could just make out a speck in the sky. "A drone?"

He nodded. "Maybe CNN, huh? Hope they'll give us their video."

"It's probably just channel five.'"

Most of the crowd was clapping now. Ruth could tell they were edgy.

"You ready?" DJ adjusted the mic. He tilted his chin in the direction of the crowd. "They are."

Ruth turned her back on the crowd. She had to center herself. Just then, the aroma of patchouli oil wafted toward her, discordant but familiar. Dena! Ruth whipped around. While the possibility of public speaking hung in the offing like a Christmas bauble, attracting and panicking her at the same time, now her anxiety melted away. Dena jogged up the steps to the stage, all energy, confidence, and red cheeks.

"Where have you been?" Ruth shouted above the noise.

"In traffic," Dena said breathlessly. "I had to ditch the car. Had to run all the way from Chicago Avenue. Give me a minute to catch my breath."

The crowd, realizing their leader had arrived, grew louder, more boisterous. Dena had *it*, Ruth had to admit. Whatever they called it now. Charisma. Magnetism. Eloquence. Ruth might be Tonto, but Dena was the Lone Ranger. An electric buzz seemed to emanate from under Dena's skin. Ruth could almost feel it make contact.

Despite his casual attitude earlier, DJ anxiously cut in. Was he feeling it too? "We have to start. Look at them." He gestured again toward the crowd.

Dena glanced out. So did Ruth. DJ was right. The crowd seemed to swell with anticipation. Ruth watched as Dena rolled her shoulders and started toward the mic. "Okay. You guys come out too. Stand behind me."

Ruth nodded. As if they knew the show was about to begin, the crowd noise suddenly dropped. In her quilted jacket, with her long black braid hanging down her back, Dena adjusted the microphone stand.

"Good morning, Resistance!!"

The crowd roared.

It was then that a crack-crack-crack spit through the air.

Chapter Two

Dena jerked. Her arms flew up, as if making a supplication. Then she collapsed on the ground. The crack and spit persisted. It was coming from above and to the side of the stage. Sweeping from the stage out to the crowd. Protestors in the front rows fell like dominoes. As the crowd began to realize what was happening, shrieks and cries erupted, and people in the front massed and swarmed those farther back in a panicked effort to escape. Protestors climbed or stomped over others, and the screams of people mowed down by their neighbors intensified. Thousands of confused, frightened people rushed the park's exits, scattering like cockroaches exposed to unexpected light.

Ruth was staring at the horrific scene when someone or something tackled her from the rear. Her feet went numb, she lost her balance, and she dropped. A tremendous weight pressed down on her. Pain so sharp she couldn't inhale. She was on her stomach, and she tried to roll over so the weight would fall off, but when she tried to move, nothing happened. She wanted to let the weight know she couldn't breathe, but she couldn't form the words. The edges of her vision grew dark. Just before she lost consciousness, she heard sirens.

Chapter Three

"Chicago's been overdue," Jimmy Saclarides said. "It was bound to happen."

Georgia Davis bristled. "How can you say that?" She rose from the couch where they were lying feet to feet watching the news. "What about the Chicago murder rate? It's up to three a day. You don't consider that domestic terrorism?"

"You have a point," Jimmy said. "But this isn't the same thing. You know that. I mean, the guy blew himself up afterwards. That's not your typical gangbanger."

Georgia headed into the kitchen of her small apartment. Jimmy was so damn evenhanded and fair. It was hard to summon up much self-righteous indignation. Probably one of the reasons she was attracted to him. She took a baby bottle out of the fridge, set it in a pan of water, and turned the heat on low.

"What are you doing?" Jimmy called.

"Heating up Charlie's bottle."

"But he's sleeping."

"He won't be for long."

As if on cue, they heard a muffled wail from the other room.

"Which came first, the bottle or the baby?" Jimmy cracked.

"Does it matter? I'll be back." She returned a moment later, cradling an infant in her arms. "Ready for your nighttime snack, Chuckie Cheese?" She raised her voice to that high pitch people used around infants. She'd sworn not to do it. It was pandering. Naturally, within a couple of hours of his birth she caught herself doing exactly that. Charlie seemed to like it, and Georgia could see him trying to make sense of sounds, tones, language. Smart kid. Now he stared at her. Georgia smiled. He smiled back.

Jimmy gazed at her. "I like the look."

"Don't get used to it. I'm just pinch-hitting for Vanna's boob."

Still, Georgia had to admit that at three months, with his hazel eyes and downy straw-colored hair, he could have been hers. She had the same blond hair, and while she had brown eyes to his hazel, there was something about his mouth and chin that reminded Georgia of herself. Then again, she and her half sister, Savannah, looked like full sisters.

"Vanna's at class, I assume?"

Georgia nodded. "I should have never introduced her to Sam." She shifted her weight so she could hand the baby to Jimmy. "You hold him while I get the bottle."

"Graphic design, isn't it?"

"Good memory." Samantha Mosele was her friend; maybe her only friend. They'd met at community college when Sam was studying design, Georgia sociology. Now Sam had her own company. Vanna, after learning what Sam did, decided she wanted to be a graphic designer too. It was a good idea. She did have a talent for drawing.

Now she felt Charlie's bottom and gave it a sniff. "Someone needs a clean diaper." She peered at Jimmy. "I don't suppose you want to change him?"

"Umm . . . I'll feed him . . . ," Jimmy offered, as if they were negotiating where to go for dinner.

"Burp included?"

He nodded. "Sure."

Georgia sighed. "Spoken like a man without kids." She hoisted

Charlie up. He started to fuss. "Hold on, little man. We gotta change you so you can poop into a clean diaper after you eat."

Jimmy's forehead furrowed. "I don't get it. Why change him now if you're just going to do it again in fifteen minutes?"

"Wouldn't you like a nice clean diaper to poop into?"

Jimmy waved her off. "Whatever."

Georgia laughed and took the baby back into Vanna's room.

. . .

Afterward Georgia plopped back on the couch. "This baby-care stuff is not for the faint of heart."

Jimmy looked her over speculatively. "How are they doing? Really?"

"Charlie's a peach. Round and happy. Vanna seems happy too. Or should I say focused. Once I introduced her to Sam, they got along like, well, two peas in a pod."

"Run, Forrest, run."

"Exactly." Vanna had studied for and passed her GED online, then signed up for drawing classes. "She's a smart cookie when she's motivated."

"Takes after her sister."

"Compliments'll get you brownie points." She snuggled closer. "It's almost like the past year was only a bad dream."

Jimmy kissed her lightly. "You went to hell and back."

"So did Vanna. But maybe it was worth it." She gestured. "Look at our lives now."

"You said it." He gazed around the room. "Only one thing."

"What's that?"

"It's crowded in here."

Georgia looked around. Her small two-bedroom apartment in Evanston used to be spare, uncluttered. She liked it that way. It helped her concentrate on important matters. Now, though, cushions, books, and baby clothes crowded into corners. Her carefully arranged furniture, what little there was, had started to look bedraggled. Vanna and the baby shared Georgia's extra bedroom, which was no bigger than a closet to begin with, and now bulged with a twin bed, crib with the obligatory mobile, baby toys, and a diaper stand. Jimmy had a point.

"I guess. Vanna didn't inherit the clean-house gene."

Eight months had passed since she'd rescued Vanna and brought her home. Two months later Charlie made his appearance. It seemed like a logical progression to Georgia. Her life, once empty and uncharted, now had purpose. Georgia wanted a family, and the universe provided. It wasn't the family she'd imagined, but Vanna was in no condition financially or otherwise to get a place of her own.

Jimmy went on. "We haven't had much time to ourselves since Prince Charles made his appearance."

"I know." The memory buzz of long, intimate nights where they couldn't keep their hands off each other swept through her.

"Well, I might have a solution," Jimmy said.

She jerked her head up. "What?"

"Remember when Luke bought that condo in Northfield after Rachel's—um—ordeal? So Ellie could keep an eye on her?"

Georgia nodded.

"Well, Rachel just moved in with her boyfriend, so the condo is empty." When Georgia didn't respond, he went on. "I thought I might rent it from Luke."

Jimmy lived in Lake Geneva, about an hour away in Wisconsin. Which was great in summer but during winter months not so convenient. They'd been commuting since they'd met.

"But your job . . . your work." Jimmy was the chief of police of Lake Geneva.

"I can drive it in forty-five minutes." He made a circular motion with his index finger. "I've got a siren, remember?"

"You'd take advantage of law enforcement perks for your own purposes?"

"If it means I can spend more time with you," he said, "no contest."

Georgia stroked his arm.

"And you could spend more time with me. Without Charlie. Or Vanna."

Georgia brightened but then frowned. "But what about money? You can't support two homes. Can you?"

"I've been offered the friends-and-family discount."

Georgia considered it. "Vanna can get her feet on the ground and experiment with life, without me in the way."

"Assuming you think she's ready."

"It's an open question. It's been less than a year."

Jimmy nodded. "I don't want to push you. Or Vanna. I just thought—"

"I know, and I love you for thinking that way." She drew her finger down his cheek. "I'll consider it."

"Well, I'm glad—"

Georgia shushed him with an index finger on his lips, then kissed him. He returned it eagerly.

"Oh, Jimmy," she whispered. He moved closer and folded her in his arms. She hoped they'd have enough time before Vanna got home.

Chapter Four

Ruth floated through the shallows of consciousness. Muted sounds that could have been chatter, an occasional bell, and padded footsteps registered through the fog. A faint antiseptic odor like the surface of a Band-Aid filled her nostrils, and she was a little girl again, her mother applying Mercurochrome to her skinned knee.

"Ruth? Ruth Marriotti?" she heard her mother ask. Not her mother. Ruth forced herself to swim through the black. As she rose, the voice grew louder, the odor sharper. She cleared her throat, wanting her mother to know she was there, but she couldn't quite speak. Still, something must have gotten through, because the woman calling her name replied.

"There you are." Her voice was cheerful. "So glad you're back, honey. Now, don't open your eyes. You're at Northwestern Hospital. Just relax and go back to sleep. You're safe now."

The next time Ruth surfaced, she cracked her eyes open. She saw the outlines of a room, curtained off in the center, the wall-mounted TV, and two plastic chairs. Then a piercing, agonizing pain obliterated everything else. She sucked in air and cried out. A few seconds later a woman in blue scrubs hurried through the door.

"You're awake."

"Hurts." Ruth mumbled. Her tongue felt furry, her lips dry and split. She wasn't sure the nurse understood.

But the woman nodded. "I bet it does." The nurse went to Ruth's IV bag on the pole beside her bed and adjusted the drip. A moment later blessed relief surged through. Ruth let herself relax.

"You thirsty?" the nurse asked. "I can get you some ice."

Ruth nodded.

While she waited, Ruth tried to piece together what had brought her to this place. A half-formed thought nagged at her, but she couldn't define it. Something bad had happened. Something really bad. She sank back into darkness.

. . .

The third time she woke, the accordion curtain separating her from the room's other occupant was pulled back. Ruth wondered what had happened. Had the patient been released? Or did they die? She reached for her water and managed to sip it through the straw. Heat wafted over her from the register under the window. The absence of light seeping around the window shade indicated it was night. She felt dirty and unkempt and wanted to ditch the hospital garb and change into a clean nightgown. As soon as she realized she'd been thinking coherently, she congratulated herself for escaping whatever netherworld she'd dipped into.

Her thoughts turned to Dena. She'd been with Dena before it happened. They'd been doing something important. Something big. All of them. Wait. Where was Dena? They'd been waiting for her. Dena was late. Ruth was especially anxious. Why? She remembered. She was panicked that she might have to speak. The demonstration! That was it. Grant Park. Finally Dena arrived. But then what happened?

For some reason Ruth recalled the first words a nurse had said to her in recovery. She was safe here. Why wouldn't she be? This was a hospital, after all. But she must have been unsafe before. In danger. What danger? In a flash, it came to her. Dena had been shot too. Ruth pressed the call button. The nurse rushed in.

"I remembered."

"What's that, honey?"

"Why I'm here."

"Everything is fine. You had surgery for a gunshot wound. The bullet is gone, and it missed your spine. You should make a full recovery."

"Dena. My friend Dena. She was shot too. How is she?"

The nurse tightened her lips.

She didn't have to say it. Ruth knew. Dena was dead.

Chapter Five

Three Weeks Later

"You want to leave?" Vanna cried. "You can't! What will I do?"

Georgia, at the kitchen sink washing dishes, shook her head. "I will never leave you. I just found you."

"But you just said you're going to move. Without me!"

Georgia had been thinking about the condo Jimmy had rented. The idea of having more private time with him was tantalizing. Even if it was just one or two nights a week. She'd just raised the issue with Vanna. Now she wasn't so sure.

"It would only be a couple of nights a week." She picked up a plate and dried it with a towel.

"But why?"

"Mostly because it's pretty crowded in here, don't you think? And Jimmy and I haven't had any private time unless I go up to Lake Geneva. Which is too far away."

Vanna worried a hand through her long blond hair. A younger—Vanna was just sixteen—more beautiful version of Georgia, her sister shared the same porcelain skin, high cheekbones, and lithe body. But her nose was smaller than Georgia's, and she was at least two inches taller. Now her brown eyes flashed with anger.

"Who's gonna take care of my baby when you're gone?"

"Excuse me?"

"You're taking Charlie, right? And what about school? Sam said I could intern with her next semester. I need you."

Georgia sighed. This was the hard part. "Vanna, Charlie is your son. Not mine. I can't babysit forever. I need to work. But don't worry. We'll find really good day care. Or a babysitter."

"I can't believe this!" Vanna's voice climbed up an octave. "You're fucking abandoning me. And my baby. Because of *your* boyfriend." Vanna's lips puckered. Georgia wasn't sure if she was going to cry or throw a tantrum. "Jimmy, Jimmy, Jimmy. It's all about him, isn't it? You don't give a shit about me. He's the one who wants you to leave. He's never liked me. He—"

"He does like you. What he doesn't and didn't like was the danger we were in. You know how I want to protect you? Well, he wants to protect me."

Vanna planted her hands on her hips, exaggerating her belligerence. Georgia almost expected her to stamp her foot. "So you're going to move out? Some protection."

"Vanna, I told Jimmy I didn't know if you were ready. But he had an opportunity to rent an apartment nearby, and I told him I'd consider spending more time with him. You've been a real trooper since—well—everything happened. You've matured a lot. And you're a wonderful mother to Charlie. I thought this might give you a chance to spread your wings." She flipped the towel over her shoulder. "See what life could be like without your sister and her boyfriend in the way."

"What if I don't want to spread my wings?" Her expression hardened. "What if I'm fine the way things are? What about me and my feelings? You just want to dump me ... like, like"—she waved her hand—"last night's garbage."

This was not the reaction Georgia had expected. Maybe she should have. Fourteen months earlier Vanna had run away from a Denver suburb where she was living with her—no, *their*—mother, from whom Georgia was estranged. Vanna came to Chicago on the bus, but Georgia didn't meet her until six months later, when

Vanna was in trouble and pregnant. Eight months later they'd created a new life together. Vanna had done well. Really well. A little more freedom, Georgia had figured, might not be a bad idea. Apparently, she was wrong.

"And what about homework?" Vanna cocked her hip. "What am I supposed to do with Charlie when I'm studying?"

"We'll figure out a solution, if it comes to that. Vanna, we're only talking one or two nights a week."

But Vanna ignored her. "I should have known. You want to get as far away from me as you can. You're just like everyone else."

Was "everyone else" a euphemism for their mother? "Oh, Vanna." Georgia couldn't decide whether to tell Vanna to quit manipulating her or to throw her arms around the girl. Her sister's words cut deep.

Just what Vanna wanted, Georgia figured. She was a former addict, a survivor of sex trafficking, and now a mother. But she was also just a teenager who thought the world revolved around her. Throw in some drama, and this was the result. Georgia wished she knew what to say to her sister, but she stood a few feet away, feeling useless. *This is how families fall apart,* she thought. Misunderstandings. Friction. Angry jabs.

"I get it." Vanna was working herself up. Her body was rigid, her eyes slits. Her skin from the neck up was bright red. "You don't give a shit about me."

"Sweetheart. That's not true."

"Don't call me sweetheart," she hissed. "You're not my mother."

Georgia had never seen her sister so angry. Pure white-hot rage with a dose of teenage prima donna syndrome. She choked back her own feelings. She'd taken a psychology class at the police academy and knew rage usually stems from a deep-seated fear. Of rejection. Or abandonment. And while she and Vanna had taken very different paths, they both shared the same mother. A mother who'd abandoned Georgia. Walked out when she was twelve and never called, wrote, or even sent a damn birthday card.

Then Vanna had walked out on *her*. Now Vanna thought *Georgia* was walking out. In her mind, the circle was complete.

She wanted to suggest they start the conversation over when two things happened at the same time. Charlie woke up with a lusty yell—Georgia was surprised he'd slept this long with Vanna's shouting—and Georgia's cell pinged.

"Let's talk about this in a minute, okay?"

Vanna turned on her heel and stomped out of the kitchen. Georgia fished the cell off the kitchen table. The screen registered an unfamiliar number, but it had a North Shore area code. Another damn telemarketer?

"Davis here."

"Is this Georgia Davis, the private investigator?"

Georgia straightened. "Speaking."

"My name is Erica Baldwin Stewart."

Where had Georgia heard that name?

The woman's voice cracked. "My daughter was Dena Baldwin."

Chapter Six

The next morning Georgia dressed in what had become her uniform: jeans, a sweater, and a blazer roomy enough to hide her Baby Glock in a shoulder holster. As a former cop, she still liked the idea of wearing a uniform. It added credibility to her appearance and, she hoped, her reputation. She drove north to Winnetka, an affluent suburb on the North Shore of Chicago, and parked across from a coffee shop that was now in its third incarnation.

Inside, the place sported dark furniture, a polished hardwood floor, and three shelves of assorted books donated by the bookstore next door. The counter could have doubled as an antique soda fountain. Georgia chose a small table against the wall.

Erica Baldwin Stewart was late. She must be on North Shore time, Georgia thought, then chastised herself for being flip. Not only had the woman lost a daughter, but she'd been reminded of it 24/7 by the media coverage. She was entitled to be late. Georgia grabbed a book off the bookcase. *Red Harvest*. Georgia thought she knew all of Dashiell Hammett's stories, whether novels or movies, but she'd never heard of this one. She tried to get into it, but reading was difficult; she had a mild case of dyslexia.

Her mind drifted to Vanna.

Maybe a therapist could help. She dug her phone out of her

pocket and was scrolling through "nearby therapists" when the door swung open and a woman entered with a younger man. The woman hesitated. Georgia had told Dena's mother she was blond and would be wearing a gray North Face coat, a birthday gift from Jimmy, over her blazer. When the woman saw the coat, she came over.

Georgia rose. "Erica?"

The woman nodded. Her black hair, threaded with gray, was pulled back into a messy ponytail. She wore jeans, a wool jacket, and snow boots despite the absence of snow. Her neck was long and graceful, but her tight expression made her otherwise smooth features look sharp and out of place, as if they were surprised to find themselves arranged on her face. She was pale and thin, on the way toward emaciated. Grief, likely.

"I'm Georgia Davis."

The woman, probably in her fifties, gave her a slight nod and gestured to the younger man beside her. "This is my son, Jeffrey. Dena's brother."

That Dena had a brother was news to Georgia. It hadn't been mentioned in the media. Jeffrey was several inches taller than his mother, but just as slim. Somewhere in his thirties. He shared his mother's dark eyes and hair, minus the gray. His face held a somber, soulful expression.

"He's as devastated as I am. We both want to get to the bottom of this."

Get to the bottom of what? Three people had died, including Dena. A dozen more wounded. The shooter had been found—dead from an IED explosion on the roof of a hotel directly across from Grant Park. An open-and-shut case, or so officialdom proclaimed. Domestic terrorism. Tick off yet another massacre to add to the legacy of American gun violence.

Georgia reined in her impatience. "Would you like some coffee? It's on me."

"I—uh—tea would be nice."

A few minutes later, with cappuccino and a pastry for Georgia, the same for Jeffrey, and tea for Erica, they settled into chairs. Jeffrey cleared his throat. Erica sipped her tea. She looked dazed, almost lost. She was clearly struggling. An unusual tug of protectiveness came over Georgia. She gentled her voice as she prompted Erica.

"You said, 'get to the bottom of this.' What do you mean?"

Erica's chest rose and fell. She took another sip of tea. "I assume you're up to speed on the events of—of Dena's death."

Georgia nodded. It was still the top story everywhere. A year had passed since the election of the most unpopular president ever, and despite a core base of supporters, millions were demanding he be removed from office. The president and his administration were incompetent, corrupt, and dangerous. The rumors were that Chicago bookies wouldn't take any more bets about his odds for survival. A special counsel was investigating.

Erica played with her spoon. "So let me tell you about Dena. She is—was—a left-wing progressive, and she supported Bernie until the convention. Afterwards, she switched to Hillary. She volunteered, rang doorbells in Wisconsin, made phone calls. She organized a rally in Evanston and even put together a carpool to drive seniors to the polls." She shifted. "The morning after the results were in, she refused to believe them. Later that day she created a Facebook group, ResistanceUSA."

"Wait. Are you saying she *founded* the group?"

A wan smile came across Erica's face. "That's right. She believed that the vote, particularly in the midwest swing states, had been manipulated by Russia. She wasn't alone: others were—and still are—alleging it too. The group exploded, and by the end of the year, there were nearly forty-two thousand members."

"Forty-two thousand people in seven weeks?"

Erica nodded. "Her energy never flagged. Within six months, she was a national figure. She was one of the first to call out every misstep by the new administration, every injustice, every example of creeping authoritarianism, every risk to our democracy. She was in the middle of expanding her 'repertoire' when she—died. She had begun to speak out about other issues. The dangers of fracking, the criminality of the new administration, the mess he's made with our foreign allies. She'd really come into her own. It's as if she was born to do this. Of course, in the process she made enemies."

"Such as?"

"There were the bots—you know—automated tweets and Facebook messages that roll out whenever a specific subject is raised. Anyway, hundreds, maybe thousands of bots trolled her online." Erica let out a world-weary breath. "Then there were the real trolls. Human crazies, I call them."

Georgia nodded. Like mutant viruses, they had invaded the Internet to sow discord and chaos wherever possible.

"They accused her of lying, of propaganda, of being a traitor to the country. Some people even accused her of being a Russian spy working undercover."

"Although how they could, given the administration's complicity with Russia, is nuts," Jeffrey cut in.

Erica nodded in acknowledgment. "Still, Dena was in her element. She thrived on allies and adversaries alike. When she wasn't appearing on TV, she was organizing, bringing new converts to the group."

Georgia's eyebrows went up at the word "converts." Erica caught it. "Yes, it may have started as a cult, but it grew so big so fast that it became a movement. Dena is—was very persuasive." Her smile held a mix of pride and sorrow.

"So, last fall she and her crew decided to organize a grass-roots demonstration. They used the Facebook group to spread the word. She called for a million people to come out. Privately, she hoped there would be at least a thousand."

"For what reason?"

"January marked a year since the inauguration, but in that short time so much of our country and policies are now unrecognizable. She wanted people to use their First Amendment rights to let the traitor know that what he's doing and what he represents are not okay."

"She succeeded," Georgia said.

Another sad smile curled Erica's lips. "It was amazing! Police estimated over two hundred thousand people came to Grant Park." Her smile faded.

Georgia understood. There was no need to repeat the rest. A sharpshooter with a .223 Bushmaster rifle equipped with a bump stock had opened up, killing Dena, group member DJ Grabiner, and a protestor in the front row. Her second-in-command, Ruth Marriotti, along with a dozen others, had been wounded. Chicago cops tracked the gunman to the roof of the White Star Hotel twenty-two minutes later, where they discovered he'd blown himself up with what they later learned was a pipe bomb. Why he hadn't used the Bushmaster to off himself was still unknown.

The shooter, Scott Allen Jarvis, had materialized seemingly out of nowhere. He was raised on an Iowa farm, but the family was forced to sell when Jarvis was seventeen. He moved to Iowa City for college but never graduated. His parents died in a house fire soon after he left home, leaving only Jarvis and his younger sister, Katherine. He enlisted in the army and survived two tours in Afghanistan and one in Iraq. Afterward he resurfaced in Rogers Park, a neighborhood on Chicago's North Side, where he lived with his sister and was unemployed much of the time.

Law enforcement and the media scoured his history in the hope of tying him to some kind of radical terrorist group but didn't find anything. It was as if the guy dropped in from another planet. That didn't deter cable news, of course, hungry for any scrap of information, meaningful or not. They replayed the video of the shooting and the simple service that passed for Jarvis's funeral so often that Georgia had to turn the TV off. She could only guess how it affected Erica.

Now Erica's eyes filled. She swiped at them with her napkin.

Georgia squeezed Erica's hand.

Jeffrey Baldwin cleared his throat. Georgia glanced over. He looked like he was struggling to control his emotions.

Erica swallowed, then picked up her teaspoon, stirred her tea, replaced the spoon on the saucer. Finally, she looked up, and Georgia asked, "Why do you think your daughter was targeted for murder?"

Chapter Seven

Slowly Erica's demeanor changed. Her spine straightened and her eyes narrowed. A fierce look came into her eyes. She reminded Georgia of a predatory cat, ready to pounce on an unlucky mouse. At the same time, her son, Jeffrey, started to squirm.

"A few weeks after the attack," Erica said, "I got an anonymous email."

"Anonymous?"

Erica nodded. "Let me tell you what it said."

Dena's mother might be bowed with grief, but she wasn't broken. Georgia wondered if Dena had inherited the same grit. But Jeffrey, for some reason, wouldn't make eye contact with her.

"The email said, *Jarvis was set up. Find the Beef Jerky.*"

Georgia leaned forward. "Excuse me?"

"That was it. *Jarvis was set up. Find the Beef Jerky,*" Erica repeated.

Georgia hoped she didn't roll her eyes too conspicuously. Conspiracy theorists had found a weird kind of stature on the Internet. People could say anything they dreamed up, and there would always be a few gullible folks who took their pronouncements as omens, or even facts. Erica was an intelligent woman. She had to know that.

"Beef jerky? Tell me you didn't take it seriously."

"At first we thought it was as crazy as it sounds. You know, just made-up crap. But Terry realized that, whatever the veracity of the message, someone had penetrated our email system."

"'Hacked' is the word, Mom," Jeffrey said.

"So, what did you do?" Georgia glanced at them both in turn.

"We—I—replied right away with *Who is this? And why are you making these claims?*"

"And?"

"My reply bounced. I got what do you call them, those mailer-daemon notices. There was no such account."

"What was the return email?"

"It was noreply@xfetw.com. But it was dead. No such account."

"When was this?"

"About two weeks ago."

"What did you do?"

"I called my lawyer, who said to call the police."

"I need to say something here," Jeffrey cut in.

"Sure," Georgia said.

"I don't agree with what Mom's doing. I think we're asking for trouble."

"In what way?"

"I don't know for sure who killed my sister. And I think it's probably better that I don't." He looked over at his mother. "We both know that we're not being told the whole story. Someone is holding back information. But I'm willing to let that go."

"Why? Do you think there's some kind of conspiracy around her murder?"

"Maybe, maybe not. I just don't want my mom in the middle of it. We're playing with fire. What if something else happens? To her?" He gestured toward Erica.

Georgia faced Erica. "You don't agree."

Erica shook her head. "She was my little girl. I need to know. I owe her that much."

Jeffrey let out a breath, his expression grim.

"So, the FBI paid me a visit. The police had already been to the house a couple of times. This time they took my computer and the router. A few days later they told me they couldn't trace the email."

Georgia wasn't surprised. "The FBI does have excellent resources. If they say they couldn't—"

Jeffrey cut her off. "Agreed. But they couldn't—or wouldn't—give us any information. Basically they told us, nicely, to forget it. And to buy new equipment. And change our passwords." His disdainful voice told Georgia how he felt about that.

"What did they say about the beef jerky comment? Did they talk about some kind of code? Or signal?"

"They said it was probably a hoax," Erica answered.

"Someone hacked into your email as a hoax?" Georgia frowned.

"Exactly. It doesn't make sense," Erica said. "There are a lot of conspiracy theories out there, you know. People from both the Right and the Left saying crazy things. The FBI said they haven't found any evidence that Jarvis was in league with any group. But that email was just so weird . . ." Her voice trailed off.

"Which is why you can't let it go," Georgia said.

"Would you?"

Like any mother, Erica was grasping for something to suggest her daughter's death was more than being in the wrong place at the wrong time. Even a bullshit comment on a mysterious email that the FBI said was a hoax was ammunition.

"Look," Erica went on, "for starters, that email came in on our private server."

"Private?"

"When Terry and I got married—he's my second husband—we set up a private server for the family. And Terry's business. The security was supposed to be first-rate. Everything encrypted and all that."

"Why do you need encryption?"

"Terry runs a hedge fund. Confidential data gets passed back and forth all the time. He doesn't trust the Comcasts or AT&Ts."

Smart, Georgia thought.

"So, whoever sent us that email went to some trouble to reach us."

"And hack in," Jeffrey added.

"But if the FBI said it was a hoax—"

A spurt of irritation flashed across Erica's face. "I didn't say that. They did. What we say is that they couldn't trace it." She hesitated. "As a former police officer, and now a PI, we thought maybe you could help."

Georgia leaned back. Erica had done some homework on her. "Why me? And who recommended me?"

"Paul Kelly. He's one of our lawyers."

Georgia and Paul went back a long way. She'd been a newly minted PI, and he sold insurance when he wasn't lawyering. He'd been responsible for her first "real" case. She trusted him. But that didn't mean she should take *this* case.

"And we wanted someone who had no connection to us or Dena. Someone who could fly under the radar, if need be."

Under the radar? That didn't inspire confidence. "Erica . . . And Jeffrey," she added, "I'm grateful for Paul's referral, and I appreciate the opportunity, but if the FBI can't trace the email, I doubt I can. My resources are minuscule compared to them. Even a large investigations or security firm could track SIGINT better than I could."

"SIGINT?" Erica asked.

"Signals intelligence. Things that involve communications signals. Electronic messages. Texts. Emails. Intercepts of conversations. That kind of thing."

"You see? You know more about this than we do. We need someone to explain what's going on. Without patronizing us."

"But I don't—"

"Paul said you'd say that. Look. We'll pay you whatever you

need. Please. We—I—really need to know the truth about Dena's murder."

"What makes you think you don't?"

Erica took another sip of tea, then set down the teacup with a clatter. "So here's what you don't know." Georgia glanced over at Jeffrey. He was watching her intently.

"You need to know who my first husband is. Was. Dena and Jeffrey's father." She took in a breath. "His name is Carl Baldwin. He is a lobbyist. In DC now. He's ultra-right wing. A member of CNP."

"CNP?"

"The Council for National Policy. It's supposed to be this secret group of right-wing politicos like Bannon, the Koch brothers, the Mercers, and more. You have to pay thousands of dollars to join. Once you're in, you're not supposed to admit you're a member or even call it by name. But the membership list leaked out a while back. Now you can see for yourself who's part of it."

"Sounds like a bunch of guys in a secret fraternity."

Jeffrey took over. "Except that they've got their hands on the money and levers of power in DC. Who do you think put the president in office? Tried to destroy health care? Rammed through the tax cut? Got him to destroy federal regulations for the sake of profit?"

"I'm not political, Jeffrey. The way I see it, the haves are always doing things to the have-nots."

"But you fight for justice, don't you?" he said. "I mean, that's what you do, right?"

Georgia wasn't prepared for a political rant, even from a grieving family. "Jeffrey, I do it because people pay me to."

It was Erica's turn. Her voice strengthened. "Okay. Carl Baldwin, along with a few others, controls a lot of people with a lot of money and leverage. He can make people do what he wants."

That Georgia could understand. "Except Dena." It slipped out.

Erica didn't say anything for a moment. "It's no secret there was no love lost between them. Or us. Carl is abusive and narcissistic.

Thinks only of his own interests. Beds a lot of women, too. Not so different from the occupant of the White House. One of his pals, actually." She paused. "We don't need resources, Georgia. We can get them for you if we need to. And money. But I just don't trust the 'official' story."

"You can't possibly think your husband—ex-husband—had something to do with Dena's murder?"

"Not directly. But what if someone was compromising him? The authorities wrapped this up fast. Almost as if it played out according to a script. The police found the shooter in just twenty-two minutes. Why don't we know more about him? Why did he blow himself up? The media says he's a domestic terrorist. Some say he was in the Klan. Others say he was a right-wing evangelical. The Left thinks he's a Russian or Chinese spy. Why don't we know for sure? Why doesn't someone from his family—an aunt, uncle, even his sister—come forward? So far, he's just a weird guy who emerged from the shadows. We don't trust anyone. We need someone who can dig around for answers."

Chapter Eight

Washington, DC

Legs together, toes pointed, just the right amount of spring, Vic Summerfield launched into a shallow dive. Once he hit the pool, he churned through the water. First one direction, then the other, as regular as a metronome. Swimming laps was not as easy as it looked. A good swimmer fought the water to advance, then used the resulting force to glide. All in the same stroke. Life was the same way, he thought. First resistance, then surrender. Yin and yang. The trick was to know when and where to apply each.

Vic had suffered the hard knocks of failure, relished the results of success. But he'd been willing to make the effort, to go the extra lap. Not many of his generation did. They grew up thinking they were special snowflakes, entitled to unlimited success and happiness just because they'd won a goddam trophy in third grade for "achievement" in soccer. Or hockey. Their only achievement was showing up, which their mothers had made them do. They were all a bunch of whiners, complaining that the world owed them greatness.

He executed his flip turns, allowing himself a touch of pride. How many other swimmers knew how to poise their body, flip over, and push off without missing a beat? You had to be precisely the right distance away from the end of the lane when you made a somersault, then apply the force of your legs to propel you forward. It took skill. And practice.

But wasn't that the prescription for success? Especially in this town. If you wanted to make it in DC, you had to know when to push and when to concede. Without showing your hand. That was rule one. Maybe the only rule, despite the chaos that had ensued from the election. He'd once dated a woman who quit her job in broadcasting because she couldn't bear the thought of walking into yet another party knowing she wanted to exploit the politicos in the room for a story, while they wanted to exploit her to get their guy on the news. She couldn't handle the cynicism. Vic was of tougher stuff. He wouldn't quit.

He performed another turn and swam his last length. He'd done almost a mile. Time to get out, shower, get to work. He made himself sprint to the shallow end, pulled up, and started to inhale a chlorine-scented breath. The acidic smell brought back happy memories of the community pool in which he'd thrashed and learned how to swim. Now, though, his reverie was cut short by a pair of Berluti boots at eye level, filling the view through his goggles. Vic looked up, ignoring the tiny rivulets of water that streamed down his cheeks. A man in an impeccably tailored bespoke suit glared at him.

"How much did the assholes pay you to fuck me over?" his boss, Carl Baldwin, hissed.

Chapter Nine

Chicago

A few flakes of snow spit sideways as Georgia left the coffee shop. She hurried to her Toyota, trying to guess whether the granite clouds overhead would produce a full-blown storm. She keyed the engine and ran the heat. Once the temperature was bearable, she made a call.

She'd been completely honest when she told Erica Stewart her resources were meager compared to the FBI's. But what she hadn't told her was that the people she relied on, whether ethical hackers, private DNA experts, or forensic fraud experts, were themselves former FBI or IC agents who had mastered their respective skills.

Her call went to voice mail. Zach Dolan, a former hacker who'd found redemption and lots more income on the right side of the law, was probably out walking his dog. She left a message and drove south on Green Bay Road.

Paul Kelly's office, no longer in the raunchy part of Rogers Park, occupied a suite in a small office building on Touhy Avenue. He'd hired a receptionist, too, a matronly woman with old-fashioned blue-white hair. She greeted Georgia with a cheerful smile.

"May I help you?"

"Hi. I'm Georgia Davis, and I'd like to see—"

"You're Georgia?" The woman's eyes widened. "The PI, right? Oh, I'm thrilled to meet you. Paul talks about you all the time." The receptionist rose from an office chair with wheels, came around, and pumped Georgia's hand. "Welcome! I'm Joan Chase. What can I get you to drink?"

Georgia felt her cheeks get hot. She wasn't used to someone fussing over her with effusive welcomes. She was saved from an awkward reply by a voice calling out from the back.

"Joan, is that who I think it is?"

"Come out and see, Paul."

The door to an office opened, and a man, somewhere in his sixties, walked out. Paul Kelly wasn't tall, but he was compact. Light bounced off his shiny bald head like it always did, but the shabby blue blazer, khaki pants, and blue shirt he used to wear had been replaced with a well-tailored suit, crisp shirt, and respectable rep tie.

Georgia ran her hands down her jeans. It occurred to her she might be underdressed.

"You're late," he said, pulling out a new iPhone. Things were clearly going well in Paul Kelly Land.

"Um, late for what? I didn't know we had an appointment."

"We didn't." His face cracked into a broad smile that crinkled the corners of his eyes. "But I knew you were meeting with Erica, and I bet Joan a buck you'd end up here before the end of the day. Didn't I, Joanie?" He spread his arms for a bear hug.

Georgia hugged him back.

"He did indeed." Joan grinned. Either he was telling the truth, or she'd perfected the art of covering for him.

Paul guided her back to his office, a spacious room. Even a large desk and small conference table in a corner didn't fill it completely. Georgia pulled up a chair at the table. An unusual amount of light flooded through the windows.

"In that case, I'm guessing I'm your insurance policy. So you can tell Erica you've done everything possible to help."

"When did you get so cynical, Davis?" But the top of his ears reddened. That was his tell. Always had been. "As you undoubtedly know by now, I told her to meet with you." He sat opposite her. "That you would give her an honest appraisal of her needs and your capabilities."

"Paul, I can't do anything for her. The FBI already told her the email was untraceable."

"And you believe them? Those bastions of truth, justice, and the American way?"

"Not you, too." She sighed. "Not everything is a conspiracy. There are times where if it looks like a duck and quacks like a duck . . ." She left the rest of the sentence unfinished.

"You're looking at it like a cop. Levelheaded. Logical. Sane."

"Someone has to."

"You know the FBI took over the case from CPD, right?"

"What else is new?" She thought about it. "Probably not a bad idea, given what Dena was doing and who her father is."

"Yeah, well, you know how well that went over with my cop buddies."

Georgia nodded. Turf battles between Chicago Blues and the feds were common, at least in Chicago.

"Erica's a nice lady. What happened to her is horrible. No mother should ever have to endure what she has," Paul said.

"Tell me about the ex-husband in DC. The lobbyist."

Paul leaned forward, interlacing his fingers. "You know how Illinois keeps sending our governors to prison?"

"Yeah . . . ," Georgia said uncertainly.

"Well, for every governor in jail, there are three lobbyists who should be but aren't. Baldwin's one of 'em."

"Why? What does he do?"

Paul unclasped his fingers and grabbed the arms of his chair. "What every lobbyist does. Bribes and threats. Google him. You'll see."

"Do you think he was involved in his daughter's death?"

"I hope to hell not. But according to Erica, the daughter sliced him out of her life like a sharp knife a couple of years back. Look.

Can you just make a call or two? It would set her mind at ease." He threw her a knowing look.

"What about the son, Jeffrey? What's his story?"

"Interesting. He was one of those entitled North Shore kids. A bully. Into everything that wasn't nailed down. He was busted a few times. Once for a B and E to steal cash for Molly. The drug. Dad got his record expunged. Then the kid moved out to Hollywood to be an actor."

"Really? He was with Erica today. He appeared to be worried. But he said he didn't want his mother to hire me. That it was dangerous for them."

"There's a reason for that."

"What?"

Kelly held up a finger indicating she should be patient. "So, Jeffrey came back after Erica started the foundation."

"Foundation?"

"She's the daughter of Franklin Porter."

Georgia flipped up a hand. "Who?"

"Old Chicago money. Lots of it. A grandfather or great-grandfather, I don't remember which, made a killing in silver mining out west. Moved here and bought their way into society. Been here ever since."

"You're saying Erica underwrote her ex-husband's business?"

"At first, but he was in the right place at the right time. And with her connections, he parlayed that into a fortune all by himself."

"Okay. What about this foundation?"

"After Erica divorced Baldwin, she started the foundation." He paused. "The Baldwin Foundation for the Future."

"What's it do?"

"What do you think? It hands out money."

"For what?"

"Basically, whatever they want. As long as it has to do with the future. You know, emerging businesses, artists, new tech ideas. The MacArthur Foundation meets Elon Musk."

"A what meets who?"

"Never mind. Not important."

"Why'd she start it?"

"Tax shelter. And to give her kids something to do. Neither wanted to work for their father."

"Dena worked at the foundation?"

"She ran the place."

"Wait . . . you said both kids."

"Right. About a year after she started it, the son realized he wasn't gonna make it in La-La Land, cleaned up his act, and came back to Chicago. Erica was thrilled. She gave him a job at the foundation."

"How did that work out?"

"Surprisingly well, I'm told."

"The kids got along?"

"Apparently. The timing was good. Dena was becoming more politically active when her brother was settling into his job. He basically took over. With everyone's blessing."

Georgia thought it over. "I still don't think there's much I can do."

"Oh, come on. You've got contacts. Your boyfriend. That Foreman woman and her boyfriend. You could poke around."

Jimmy was in law enforcement, and Ellie Foreman's boyfriend was probably as rich as Erica Baldwin. They probably ran in the same circles. "You've done your homework."

"Just dotting my i's and crossing my t's. Gotta justify my outrageous malpractice premiums." He grinned and leaned back. "So, how's tricks with you?"

Georgia suspected he already knew, but she filled him in on her news. In another life Paul Kelly might have been her favorite uncle. And she did owe him her start. When the small talk was over, he inclined his head. "So?" he asked.

"Okay. I'll turn over a few rocks. But the cops and the Bureau have been all over this. Don't expect much."

"That's my gal." He beamed.

How did he always manage to get his way?

Chapter Ten

Fifteen Months Earlier

Things began to go south around nine thirty pm on election night. Dena had commandeered a booth in her Lincoln Square neighborhood tavern with a few friends. Normally sports channels blared on the half dozen flat-screen TVs, but tonight the screens were tuned to the networks and CNN. Early returns reported East Coast states falling pretty much as expected; her candidate had been piling up votes. Early calls had been proclaimed, accompanied in the pub with congratulatory cheers and drinks on the house. The crowd, mostly millennials, was in a good mood. The torch was passing in the expected way.

"Let's have some wine," Dena said. "We deserve it." She ordered four bottles.

The first hint something was amiss happened during the second round of poll closings. Reports from Florida, always a thorny state, indicated the race was much closer than expected. Then came Virginia. Then a slew of too-close-to-call rust-belt states. When Michigan, Pennsylvania, North Carolina, Wisconsin, and even New Hampshire showed a lead for the Republican, the bar went quiet. Dena felt queasy. An hour later, she developed full-fledged nausea. And by the time they called the election, Dena joined ranks with the other shell-shocked voters who hadn't seen it coming.

Her gut tightened with rage. How could this have happened? Bottom line—it couldn't have. Something had gone horribly wrong. Someone or something had rigged the system. Ironically, that's what the Republican candidate had been alleging throughout the campaign. Projection, maybe? He was as easy to read as a crystal bowl. Always blaming others for whatever didn't go his way.

But this was a travesty. A miserable misogynistic narcissist had no right to the presidency. Like a pilot light that's been lit, Dena's rage exploded. She swilled the rest of her wine fast and hard.

As she did, the man she was currently sleeping with shot her a sympathetic glance. She eyed him with revulsion. How dare he feel sorry for her? She fucking wanted to belt him. This couldn't go unanswered. In fact, this was war. She got up, went to the bar, and positioned herself next to a man she'd never seen before. He was drinking alone. She signaled for another glass of wine and ordered him a draft. When their drinks came, she took stock. Nice body, clean clothes, bedroom eyes. He would do.

She tossed back her drink in one go.

"That was fast," he said.

"I dare you," she said.

"Dare me what?"

"How fast can you swig that draft?"

"Why would I want to?"

"Because I want to get out of here, and I want you to come with me." Even though it almost always worked, Dena braced for that split-second judgment every man made about her. She was attractive, she knew, with long, wavy black hair and big blue eyes. She still had a willowy figure, as well as a unique hippie-gone-straight style. She could have been a social worker, a millennial lawyer, even—she chuckled—a dedicated nonprofit executive. But this guy looked young. Happily, in the dim lighting of the bar, he couldn't see her crow's-feet, the permanently carved lines on her forehead, or the just-a-bit-too-flabby tummy that nature conferred on a thirty-fiveish woman.

A knowing smile came across the man's face, and he threw back his beer. Dena smiled too. She threw a twenty on the bar, took his arm, and made sure her now former lover saw her before she sashayed out of the pub.

By the time they got back to her condo, they still hadn't called Florida, but Michigan was looking grim. She retrieved the celebratory bottle of champagne from the fridge, poured them two glasses. Then she smashed the bottle into the sink. A flying shard nicked her finger. She sucked the blood off, picked up the glasses, and led him into her bedroom.

Chapter Eleven

The Present

Three inches of snow would hide a lot of ugliness, Georgia thought as she climbed into her Toyota. It wasn't coming down yet, but the skies were gray and threatening. She stopped into the supermarket for baby formula, a cooked chicken, and salad. She was about to go to the checkout lines when a greasy, sugary aroma made her backtrack to the bakery, where she picked up a box of cookies just out of the oven.

Back home she nabbed a parking space in front of her building—the gods were granting her parking karma today. Inside, she headed toward the kitchen, calling out, "Hey, I'm home."

There was no answer. She put the food away and checked Vanna's room. No Vanna. Or Charlie. She grabbed her phone and texted, "Hey. Where are you?" Vanna usually replied right away.

Georgia checked the calendar in the kitchen. Vanna didn't have class on Tuesday. When Vanna didn't respond after five minutes, a tiny prickle of worry edged up her spine. She called Sam, but her friend's voice mail picked up. She left a message. "Hi, Sam. Is Vanna with you?"

She was just disconnecting when her cell buzzed. Probably Vanna. She checked the incoming number. It wasn't. She picked up.

"Oh, hi, Zach."

"Gee. I've had warmer welcomes from a statue."

"I'm sorry. I was—"

"Don't worry about it."

A high-pitched canine bark spilled from the phone's handset.

"Doesn't sound like Joshua. New puppy?"

Zach, and his brother Mike, had been rescuing big dogs for years. Shepherds, Rottweilers, retrievers. Despite their size and seeming ferocity, they were well trained and gentle, at least to the brothers' friends.

"As a matter of fact, Jeremiah has joined the family."

"Still with the biblical Js," she said. Their other dogs, Joshua and Jericho, had crossed over the Rainbow Bridge.

"We wouldn't want to tempt our higher power. Whose name, Jehovah, we say in all reverence."

She hesitated. Was he kidding? Because Georgia didn't believe in anything she couldn't see, hear, touch, or taste, the fact that others could, especially those she respected, baffled her.

He laughed, as if he knew what she was thinking. "So. What is it today?"

"Can I buy you a beer? I'd rather talk in person."

"Come on over. Bar's open."

Thirty minutes later, Georgia was sitting inside Zach Dolan's office tucked away in an industrial park in Northbrook. Zach still looked like the brunette son of Santa Claus: burly, with dark eyes and long hair that blended into a full beard. He was attempting to nurse a beer, but a curious shepherd puppy kept nosing its head into Zach's lap, demanding to be part of the conversation.

"Meet Jeremiah," Zach said.

Jeremiah pricked up his ears at the sound of his name, and his tail began to swish like a windshield wiper on high speed.

"Smart guy."

"Can you believe he was a rescue? Who would abandon a beautiful dog like that?"

Despite her cynicism, her heart pinged. Why was it so easy to have more compassion for an abandoned dog than for a person? Was it that dogs were intrinsically innocent creatures, who through no fault of their own had landed in ill-fated circumstances, while humans were supposed to have free will and were, at least partially, responsible for their lots? Then again, humans were supposed to be God's creatures too. It was a no-win argument.

Zach fondled the dog's ears. "So, what brings you to my lair?"

She glanced around. The room they sat in was occupied by four computers, each flashing a mysterious light or two. Still, as she'd learned before, Zach's security protocols were first-rate. No hot mics, hidden cameras, or other surveillance toys would monitor or record their conversation.

"In nontechnical terms, can you explain how someone might set up an email account and then delete it without leaving a trace?"

"Hmm. Tell me more."

"Oh, and whoever did it was able to hack into a private server. But here's the thing: as far as I know, that account only sent one email while it existed."

"Interesting."

"The person who received the email tried to reply but got the 'there is no such account' message."

Zach stroked his beard for a moment. Then: "Well, off the top of my head, I can think of two ways to do it."

Georgia inclined her head.

"You could buy a hacked account on the dark web with bitcoin."

"How does that work?"

"You use bitcoins to buy an account that's already been hacked and is for sale. Then you send the email and tear everything down afterwards. It's complicated but very doable, if you know what you're doing," he said. "The other way would be just as safe. Basically you would need a VPN, Tor, and an—"

"Tor is the browser that lets you surf anonymously, right?"

"Exactly. And a VPN is a virtual private network that lets you send information securely, without being monitored. You could set up your own account that way."

"How much knowledge would a person need in order to do either of those things?"

"It's not rocket science." He paused. "But I guess it does take some skill in hacking."

"And there would be no way to trace it."

"Right. Unless the device being used had malware or a virus already on it. Which wouldn't be the case if someone knows what they're doing."

Jeremiah padded over to Georgia and tucked his face in her lap. She petted him.

"He likes you."

"I like him."

"You should get a dog."

"I have a baby instead. Which reminds me." Georgia dug out her cell and checked for messages. Nothing from Vanna. "One other question. If you have a private server, do you have a VPN?"

"Undoubtedly."

"So theoretically whoever hacked into that server and/or VPN had the proper credentials?"

"With the right encryption software it's a piece of cake."

"What if they didn't? Have the encryption keys."

He blew out a breath. "Wow. That would be hard."

"How hard?"

"To hack into a VPN without the key would take me a long time. Days. Weeks. Even months. The NSA did it, but look at their resources. It would be a whole lot easier just to steal the encryption keys."

"How?"

"Easiest way would be to know someone who had the key and get it from them. Knowingly or not."

Georgia mulled it over. Did whoever send the beef jerky email know the Baldwin family? Or Dena? Jeremiah nosed her lap again, demanding attention. She stroked the top of his head.

"So, you want to tell me why you need to know all this?" Zach asked.

"I can't. Not yet." Georgia bit her lip. "But does the term 'beef jerky' mean anything to you?"

"My favorite is Sweet 'n Spicy."

"Not in that context. What if I sent you a message that said, 'Find the beef jerky'?"

Zach frowned. "Uh—"

"I take it you have no idea."

"Not a clue," he said. "But when you figure it out . . ."

She stood. "You'll be the first to know."

Chapter
Twelve

A winter dusk descended, bringing with it lazy bands of snow as Georgia drove back to Evanston. At a red light she punched in Vanna's cell. It went to voice mail. Where was she? The tickle of anxiety in her gut expanded. Although the nightmare a year earlier was over, her connection to Vanna was still tentative and fragile. Like the delicate web of a spider, family bonds could be destroyed by the slightest breeze or movement.

Back home, Georgia called Erica. She told her she'd look into the mysterious email but not to expect much. She'd work on the case for a week. Then they could reassess.

"Great," Erica said. "What do you need from me?"

"A key to Dena's apartment and permission to go inside. The passwords on her computer, if you know them. Emails, Facebook, other social media accounts."

"I don't know her passwords, but it doesn't matter anyway. The FBI has her computer."

"Do you have the names of the agents who took it?"

Erica told her. The names weren't familiar. Georgia wrote them down.

"What was her email address?"

"She had a few. Her main one was Denaeaglewin@comcast.net."

"Eaglewin?"

"Bald eagle. Baldwin."

"Got it." Georgia wrote it down. "And the others?"

"Dena@ResistanceUSA.org and DenaIQ160@comcast.net. Dena never dumbed herself down."

It took Georgia a few seconds to get it. When she did, she kept her mouth shut. "So, let's talk about 'beef jerky.' To your knowledge did she know someone who loved beef jerky? Did she like it?"

"Dena didn't eat the stuff. Too many chemical additives, she said."

"Okay. What about her brother? Would Jeffrey by any chance know?"

"I'll ask him. Call you back."

"Thanks. One other thing . . ." Georgia proposed her fee for the week. Erica accepted without hesitation.

Georgia checked her phone. A text from Jimmy; he was on his way down, but with the snow, he probably wouldn't be there for another hour. Nothing from Vanna. She swallowed, then forced herself back to the case. She made herself comfortable on the sofa, booted up her computer, and went to the Facebook group.

ResistanceUSA was a public forum. Anyone could join. So she did and was told she needed to be approved by an administrator. Still, all the posts on the Facebook group were public. She read through them.

At the top of the page was a flood of condolence posts about Dena's death, plus some panic-laden notes asking what they would do now. A few messages asked about Ruth Marriotti's condition. The name sounded familiar; Georgia googled it. She was one of the people wounded at the demonstration. A few generic responses said Ruth was on the mend and she'd be back.

She scrolled down. Most of the posts were highly critical of the president; some were bitingly funny. She read a decree from

Dena not to post memes, which, judging from all the quotes and graphics, had been ignored. A chorus of comments typically followed every post—with forty-two thousand members, that wasn't surprising. But the rage bubbling just below the surface of many posts was. Georgia hadn't realized how bitter people were that the political pendulum had swung away from them.

Not all, however. One poster wrote, *This is the only place I can get accurate information. Thank you, Dena.* Another wrote, *This is my refuge from the insanity. It's the first place I check in the morning and the last place at night. I don't know how I'd survive without all of you.* Dena must have been pleased—and proud—of what she'd created, Georgia thought.

She scrolled to posts dated before the demonstration. An air of excitement and resolve came through the page. Plans were crafted, critiqued, adopted or rejected. Earnest discussions about nonviolence and what to do if someone—God forbid the Chicago police—started using aggressive tactics. Many of the posts were barely articulate and were rife with misspellings, but their passion for becoming crusaders against injustice, if only for a day, was clear.

Dena posted more than anyone, sometimes a dozen times a day. Her comments were usually the last word on a subject, although to her credit, Georgia noted, she let the conversation keep going until posters started to repeat themselves. She also shared ideas; for example, she encouraged people who knew A-list celebrities to invite them to the demonstration. Some, according to comments, were actually coming. Dena applauded each member who'd made an effort. Good leadership skills, Georgia noted.

She clicked on the tab for "Members." Besides Dena, there were three administrators, two women and two men. One of the women was Ruth Marriotti. Georgia's eyebrows rose. A list of members in Chicago followed. She scrolled down. Almost six thousand. She scanned the list quickly and found Ruth's name again. A stroke of luck.

She jotted down some notes, beginning with Dena's family:

- First, Dena's father, the big wheel in DC. Did he have enemies? Were they coming after him through Dena? Was he enraged about his failed marriage?

- What about Jeffrey, Dena's brother? Erica claimed they were close, but kids often put on a show for Mom. Plus, the guy was a deadbeat for a while, out in LA trying to break into Hollywood. What else was he doing before becoming the prodigal son? And why was he less eager than Erica to hire Georgia? She needed more.

- Then there was the foundation. Was anything irregular going on financially or otherwise? Any organization or person who thought they were entitled to a contribution but didn't get one?

- Did Dena have a boyfriend? Or girlfriend? She'd have to investigate.

- Then there was the fact that Jarvis used an IED to blow himself up. Most terrorists ate their guns. Why did he go to the trouble of building an IED, which limited the crime scene evidence that could have been collected after the fact? Was he sending a message? Protecting an accomplice?

- She'd have to look into Jarvis's world. His sister, Katherine, was mentioned but not quoted in the media. Did she or someone else close to him set him up? If so, why?

- Georgia even wrote down Erica's husband and his hedge fund. Did anyone there hire Jarvis? It bore looking into. In fact, she needed to run background checks on everyone associated with Dena Baldwin, her family, and her killer.

- Most important, however, was the Facebook group. If Jarvis was a gun for hire, did someone in the group hire him? Were there members of the group who didn't support Dena? And if there were, how was she supposed to find them? Technically she now had forty-two

thousand suspects. The social media behemoth had
created a giant haystack. Moreover, the needle she was
searching for might not even live in the US; she'd noted
names like Pierre, Julio, Simone, and Lao-Chu in the
group. While it would be impossible to track all forty-
two thousand members, she assumed the FBI had culled
data from Facebook. At least run their names through
NCIC. And if they'd zeroed in on any suspects, their
names would have leaked by now. She would interview
the group admins, but what about the other 41,997
members?

She got up and started to pace. The seventeen alphabet
intelligence agencies used to be the only institutions that could
pull off a huge data search. But now, with companies like
Cambridge Analytica or that Israeli outfit, private organizations
with just a few people were data mining regularly. Maybe there
was a way for her to plug into one of them.

Georgia had a lot of work to do. But first, she needed Dena's
computer from the FBI. Or a flash drive with its contents. Jimmy
knew someone at the Bureau. He'd have the guy's contact info.

The meaty aroma of the cooked chicken in the kitchen wafted
over her. She checked the time. After five. She hadn't eaten since
the coffee and pastry she'd downed that morning. No wonder her
mouth was watering. She was setting the table in the kitchen
when Vanna, Charlie, and Jimmy came in together, shaking snow
off their boots.

Relief washed over her at Vanna's return, but she tried to be
casual. "Hi, guys. Did you drive home together?"

Vanna stared at her with dead eyes.

Georgia felt lost; how was she supposed to treat an angry
sixteen-year-old? Fortunately, Jimmy took over.

"We bumped into each other out front. Where were you,
honey?" he asked Vanna.

"Out." Vanna whirled around and headed to her room. "I'll go change Charlie. Is dinner ready? I'm starved."

Georgia and Jimmy exchanged glances. Jimmy held up his hand, a signal for Georgia to let it go.

She did. For now.

Chapter
Thirteen

The next morning, Georgia ran the engine with the defrost on high and scraped four inches of snow off her car. While she worked, she punched in the number of the FBI contact Jimmy had given her.

"LeJeune . . ." In the two syllables he spoke, Georgia could hear his Cajun lilt.

"Good morning. This is Georgia Davis. I'm an investigator, and Jimmy Saclarides gave me your number."

"Mornin', darlin'." Georgia rolled her eyes. "How is my favorite chief of police?"

"He sends his regards. The reason I'm calling is that I'm working for the family of Dena Baldwin, the young woman who—"

"I know who she was."

"Did you work on the case?"

"Not directly. But I am familiar with it."

Georgia stopped scraping. "I'd like to get Ms. Baldwin's computer. I've been told the case is closed as far as the FBI is concerned, or at least inactive. If the agency isn't willing to return the actual computer, perhaps you could copy the hard drive and give me that. I'm hoping you'll put in a good word with the agents involved."

"Not gonna happen," he said crisply. "It's an open criminal investigation, and her computer may contain important evidence for us."

"But from what I'm reading, the Bureau doesn't consider it a heater case. The guy who killed her is dead."

"What about the fact that you've been hired by the family? That would indicate to me that something *has* changed, *n'est-ce pas?*"

Christ. French too? Jimmy had warned her it could be a long shot, but she had her answer ready. "Nothing's changed. The family just wants to close the book on it, and this would help."

"Nice try, angel."

Despite the cold, Georgia felt her cheeks get hot.

"But since Chief Saclarides and I are such good friends, tell you what I'm gonna do. You get a court order or a Freedom of Information Act request approved, and I'll be the first to give you that flash drive."

"Oh, come on. That's going to take way too much time, and most of what's there will probably be redacted."

"Yeah. I've heard that."

Georgia couldn't understand why Jimmy respected LeJeune. He was acting like an asshole. She hated to pull rank, but she needed Dena's laptop. She didn't have a choice. "You do know who her father is, right? I can probably get it that way if I have to."

"Be my guest, *cher*," LeJeune said. "And when you do, it will give me great pleasure to meet the woman who wrapped Chief Saclarides around her little finger."

She stabbed the "end" button harder than she needed to. LeJeune was a cliché from one of her Dashiell Hammett novels, misogyny and all. Then again, if she was being honest with herself, she had to admit he was just doing his job.

Once the Toyota was free of ice, she climbed in and headed over to Zach Dolan's office in Northbrook, stopping at a bagel place on the way. He was outside walking Jeremiah when she pulled up. He stopped. Jeremiah barked.

She rolled down the window and held up the bag of bagels. "I brought breakfast."

Zach lifted his eyebrows. "Cream cheese too?"

She grinned. "And jelly."

He shushed Jeremiah and swept his arm in a welcoming gesture. "Then you may enter."

Inside Zach toasted a couple of bagels. He loaded his with both cream cheese and jelly and dug in. Halfway through he sighed with satisfaction. "They're fresh."

"Only the best for the Dolans."

He threw her a side-eyed glance. "And what impossible task brings you back so soon? With bribes?"

Georgia cleared her throat and explained what she had in mind. As she did, Zach's expression changed from contentment to surprise to disbelief.

"You want me to run forty-two thousand names through a background check?" He rubbed a hand against his forehead. "And I suppose you want it yesterday."

"That's about right."

"Impossible."

"Really?"

"I'd need a team of people. First to pry out the real names of the Facebook members. Then to run them through criminal background checks."

Georgia didn't blink. "A team is fine."

"Oh. We have money for this?"

"Whatever you need."

Zach whistled. Jeremiah, who'd been lying at Zach's feet, pricked up his ears. When he saw Zach with a bagel, he got up and pushed his head into Zach's lap. "See what you made me do?" He tore off a piece of bagel and handed it to the dog, who snapped it up, swallowed it in one bite, and drooled just enough that Zach gave him another piece.

"Somehow I think this is going to be one spoiled puppy," Georgia said dryly.

"Two points for the lady." Zach's forehead furrowed. "You know, I do have a friend who says he can match Facebook user names to their account IDs and real names."

"I didn't hear that," Georgia said.

"Hear what?" Zach grinned. "Although Facebook is pretty much a sieve these days since Cambridge Analytica stole all their data. You can find stuff all over the dark web."

"The timing is what's critical," Georgia said.

Zach nodded. "How fast do you need it?"

"You were right when you said yesterday."

"Can't do it, Georgia. Even if I divide up the list, say, between five or six guys, it's gonna take longer."

"How much longer?"

"For forty-two thousand names? A month at least. Maybe more."

Georgia bit her lip. "That's too long. What if you had ten or twelve guys working on it?"

"Even if I knew ten or twelve guys, it would still take a month." He shook his head. "And at least twelve grand."

"Can't you come up with some program that can automate the whole process?"

He didn't say anything.

"Okay. A month. We'll make it work. I have things to do in the meantime. Let me check with the client to make sure twelve is okay." She called Erica, who agreed to the fee, then turned back to Zach. "Can you flag the people with issues and send them over as you work your way through the list? At least that way, I could start in on a few."

"We could do that."

She smiled. "Great. Well then, what are you waiting for?"

Chapter Fourteen

Ruth Marriotti lived in a two-bedroom condo on the northwest side of Chicago, Georgia discovered when she visited that afternoon. It was a small eight-unit building on a one-way street off Lawrence. Inside everything was so clean and neat it reminded Georgia of the formerly spartan look of her own place.

Ruth herself was tall and gangly, with long curly brown hair tied back with a clip. Her hooded eyes gave her a suspicious cast when she smiled, which she was trying to do now. Above her forehead was a widow's peak. Her pallor added to her drawn look, which, given that she was still recovering from a bullet wound, wasn't surprising.

"I'm so glad you're out of the hospital," Georgia said.

Ruth nodded, clumsily manipulating a walker from the door toward a brown leather La-Z-Boy whose cushion was covered with a pillow.

"Can I help you get settled?" Georgia asked.

"I can handle it." She lowered herself into the chair with a soft thud, looked around, then focused on Georgia. "Sorry I can't offer you anything, but if you want something, be my guest." She gestured vaguely in the direction of what Georgia saw was the kitchen.

"I'm good. Thanks for seeing me. I'll try to be brief; you can't be very comfortable."

Ruth took her time arranging herself. Then: "I was hoping all the interviews and questions were over. Most of the press and social media already have what they need. I must have talked to fifty people, all told."

"I'm not with the press. I'm an investigator."

"You with the police? The FBI?"

Georgia sat on a sofa upholstered in an ugly pink, brown, and green floral print. A scuffed coffee table sat in front of it. "I'm working for the family."

"Dena's?"

"They hired me to dot the i's and cross the t's." Georgia waited. Ruth didn't say anything, just stared at her with those hooded eyes. Georgia had to remind herself she was the one asking questions. She pulled out a spiral-bound pad. "So, you were an administrator for the group. One of three besides Dena, right?"

"That's right."

Talkative, this one. "What does—did—an administrator do?"

Ruth arched her eyebrows. "What didn't I do? The group was huge. We really needed more admins, but we took what we could get. First off, we had to vet all the applicants. That took time. Then we had to monitor—"

"How did you vet them? And why?"

"We didn't have to at first. After a month or so, though, hundreds of people joined the group every day, and a lot of trolls slipped through."

"Trolls?"

Ruth waved an impatient hand. "You know, supporters of the president who gave us a hard time. Telling us they won and to deal with it. That we were special snowflakes." She shook her head. "Dena would cut them down to size, of course, but a few of them were pretty aggressive. So Dena and I decided we needed a way to keep them out."

"What do you mean 'cut them down to size'?"

"Dena didn't let any grass grow under her feet. She would call them assholes, kick them out, then block them for good measure. That's one of the reasons I liked working with her. She was direct. You always knew what she was thinking."

"Got it." Georgia smiled. Ruth seemed to loosen up. "So, how did you vet them?"

"It wasn't scientific. We'd check out their Facebook profiles. If there was some sign they were against the president or had doubts about the election or were a member of the Resistance, that was good enough. Sometimes if we weren't sure, we'd check their Facebook friends."

"Smart. What if they didn't meet the criteria?"

"We didn't let them in." She paused. "But that was just one of our jobs."

"What else did you do?"

"Well, we each had a shift where we kept an eye out on posts. If anyone advocated violence, that was an automatic removal. Oh, and there were no memes allowed. Dena thought they detracted from more substantial messages. Only articles. And editorials." Her lips tightened.

Georgia picked up on it. "You didn't agree?"

Ruth shrugged. "It wasn't that important."

Georgia sensed she was holding back. "Did you know Dena before the group started? Seeing as how you're both from Chicago."

She shook her head. "Just coincidence. Of course, she grew up on the North Shore."

"What about you?"

"Bolingbrook. The other side of the tracks." She snorted. "Well, not really. But you know what I mean. Buying this condo cost me almost more than I could manage."

Georgia tapped the pencil against her pad. She'd done a background check on Ruth before the interview; Ruth was telling the truth. She knew the answer to her next question but asked it anyway. "Where do you work? Your day job?"

"I'm a middle school math teacher." She paused. "But I'm on sick leave for another two weeks."

A moment of silence passed between them. Then Georgia said, "Big difference between the North Shore and Bolingbrook."

Another pause. "That's true, but when you believe in the same things, you can be friends with someone who's very different than you." Ruth shifted uneasily. Then she gazed at Georgia as if a thought had just occurred to her. "Why are you really here?"

"What do you mean?"

"Look, I worked with Dena over a year, and I learned there was always an ulterior motive where her family was concerned. What do they want?"

Georgia inclined her head. "I told you. I'm working for Mrs. Baldwin."

"Mrs. 'my daughter can do no wrong' Baldwin." Ruth scoffed.

"Is that what you thought of her?"

"Dena's family—how do I say it—are opportunists. They use people. Dena was that way herself sometimes."

"I thought she was guided by her politics."

"Mostly. But when she saw an opportunity, well . . ." She rubbed a finger underneath her nose.

"For example?"

Ruth released the lever on the La-Z-Boy and sat up, leaning to one side. "Well, for one thing, we needed a tech person early on. To help us manage the site. You know, set up private folders for files, articles, a calendar of events. Things like that. We asked for volunteers, and this guy offered to help. Everything was fine for about a month. Then I got a message from her saying the guy disappeared."

"Disappeared?"

"That's the way she made it sound. That he disappeared into thin air. But I kept asking questions. Eventually she admitted he claimed he was in love with her and wanted her to meet him in Vegas."

"What? Did they know each other?"

"No. Sounds crazy, right? Knowing Dena, my guess is that she probably flirted with him online and led him on so he would work for her." Ruth turned wistful. "And the thing was . . . I'm sure it worked. She could cast a spell over people when she wanted." A noise that could have been a laugh if she'd let it. "Look at me. I worked for her for free for a year. On top of my day job. And all I got out of it was a bullet in my ass."

Georgia shot her a look.

She ran a hand through her hair. "Well, okay. I was just being flip. I got the satisfaction of working against the monster in the Oval Office."

"Has it been worth it?"

"Absolutely." She leaned back again. "You know, after the guy 'disappeared,' I checked him out. Turns out he was married."

Georgia blinked. "Did Dena know?"

"She says she didn't. But pictures of his family were plastered all over his Facebook profile. He wasn't hiding it." She hesitated. "Not that it matters."

"What do you mean?"

"Dena already had a boyfriend."

"Is that so?"

"Like I said, she has . . . had . . . kind of a magnetic personality. She was hard to resist."

"Who was her boyfriend?"

"One of the other admins. Curt Dixon."

Georgia wrote it down, wondering if Ruth was jealous of Dena. From what she'd said, it was hard not to be.

"What about the tech guy who was married? What was his name?"

"Hand me my laptop. It's over there." She pointed to a table in the corner of the room.

Georgia retrieved it. Ruth busied herself, tapping keys, then said, "Willie Remson. He's on Facebook. From Maryland."

Georgia wrote it down. "Thanks. Whatever her motives, it sounds like Dena trusted you."

"We were close. But, like I said, that doesn't mean we always agreed. We'd have arguments about how the group should be run. I've worked so hard, it's hard not to feel proprietary, you know? And I'm sure Dena felt the same way. But we made it work."

"So who do you think killed Dena?"

Ruth looked startled. "Jarvis did, of course. An act of domestic terrorism. And when I'm recovered, you can bet your bottom dollar I'm going to get back at those right-wing assholes."

"What are you going to do?"

"Well, I'll probably run the group. That is, if Curt's okay with it."

"Curt Dixon."

"Right. DJ and Dena were the other admins, but—well—they're not here anymore."

Georgia nodded. "You said 'assholes.' Does that mean you think someone put him up to it?"

"You know, the police asked me the same question. I'll tell you what I told them. I didn't have anything to do with her death. Shit. I almost died myself. And—and I miss Dena. Things—things just aren't the same."

That wasn't the question Georgia had asked. She noted it down and changed the subject. "Did she have any enemies?"

"Oh yeah." Ruth rolled her eyes. "We all did."

"Such as?"

"Even though we were always on troll patrol, one or two slipped in. And, of course, she hated her father."

"Why?"

"She blamed him for her parents' divorce. Said he was cheating on her mother. Ironic, isn't it?"

Georgia let it go. "What about her brother?"

Ruth seemed to think about it. "She didn't talk about him much. Just things like 'we had dinner,' or 'we took Mom to a movie.' Oh. There were a few creepy phone calls, Dena said. But she didn't seem too bothered by them."

"Creepy phone calls?"

"Hang-ups, she said. I told the police about them."

Georgia made a note.

"I see. So what are your plans now?"

"Not sure. The group will go on as long as Cheetoman is in the White House. And, like I said, Curt and I will have to talk about who takes over." For the first time in their conversation, Ruth flashed Georgia what looked like a smile.

"One more question. Do the words 'beef jerky' bring anything to mind?"

"Huh?"

"Beef jerky."

A faintly irritated expression flitted across Ruth's face. "Not a damn thing. Hate the stuff."

Chapter Fifteen

Georgia made her exit a few minutes later and started back to Evanston. Ruth wasn't the most likeable person: she was bitter at times, even catty. Georgia wondered if she was lonely—she hadn't seen any get-well cards or flowers. She claimed she liked Dena, but she was judgmental about Dena's personal life and the way she ran the group. Was Ruth a person who always found fault with everything? Or was she envious of Dena's success? Maybe she had a crush on Dena, platonic or otherwise, that Dena did not reciprocate. She was ambitious too, based on her desire to take over the group.

Georgia glanced out the Toyota's window. A guy in a BMW sedan zoomed past her in the wrong lane. He gave her the finger as he passed. She almost replied in like fashion but at the last second managed not to.

A news clip of Dena's death flashed through her mind. Anyone who hired a killer had to have guts. And a burning hatred. Was Ruth capable of that much passion? Where would she have met Jarvis, anyway? Georgia made a note to cross-check Ruth's background with Jarvis's to see if there were any intersections.

Driving north, she passed her old gym in Andersonville. On the second floor of a small building, it used to be an overheated, smelly place to which only serious lifters flocked. But it had recently changed owners, and they'd remodeled. Now, judging from the custom lights hanging from the ceiling, it was suspiciously trendy. She'd found another overheated, smelly gym.

At the next red light a pang of worry struck her. What if she came up with nothing? She'd only been a PI four years; she had a lot more to learn. That meant investigating the way she'd learned to as a cop. Start with family members, widen out to friends, significant others, then work and professional associates. But that was the problem. With forty-two thousand people in the ResistanceUSA group, she could spend the rest of her life running down suspects. She hoped she was up to it.

· · ·

She stopped in at the Jewel in Evanston and asked where the beef jerky was. The checkout girl pointed to another aisle. Georgia scanned the cashier's lane first. There were three different brands. One looked like the kind of stale, cardboard meat strips from her childhood, but two had labels promising a softer, fresher chew. She picked up Applewood Smoked Beef. Looked interesting. She read the front and the back of the package, and dropped it into the handbasket she'd picked up at the front door. She grabbed a Smoked BBQ as well. Then she headed to the aisle, where there were half a dozen additional brands and flavors and chose several more. Back in the car, she popped one of the applewood strips in her mouth.

Some people loved the peppery, tough texture, but Georgia wasn't "partial to it," as her mother used to say. Beef jerky reminded her of chewing tobacco, truckers, and country music. She knew she was stereotyping, but it was a part of Jarvis's world. "Find the beef jerky?" She took another bite. The email was too unusual to ignore. What did it have to do with Dena's murder?

Back home, Vanna was in the kitchen, her papers spread over the small table. She was sketching a logo for an imaginary company the teacher had invented for a homework project. Charlie was in his baby seat, swatting a plastic giraffe and monkey that hung above his head.

"Hey, sweetheart," Georgia smiled.

"Hi." Vanna's voice was soft and bright, their spat from the other night apparently forgotten.

"Here's a snack." Georgia dug out one of the packs of jerky and tossed it to her.

Vanna picked it up with a puzzled look.

"You don't like it?"

Vanna screwed up her face as only a teenager could. "Some new fad?" she said disdainfully.

Georgia shook her head. "It might be related to a case I'm working on."

"Oh." Vanna tossed the beef jerky on the table and went back to work.

Charlie cooed at Georgia with the contented "I've just been fed" babble that came with a full stomach. *If only life was this good all the time.* Georgia leaned over and kissed them both on the tops of their heads.

Chapter
Sixteen

Washington, DC

Vic Summerfield climbed into a cab with Carl Baldwin. Their office was only a short hop away. After Carl's appearance at the health club, Vic showered and dressed in a hurry. His boss often went nuclear, attacking everyone, Vic included, for imaginary betrayals. But Vic had been working for Baldwin eighteen months now, and he'd learned not to take it seriously. His rants were frequent and furious, but they subsided quickly. Vic, who harbored a grudge for years, was often surprised at the ease with which Baldwin embraced someone he'd disparaged only hours before. It took immense self-control to pull that off, Vic thought. Which made it even more bizarre that Carl allowed himself to lose control in the first place. A fascinating, dangerous paradox of a man.

And yet, Baldwin's outbursts made Vic wonder if the lure of money—and there was lots of it in lobbying—was worth the drama. Assuming you had the right clients and contacts, lobbyists could rake in enormous amounts of dough. Carl Baldwin had both, and his contacts stretched into the Oval Office and beyond. At twenty-nine Vic was making more money than he'd ever imagined. He'd bought a town house just outside Georgetown, a Benz S-Class, and still had enough to send money to his parents.

Riding through Rock Creek Parkway, Vic counted four joggers and three bikers. Back home in South Dakota, February was locked in the relentless grip of winter. Hell did freeze over in the Black Hills, his father would laugh. In DC, though, a temperate climate permitted outdoor activities all year. Another benefit.

"Why didn't you get back to me last night?" Baldwin's tone was accusatory.

Vic looked over, frowned. "I did."

Baldwin shook his head. "I never got a voice mail."

"I met Dimitri at the embassy cocktail party. I couldn't use my phone. I sent you a text."

Baldwin's eyes narrowed as if he wasn't sure whether to believe him. That went on the negative ledger. Baldwin demanded abject loyalty from those around him, but he could turn on you in an instant. Even after eighteen months. This time, though, Vic gave Baldwin some slack. His daughter had been gunned down in a horrific terror attack a few weeks earlier. She'd been his favorite child, though they hadn't spoken in years, and he'd still kept tabs on her. In fact, part of Vic's job was to monitor the ResistanceUSA group and report back on Dena's activities.

"So, are they fucking me over?" Baldwin asked. "The Russians?"

Vic glanced at the cabbie before answering, but the driver, bobbing his head to some unheard music streaming through his headphones, seemed oblivious to their conversation. Still, Baldwin should have been more cautious. Was he losing it?

Vic lowered his voice. "Dimitri said he would run it by the ambassador and get back to me."

"That's what he said the last time."

"I know."

"That means the FSB pricks are running the show."

Vic nodded. Their steady stream of "clients," sanctioned by the FSB, the successor to the Russian spy agency KGB, were oligarchs from Russia and its former satellites. They had made Baldwin's career. Sure, they wanted a financial break here, a tax break or favor—usually a lucrative one—there. But everyone had the right to ask. That was the essence of lobbying, Baldwin had taught Vic. If the client's request had merit—and occasionally it did—it was a win-win for everyone. Still, the FSB was Putin's eyes and ears, and its agents kept watch over all the oligarchs' dealings. Nothing happened without Putin's tacit or explicit say-so. And, apparently, he was saying no.

The cab wound uphill on the Massachusetts Avenue exit and promptly got stuck in traffic. Why was this exit always backed up? Vic wondered. It didn't matter what time of day it was; he always had to wait through two red lights.

Recently, though, the Russians' businesses, and consequently Carl's business, were suffering. The weak American president, unable to lift Congress's economic sanctions, had stymied the exchange of illicit financial favors. Times were tough on both sides of the pond. The problem was that the FSB and the oligarchs conveniently ignored reality, demanding more from Baldwin. And Carl didn't have enough intel or profitable deals for them. The vise was tightening—inexorably.

"After all I've done for those fuckers." Baldwin drummed his fingers on the rear-seat armrest.

The cab pulled up to Baldwin's house, a tan brick mansion with white columns on Wyoming Avenue in Kalorama. A street, Baldwin never failed to remind Vic, on which Woodrow Wilson once lived. With William Taft on the next block. As if he expected Vic would someday point out to his children that Carl Baldwin had lived here too.

Inside, a large central foyer with marble flooring was flanked by formal living and dining rooms. White columns separated those rooms from the rest of the first floor, which had been remodeled to house Baldwin and Associates. Only a few minutes from the K Street corridor and the Hill, the house was a shrewd buy. Kalorama offered much more for your money than Georgetown,

Baldwin proclaimed, implying the congressmen, journalists, and VIPs who bought on N Street were fools.

"Well, I'm not waiting around for the SOBs," Carl said. "We're still good with the arms deal. And fracking legislation. Let's move those forward. Set up a lunch with the chairman of Energy and Commerce at the Four Seasons."

Vic paid the fare, and the two men exited the cab. The cabbie was still jabbering away in an unknown language on his cell.

Chapter
Seventeen

Seven Months Before the Demonstration

Dena sat behind her desk in the sprawling digs of the Baldwin Foundation in Chicago, located in River North. Her mother, Erica, had spared no expense on the office décor. Sleek cherry furniture was accented by old Pueblo tapestries, polished hardwood floors, and the ubiquitous bright white HVAC pipes that looped around the ceiling. LaSalle Street exec meets hippie Lakeview. Just Dena's style. *Chicago* magazine had done a spread on it.

But Dena felt as if she was trapped in a hamster wheel. She never enjoyed the work and disliked coming downtown, preferring to conduct business from her condo in Lincoln Square. Hell, since the election, she'd lost interest in foundation business altogether. At first her plan was to hunker down and wait for the nightmare of an illegitimate president to fade. But then she started ResistanceUSA. Its explosive growth, at ten thousand after only three weeks and now 42,000, was proof she'd tapped into something huge. Her time would be better spent managing and expanding the group. Who knew where it could lead?

But today was a meeting with the foundation accountant, so

she'd had to change from shorts to business casual and make her way to the River West building. She absentmindedly flipped her long braid and tried to focus on the documents in front of her, but they didn't make a lot of sense. Her father had taught her how to read a P&L years earlier, along with the racing form. He laughed when she admitted she wasn't sure which she liked best.

"The apple don't fall far from the tree," he said.

"Doesn't, Dad. The word is 'doesn't.'"

"Who the hell cares, baby?"

She would frown at him in mock annoyance. Back then. Before.

Now her gaze slid to a framed photograph taken five years earlier of them on her father's sloop on Lake Michigan. She was hoisting the mainsail in her favorite blue bikini. Her father saluted as she did, as if she was raising the American flag. A hot Chicago sun beat down, and puffy white clouds in the distance signaled their approval. The world was good. It was a sweet moment, one of the few they'd shared. She'd thought many times that she should get rid of the photo. She didn't want the reminder. He was the enemy now.

She turned back to the financials. She didn't quite grasp things, for example, how cumulative depreciation affected income. Hell, she wasn't even sure what depreciation was. But Jeffrey would be studying the same documents; he'd catch any anomalies. He was good that way. In fact, she was glad when her brother gave up his acting career and came home to work at the foundation. Even more now that her own interest had waned. He seemed to be making up for lost time.

She spun in her chair and peered out the window. The noontime July sun bounced off the sparkling water of the Chicago River, making everything look dazzlingly clean. Jeffrey's acting career in LA had been a cover, a carefully constructed lie held close within the family. The truth was Jeffrey had been in prison. He'd majored in opioids, then heroin at Indiana, flunked out, and moved to LA. Half a dozen busts for possession with intent to sell had used up whatever clout came with the Baldwin name, and the family could no longer keep him out of prison. Sentenced to two years in a medium-security facility, Jeffrey had officially become the black sheep of the family, conspicuously expelled and ignored by their father.

The Chicago media had discovered Jeffrey's crimes, and to this day the family hated the reporter and newspaper that published the story. At the time, the coverage emphasized how wealth and prominence couldn't shield a "bad seed." Now, of course, the media was back, this time prowling for stories about Dena's Resistance activities. She had learned to be cautious.

But their mother never gave up on her son. Erica made the awkward visits to the California state prison in Solano, always optimistic and supportive. She encouraged Jeffrey to get his associate's degree online. He studied finance and did so well that his last job in the prison before parole was "inventory manager" for the warden, keeping track of the prison's kitchen and job-training equipment. Kind of a junior bookkeeper, he'd explained in a letter.

The intercom buzzed and snapped Dena back to the present.

She tapped a key on her phone "Yes. Lori?"

"Jeffrey and Iris are here."

Iris kept the books for the foundation. "Show them in."

A moment later Iris came in. Petite and blond, she just missed being pretty—a forehead too high, eyes too small, a chin too pointy. Jeffrey followed, his face pinched with worry. They took their time seating themselves in the chairs opposite Dena. Once settled, they glanced at each other. Jeffrey nodded, giving Iris the okay.

Iris cleared her throat. "We have a problem."

• • •

Dena's cell chirped that night just as she and Curt were drifting off. Dena opened an eye. A doobie lay in an ashtray, two empty bottles of beer flanking it. Behind the bottles lay her cell, its screen flashing.

"Don't get it," Curt groaned.

"I have to." Dena groped for the cell and knocked over one of the bottles. "Shit." She pulled the phone toward her. "Hello?"

There was silence.

"Hello?"

Nothing.

"I hope you never get sucked off again, you asswipe. Stop calling me."

The connection dropped. Dena silenced the phone and slammed it back on the bedside table.

Curt rolled over. "Again?"

She grunted.

"That's the third time this month. You need a new number. Unlisted this time."

"That doesn't stop anyone these days."

He propped his head on an elbow and tried to shrug.

She was quiet for a moment. "But you're right. It's time I did something. I've had it. I'm going to find out who it is."

Curt rubbed her back. "You okay?"

"Everyone wants a piece of me."

"What do you mean?"

She sighed. "Today at the foundation . . ."

"What happened?"

"I can't go into it. Family business. But I don't know how much longer I can do two full-time jobs. Every time I turn around, someone wants me to do something for them."

"Ahh." He took a lock of her hair and twirled it in his fingers. "But not as much as me."

She turned onto her side. "Is that right?" She gave him a sly smile.

He took her smile as an invitation and scooted closer. She didn't resist. He curled his arm around her and began to massage her butt.

She arched toward him and slowly circled her hips.

He lowered his voice to a whisper. "That's right. Give it to me, Dena."

She kept rolling her hips, establishing a rhythm that Curt mimicked with pretend thrusts. On their sides, only inches apart, their bodies didn't touch. But their eyes were locked on each other. Dena's pulse sped up, and her body tightened, vibrating like a tuning fork. She kept rocking and reached for him. He was hard. She wanted him. Wanted him to take her. To drive everything out of her mind except the feel of him inside her. He clearly felt the same way because he suddenly, violently rolled her onto her back and shoved himself in deep.

Chapter Eighteen

The Present

The next day Georgia inserted a flash drive containing the contents of Dena's laptop into her own computer. Dena's data was now in her possession. She'd had a brainstorm the night before and called Jeffrey Baldwin.

"Hi, Jeffrey. Georgia Davis."

"Yes . . ." He didn't sound enthusiastic to hear from her.

"Did Dena have a computer at the foundation? Or did she bring her personal laptop to the office?"

"She had an iMac, just like me."

"Really?"

"Mom went all out when she set up the foundation."

"Would you know if it was synced to her laptop or iCloud?"

"It was. Mine is too."

Georgia could hardly suppress her elation. "Can I come down first thing in the morning and make a copy of her hard drive?"

"Sure, but if you don't mind, let me make the copy. I'll have a flash drive ready for you."

Georgia wasn't sure why he'd want to make it himself, but she couldn't think of a reason why he shouldn't. "What time do you get in?"

"I'm there by eight."

"Okay. I'll be there by eight too."

She smiled. Score one for the PI. Still, she couldn't help but wonder why LeJeune had been so brusque with her yesterday. Part of it was likely an attempt to make her feel like a second-class citizen because she was a PI with no official standing. But was part of it—even a little bit—because she was a woman?

Whatever it was, she forced herself to let it go and booted up her laptop. Vanna had taken Charlie to a Moms and Tots class, and a few solid hours examining Dena's data might reveal some authentic clues.

Her first surprise was the absence of a password restricting access to the laptop. Georgia had assumed Dena was a sophisticated user. She had to know about all the security breaches that had exposed the information of millions of Americans. Did she think she was immune? That she had special dispensation from the hacker gods? Georgia sighed. Generation Z was supposed to be tech savvy. Was Dena playing with fire? Or did the FBI disable her password for easier access?

Georgia clicked on Chrome, brought up all of Dena's other passwords, and printed out the list. Then she logged into Dena's Facebook account. Twenty-five hundred twenty-two unread messages. Christ. It would take days to go through them. As the group's founder, Dena was also one of the administrators. She'd probably configured the settings so that in addition to herself, the other administrators got every message and comment generated by the group so they could monitor and approve them before they posted.

She was scrolling through the subject lines of the messages when she realized Ruth had already given her a lead. The guy who said he was in love with Dena. Georgia checked her notes. Willie Remson. From Maryland. She typed his name into the search box, which took her to his Facebook page. The page was public, which meant anyone could see his profile. The first thing Georgia noticed was dozens of family pictures. She clicked through them: an attractive dark-haired woman and two towheaded kids at a swimming pool. The same group standing in front of a minivan, the kids dressed for Halloween. Was Remson trying to prove what a family man he was?

She went back to Dena's messages and scrolled to the first one from Remson. They started in February and ran through May. The early notes were friendly but distant. Remson asked about the group, told her he was experienced in social media, and offered to help. Within a couple of weeks, however, Dena started to ask him provocative questions and leave comments with double entendres. Flirtatious. It only took him a minute to reply in equal fashion. Georgia leaned forward. Dena must have checked out his Facebook page and seen the family pictures. But she still went after him.

Which was Georgia's second surprise. According to Ruth, Dena had claimed Remson initiated the relationship. But Dena seemed to be the one leading him on. If Ruth was wrong, and it was Dena who pursued the relationship, knowing he was a married man, why tell Ruth something different? In fact, why tell Ruth at all? People usually kept an affair secret. Especially since Dena was already in a relationship with Curt. It didn't make sense.

The following week the message chain grew more personal and erotic. Both made pronouncements about the lack of trust and love in their lives, pronouncements they claimed they had never told anyone until now. Within a week they talked about meeting in a neutral city like Vegas.

Georgia blew out a breath. Why was Dena toying with this man, a married man at that? And then revealing it to another member of the group?

She read on. Dena had written:

Now, go with me on this. Imagine we meet for the first time in the lobby of a hotel on the strip. We decide to share a drink at the bar. Even though it's mid-afternoon, the bar is dim and quiet. I order a Chardonnay. You have a draft. Both of us check out the other. I decide you're hot. I tell you so. Then you—

Then she stopped. *Your turn now . . .*

Remson picked up on it right away. *I can see your breasts through your T-shirt. You're not wearing a bra. I want to touch your nipples.*

Dena wrote back. *I want you to. And I want to touch you too. I want you to want me.*

The conversation grew pornographic. When Georgia came across a message that began with *I lick . . .* , she got up from her computer for a glass of water.

As she swilled it down, she found it curious that they'd never met. Ruth said Dena claimed Remson "disappeared" when Dena discovered he was married. But Dena had to know he was married when she checked his Facebook page.

She went on. By November they pledged undying love for each other. But there was no mention of him being married. It appeared as if Dena assumed he was single.

The last message was from Remson. Apparently two days had passed without any word from Dena. He sounded worried. *Why haven't you written? What's going on? Are you sick? Please let me know you're okay.*

Georgia sensed his distress. To go from the height of passion to brooding silence was a blow, even in a virtual relationship. But it wasn't unusual. Anyone who played the online love affair game knew that a partner could disappear when they grew bored.

Dena never responded.

Not surprisingly, Remson's subsequent posts turned nasty. She'd been leading him on. How dare she? What about the hotel on the strip? Didn't that mean anything? Was her come-on just a game? Even though their entire relationship had been a fairy tale, he sounded like a genuinely jilted lover.

Then his messages took a different turn. With still no word from Dena, Remson began to make threats. *You can't do this. And don't tell me you didn't know I was married. All you had to do was look at my Facebook page. It's all there. You're a cunt. You'll pay for this.*

Georgia started to pace. People who created relationships—no—affairs out of whole cloth were crazy. How could they pledge undying love to someone they'd never met? And then hurl threats when the fantasy didn't play out? Georgia was grateful to have found Jimmy. She stopped pacing and sat down again. This time she pulled up Dena's Facebook block list. There were hundreds of names, mostly trolls, Georgia assumed. She scrolled down the list. There it was. WRemson. He didn't "disappear" like she'd told Ruth. She'd *made* him disappear. The question was why. Dena clearly knew he was married. The spray of photos on his Facebook profile was proof. Unless—what if the photos were posted after Dena was killed? She quickly checked his Facebook page. No. They'd gone up several years ago.

She stood up. Georgia didn't "do" conspiracy theories. The most logical explanation was that Remson was just a guy swept up in the illusion of adultery, like every other man on the planet. So why the threats? Retribution?

There was something else, too. Based on what she'd been able to uncover, the FBI had to know about Remson. She wished she had an inside source who could fill her in; without it, she would be forced to duplicate the FBI's work. She tapped a finger on the mouse. One thing was sure. Willie Remson had just shot up to the top of her suspect list.

Chapter Nineteen

It was after five when Georgia closed the lid of her laptop. Vanna and Charlie would be home soon. She should think about dinner. When she opened the refrigerator, the rancid, acrid odor of sour milk overwhelmed her. She pulled out a mixing bowl loosely covered with tin foil. Damn Vanna. She was expressing milk right and left; didn't she know it had to go into bottles right away? Now it was ruined. Georgia dumped it out, ran the garbage disposal, and spritzed the air with room deodorizer.

She pulled out stewing meat from the freezer and started peeling potatoes. Were Remson and Jarvis, Dena's killer, connected? She'd run a background check on Remson last night. He was from New England and moved to DC for law school at George Washington. No connection to Iowa or Rogers Park. Still, it was possible they'd met at some random bar if Remson had come to Chicago or Jarvis had gone to DC. Hell, they could have met anywhere.

She threw the meat into the microwave and pushed auto defrost: "1.0 lb." Something else was bothering her. The FBI had access to the same data as Georgia. Dena's Facebook history was an obvious place to look for suspects. If Remson's threats were any indication, he was a dangerous guy. The Bureau had to be all over him. They must have gone over every detail of his life. Surveilled him. Maybe interviewed him.

But his name never came up as a suspect. Of course, suspects didn't always surface in the media. But for something as big as Dena's murder—with CNN and every other media outlet crawling all over it—there would have been a leak. Someone would have reported Remson's name. It wasn't adding up. She checked his current location. Chevy Chase, Maryland. Just outside DC. Dena's father was in DC too.

She took the meat out of the microwave and started separating the little cubes. Halfway through she realized she didn't have any onions. Or carrots. She left everything on the counter, threw on her coat, and headed out.

Twenty minutes later she tossed the grocery bag of carrots, onions, and milk on the passenger seat. The only way to get a handle on Remson would be to find him and ask him about Dena herself. She thought about calling Paul Kelly to tell him this case was too complicated for one person. She needed a team of investigators in both Chicago and Washington. For the first time since going out on her own she regretted leaving the police department. They had resources.

On the way home she blasted the heat, but the Corolla was slow to warm up, a danger in this frigid weather. She should take it into the shop tomorrow to make sure Vanna wouldn't have any trouble when she drove it to class. Checking the side-view mirror, she noticed a man on a motorcycle behind her. His helmet and visor concealed his face, but he was bulked up in a jacket with plenty of padding. Bikers were rare on Chicago's North Shore in winter, and today wasn't mild.

She veered off Green Bay Road onto Asbury. The biker did too. That was unusual. Just to be safe, she drove farther south than she needed to and turned left on Church. So did the biker. Damn it, she was being tailed. The light at Church and Green Bay was yellow, but instead of stopping she gunned the engine as the light turned red. Horns blasted, but the motorcycle was forced to stop.

Georgia kept going, circling randomly around Evanston streets until she was sure she'd lost the biker. Who the hell was he?

Back on her street, parking was at a premium; she finally found a space two blocks away. She made her way back to her building and shuffled up the stairs. As she fished out her key, she heard two female voices. Probably a student from one of Vanna's classes. She stopped digging and listened. The other voice was familiar.

Georgia kicked off her boots, slipped the key in the lock, and opened her door. There was no sign of Vanna, but a woman sat on the sofa bouncing Charlie on her knee. Older. Late fifties. Blond. Attractive. She prattled on to Charlie in baby talk, then paused, grinning, waiting for him to babble back. As Georgia approached, Charlie turned toward her. His expression brightened, and his little body squirmed in pleasure the way babies do when they recognize someone.

The woman looked over at Georgia. Her chatter stopped and her smile disappeared. Georgia stared back. Her mouth dropped open. Silence swallowed the room. Charlie sensed something and stiffened. Then Vanna called out from the kitchen. "You're really quiet all of a sudden, Mom. Is everything okay?"

Chapter Twenty

"Hello, Georgia," the woman said.

Vanna hurried out of the kitchen and lifted Charlie off her mother's lap. Georgia turned to her sister, but she refused to make eye contact.

"What's going on?" Georgia managed to croak.

Vanna swallowed. Charlie whined.

"Don't you recognize me, sweet pea?"

Georgia wanted to flee, to run as far as she could as fast as she could. But her body wouldn't cooperate. She felt paralyzed.

The woman caught Georgia's icy reaction. Her brows drew together, revealing deep lines on her forehead that indicated worry was her go-to expression. She gazed at Vanna, then at Georgia, then sank back on the sofa, less sure of herself. "Vanna called me a few days ago. I—I hadn't heard a word from her in over a year. I didn't know where she was, if she was even alive."

"That's about par for the course, isn't it?"

The woman's lips tightened. Georgia expected her to say more, but she reined herself in.

"Is this true, Vanna?" Georgia asked. "Did you call her?"

Vanna's face paled and grew pinched. A terrified expression

came over her. "We were fighting. You and Jimmy were gonna leave me. I didn't know what to do."

Georgia squeezed her eyes shut. She'd been sucker punched. By her own sister. "So you decided you'd show me and bring Mommy in to take my place."

"No, that's not—"

"Sure it is, Savannah. That's what we girls do. Break each other's heart and run away before the other does it to us. After all, we learned from a pro. JoBeth Crawford. Our mother." She spit out the word.

"It's different now," their mother said. "Everything's changed."

"You bet it's different. We're grown up now. And you're old. You probably figure you can mooch off us, instead of the men who used to give you the once-over. How many have there been, *Mother*?" She emphasized the word. "Four? Seven? Ten? Oh yeah. Are there any other kids you want to tell us about? Brothers or sisters you walked out on without saying good-bye?"

"Georgia . . ."

"No. Keep your mouth shut. This is *my* home. And you can't waltz back into my life after twenty-five years as if you've only been away for a week. Did you think I'd be happy to see you? A mother who never even sent me a fucking birthday card? Or made a phone call? Sent an email? Or a text for twenty-five years?"

At least JoBeth was embarrassed enough to hang her head.

"Georgia," Vanna cut in. "I needed her." It sounded like a plea.

"Because I wasn't enough." It was a statement, not a question.

"You were going to leave me."

"You know I would never do that." Georgia turned to her mother. "You have twenty-four hours to get out of my apartment. And you too," she said to Vanna, "if you go with her. But if you do, I never want to hear from you again. Do you understand? Never."

She was still clutching the paper bag from the grocery store. She looked at it as if it was suddenly a strange, unfamiliar object. "Here. You finish making dinner, JoBeth. You know how to make stew, right? Meat. Potatoes. Carrots. Onions. It's more than you ever did for me."

She dropped the bag, spun around, and stomped out.

. . .

She was driving aimlessly around the North Shore when the tears came. Long-overdue tears. The tears of a little girl whose mother didn't want her. Tears of a daughter whose father abused her because she wasn't her mother. Tears from a job she loved but ultimately lost. And a relationship gone bad. She careened around streets and plowed through alleys, not knowing or caring where she was. She didn't know how long she'd been driving when she passed the lake, a dark, stolid reminder that the universe would never trouble itself about little Georgia Davis. The universe would go on whether she was happy or sad, alive or dead. She wasn't on its radar. Would never be.

The last time she'd felt so desperate she'd crashed into a concrete viaduct near Greektown and nearly died. She was drunk then, and the shame of where life had taken her was unmanageable. She was close this time too.

She called Jimmy. Two hours later she met him at the apartment he'd rented from Luke. Hollow and hoarse, she fell into his arms, sobbing. He stroked her hair until she finally fell asleep.

Chapter
Twenty-One

The Next Day

The only green at the Green Mill Lounge was in the letters of the neon sign outside. Otherwise, the faded brown walls, dimly lit booths, and white-tablecloth-covered tables reminded Georgia of a woman trying to hide her age. There was a reason for that. The bar, first known as Pop Morse's Roadhouse but renamed the Green Mill in honor of the Red Mill, or Moulin Rouge, in Paris, opened in 1907 on Broadway. Over its hundred-year lifespan, it had become an iconic landmark for serious jazz as well as a hangout for mobsters. Al Capone had his own booth with a view of two doors so that he could, if necessary, make a speedy exit through one when the cops raced in the other.

There was also a secret escape route in the basement that led through a series of tunnels, originally built to ferry coal. During Prohibition not only were the tunnels used to flee the cops, but they also stored alcohol and provided a place for poker and craps.

Georgia waited in a booth along the sidewall for Curt Dixon, Dena Baldwin's boyfriend. Drawing on all her Darwinian self-will, she'd managed to paste on an expression of composure and competence. She sipped a Diet Coke with lemon.

The front door swung open, and Curt entered. She recognized him from TV. He was the shaggy bear. He'd come through the ordeal without a scratch and was the unofficial group spokesperson after the event. Georgia raised her hand and waved. He saw her and ventured over.

"Hi," he said. "You're Georgia."

She tried to smile, but she knew it wasn't much of one. " Grab a draft if you want. On me."

He went up to the bar and came back with a tall glass stein.

"You hungry?" she asked.

He shook his head and sat across from her. "I thought all the interviews and press were over."

"I'm a private investigator. Dena's family hired me."

His eyebrows shot up. "Is that so?"

She took a sip of her drink. "Does that surprise you?"

"Not at all. I'm kind of wondering why it didn't happen sooner."

"Because . . ."

"Well, mostly because of the calls."

"Calls?" Ruth had mentioned calls, Georgia remembered.

"Dena would get these strange calls. Usually at night. No one spoke. But they'd hang for a while. Then disconnect when she pressed them."

"Press them?"

"You know, ask who was there and what they wanted."

"Didn't you star-sixty-nine them afterwards?"

"We tried once or twice. But we got a message that said the number was unavailable."

"They worried you."

He nodded. "At first they were just once every few weeks, but right before the demonstration we got calls two or three times a week."

"Was Dena worried?"

He picked up his mug. "You know—well, you didn't

know—Dena. She acted pretty casual. Eventually, though, she called the cops."

"Did they ever find out who was making the calls?"

"Never heard."

"Do you have any idea who it was?"

"If I did, I would have torn them to pieces."

"Easy, boy," Georgia wanted to say. "You cared for her."

He set the stein down, and when he looked at Georgia, she saw his pain. "She was—she was a handful, but she was *my* handful."

Proprietary. "Tell me."

"She was smart, dedicated. Charismatic. Loyal. A natural leader. She really cared about the Resistance. And the group. Oh, and she was a born speaker. She could bring a crowd to their feet in thirty seconds. Frame everything that happened over the past year in a few sentences."

Curt Dixon was clearly smitten. "How did you meet her?"

"I was living in Tennessee, but I—"

"You're from the South? You don't have an accent."

"Dena didn't like it."

Georgia had been born in Georgia but moved to Chicago when she was just a toddler. Still, it wasn't easy to ditch an accent.

"Anyway, once I found the group, I volunteered to help with admin, mostly moderating posts. I created some graphics too. It got so that we were in touch every day. We talked—messaged—about everything. A week or so later she asked me to come up and help her scout locations for a possible demonstration." The lines on his forehead smoothed out, and a faraway look came over him. "I never left."

Georgia thought about Dena's online relationship with Remson. Did she come on to Dixon the same way? Were the men two of many? "Did she feel the same way?"

He hesitated. "Dena was a worrier, and she always found something to worry about. She tried to hide it, you know. She pretended to be the competent, always-in-charge leader. And she could be bossy. Even arrogant. But I knew that underneath that tough exterior was a sweet emotional marshmallow. She was vulnerable. I was there to support her. Ease her mind. Night and day."

Was that the reality of the relationship or just wishful thinking? "And did you?"

"I did the best I could." He swallowed, and his Adam's apple bobbed. He took a swig of beer to mask it.

"What kinds of things did she worry about?"

"You name it. The group, the demonstration, safety, permits, security, the money to run everything, all that."

"What about personal things? Like her family?"

Curt sat back. He went quiet. Then, "Well, she was worried about the family foundation. Do you know about it?"

Georgia shook her head. "Not much."

"She said there was a problem. But she wouldn't tell me what it was. Said it was family business."

No big surprise there, with her brother a public embarrassment. But Georgia noted it down. "What about enemies? Did she have any?"

"Not really."

He couldn't be that naïve. "Come on, Curt. A woman who stakes out radical political positions like Dena had to alienate some people."

"Well, of course. We had trolls. And bots," he said. "I thought you meant personal enemies. People she knew."

Georgia eyed him carefully. Was he holding back? "Did she ever talk about anyone on Facebook, like, for example, other members of the group? For better or worse?"

"Well, we talked about the admins sometimes. We were sort of the nucleus of the group."

"You, Dena, Ruth . . . "

"And DJ."

DJ Grabiner had been killed in the attack. "Tell me about DJ."

"He was from New York. But the most laid-back New Yorker I've ever met. He was a musician. Played the flute and keyboard.

Part of a band for a while." Dixon paused. "But then, after the election, he got political. Like a lot of other people."

Georgia had run a background check on Grabiner. Dixon was telling the truth. "So. Back to Dena's enemies. Anyone else you can recall?"

He shook his head and took another swig of beer.

So Dena hadn't told him about Remson. Georgia wasn't surprised. And Ruth, who knew about Remson, hadn't said anything to Dixon either. Interesting.

"Hold on. I do know she was spitting mad at her father. I sometimes . . ." He bit his lip.

"What?"

"I sometimes wondered if her rage at the president was tangled up in her relationship with her father. You know."

It was well-known that the current president had numerous affairs while he was married. Many accused him of being a sexual predator. "Because of the women?"

Dixon nodded.

Erica had mentioned affairs as well, Georgia recalled. "What about dissension in the ranks? Within the group?"

He hesitated, took a pull on his draft. "Dena was a strong leader. And I guess there's always someone who thinks they can do things better."

"Someone in the group?"

He looked up, as if thinking about it. "No, not really. I mean, we quarreled about little things. But we all knew we couldn't have come as far as we did without her."

"Who quarreled the most?"

"If you're asking if someone had a grudge against Dena, I don't think anyone did. I mean, we would sometimes discuss whether something was the best solution, the best plan. But nothing major. At least not to my knowledge."

"What about Ruth Marriotti?"

"Ruth? No way. She and Dena were close." He squinted and leaned back against the booth. "Why? Do you think Ruth was—

No. No way. On the day of the protest, Ruth was panicked when Dena was a few minutes late. She thought she'd have to speak to the group instead. She looked like she wanted to throw up."

Georgia picked up her glass, mostly empty now, and sloshed the crushed ice around. The soft, crunchy sound was satisfying. "Does the name Willie Remson mean anything to you?"

He thought about it, shook his head. "Should it?"

She gazed at him, trying to suss out the truth. "No." She put the glass down. "So, what are you going to do now?"

"Go back to Tennessee, I guess. Try to pick up my life."

"Did you send an email to Erica Baldwin?" Georgia asked.

"No."

"Do you like beef jerky?"

He straightened up in a hurry. "What?"

Georgia repeated the question.

"What a weird question."

"Why is it weird?"

"I dunno. Going from email to beef jerky? I don't get it."

Georgia watched him carefully. "When was the last time you ate or thought about beef jerky?"

"Never . . . Well, I don't remember."

She didn't see a tell. He was probably being honest. She asked for his number in case she had more questions, wrote it down, and gave him one of her cards, in case he recalled anything else. "Thanks for coming."

"I miss her." His face was sorrowful. A twinge of guilt stabbed Georgia. She wished she could offer him more support, but she was running low on compassion.

. . .

After visiting the ladies' room, Georgia headed to the front of the bar to leave. But when she saw what was happening outside, she froze. Vanna, with Charlie in tow, and JoBeth had just pulled open the front door of a parked car and were heading into the bar. Georgia's pulse sped up, and her body flooded with adrenaline.

What were they doing here? The only person who knew where she was going was Jimmy. What had he done? Frantic, she gazed around the room. No way could she deal with them now. She needed to escape. She thought about the tunnels in the basement, but the only way to get downstairs was through the trapdoor behind the bar. That wasn't going to happen.

She spun around and hitched up the collar of her jacket to hide her face, but she felt them looking her way, trying to pick her out of the few customers already in their cups. Thankfully, the door leading to Lawrence Avenue was only a few yards away. She hurried over and pushed through. Once outside, she sprinted down the street, wondering if Al Capone had felt the same panic when he bolted from the law.

Chapter
Twenty-Two

"Why the hell did you tell them where I was?" Georgia verbally pummeled Jimmy that night. They were in the apartment Jimmy was renting from Luke. Sparsely furnished, it had a transitory air to it, as if on some level there was an awareness of impermanence.

He stood with his hands in his pockets, staring as if he didn't understand her anger. "They really wanted to talk to you. Patch things up."

"Bullshit," she seethed. "I don't believe you. You knew how I felt last night. You had no right to get involved."

"As you remember, we didn't talk much last night."

"So you figured today would be a better time for a confrontation?"

He gazed at her with what she guessed was wonder at the raging lunatic in front of him. If she'd been in her right mind, she might have been surprised, too, at her raw fury. She felt her eyes narrow, her breath go shallow. It didn't happen often, and when it did, she could usually control it. But this time she couldn't wrap her arms around it. This was a rage that had been suppressed for years.

Jimmy leveled a steady gaze at her. Not aggressive, not passive. "What do you want from me, Georgia? If it's an apology, you got it. But if you're looking for approval, well . . . I don't know."

"What am I looking for?" She flipped her hair behind her ears. "How about loyalty for starters?"

"You think I betrayed you?"

She didn't, not really. But she wasn't ready to admit it. She tossed it back to him. "Do you?"

Jimmy shook his head. "No, Georgia. No cop-suspect interrogation games. We both know how that turns out." He folded his arms. "Whatever you think, they are your family. You rescued Vanna from certain death. You are helping raise your nephew. They matter. I know that. And so do you."

"But not JoBeth."

"No. Not your mother." How could his gaze penetrate her soul like that? He knew her at her ugliest. But he didn't run away. He could deal with her. Her rage began to dissipate, and she wanted to throw her arms around this man. This strong, complex man, whose love was the most precious gift she'd ever been given.

"They're gone, you know," he said.

"What do you mean 'gone'?"

"They left your place. They rented an apartment in Arlington Heights."

"Why there?"

"Your mother couldn't afford the North Shore."

"Vanna went with her?" She hesitated. "Charlie too?"

He nodded.

"Where did she—oh, never mind. I don't care."

But Jimmy knew what she was going to ask. "She says she's different. She stopped drinking. Got a job. Cleaned up. Put some money away for the day that Vanna called."

What about me? She never put away anything for me. "Right," Georgia snapped. "And you bought that?"

"Maybe she's telling the truth. Maybe she wants to make amends. With you *and* Vanna."

"How do you make amends for ignoring one daughter and not the other?"

"You have to start somewhere."

"I don't. Not my problem."

Jimmy didn't reply.

"I think I'll go home tonight," she said.

Disappointment flooded his face. "You don't have to."

"I know." She hoped she sounded conciliatory.

"If you're going home because you need to punish yourself . . . by not spending the night with the man you love, who loves you back . . . you might want to reconsider."

That was exactly why she was going home. But she'd never admit it.

Chapter
Twenty-Three

Owen Dougherty snapped the towel that normally hung over his shoulder. "Where you been, Davis? Place hasn't been the same without you."

Mickey's, a bar and grill in Evanston, was way past its prime but still managed to pack in a crowd. And the owner, Owen, only snapped his towel for special customers.

Despite her black mood, Georgia grinned. "I can tell." She glanced at the scarred bar, scuffed booths, and dim lighting. "It's aged another five years."

Owen, a rotund sixtyish man who reminded her of Jackie Gleason, glanced around as if noticing the furnishings for the first time. "Then it's a good thing no one wants to take it off my hands."

Georgia let his little white lie pass. She knew the offers were stacked up sideways. Evanston had been inundated by empty nesters with disposable income who were catered to by high-end establishments and restaurants. It took guts for Owen to hold on to Mickey's. Then again, the bar was full. Maybe aging boomers needed a shabby Chicago tavern to remind them of their wild and wooly youth. Which would make Owen a marketing genius.

"Hey," Georgia said, "aren't you supposed to be in Arizona, soaking up the sun?"

"Yeah. But my daughter and her no-good husband went to Cabo, so . . ."

His son-in-law usually ran the place when Owen was away. "What's wrong with this picture?" she bantered.

"Tell me about it," he grumbled. "So. What'll it be, gorgeous?"

She should order a Diet Coke with lemon. She usually did. She asked for a Chardonnay.

Owen didn't react. He fished under the counter for a wineglass, set it down, and filled it with wine.

"Anything to eat?" Which was Owen-speak for "If you're gonna drink, you better eat."

It was way past dinnertime, but Georgia hadn't eaten. "I'll have the usual."

"Burger, bloody as hell, with fries, crunchy as bones."

"You got it."

He wrote down her order and waddled off to the kitchen. Georgia eyed the wine. Even after all these years, that first sip was pure heaven. She twirled the glass as if looking for the perfect spot on the glass to place her lips, found it, and took a sip. She shut her eyes and felt it slowly slide down her throat. She might even have let out a tiny sigh of bliss.

But the contentment that came with the wine was short-lived. In lighter moments she called it the other-shoe theory of life. For every brief moment of joy, she would suffer an equally intense amount of misery. She never knew how, when, or why it came, but it always did. She felt destined to slog through life with one foot in the muck.

Sipping her wine, she wondered whether Jimmy had a point. Could her mother have finally atoned for her shortcomings? Become responsible? Georgia doubted it. JoBeth was incapable of growth. But what if she *was* sincere? Maybe she wanted to be part of a family again. People did change as they aged.

Nope. It wasn't going to happen. Georgia wouldn't let it. JoBeth would never be part of her life. Not after what she'd done. Georgia downed the rest of her wine and ordered another glass. Despair, her old friend, draped its arm around her shoulders.

. . .

She was three bites into her burger when her cell vibrated. Georgia fished it out of her bag. "Davis here."

"Georgia, it's Erica Baldwin."

"Hi, Erica. I was going to call you tomorrow and give you an update."

"Listen. Something happened this afternoon, and you need to know."

"What?"

"A significant amount of money is missing from the foundation."

Georgia slid off her barstool, shrugged into her coat, and went outside where it was quieter. "How much?"

"About thirty thousand. It doesn't sound like much, but—"

"It's not peanuts. How did you find out?"

"We've got a new accountant, and she told us."

"New?"

"She replaced Iris, our bookkeeper. She left about six months ago."

"You've been without a bookkeeper all this time?"

Erica's voice went small. "Jeffrey didn't think we needed one."

"Oh." Through the glass door Owen pointed to her plate of burger and fries and gestured for her to come in. Her mouth watered.

"Who's been doing the books?"

"Jeffrey thought he could handle it. Until he turned everything over to the accountant for our quarterlies. That's when they found the discrepancies." Erica hesitated. "Georgia, I know we said you'd work a week and then reassess, but would you stick around for a while? I need your help."

"You want me to talk to your son."

"Yes." Erica's voice was barely above a whisper. "I just don't think I can deal with this, too. Not right now."

Erica's world had collapsed. Her daughter had been murdered, her ex was an adulterer, and now her son might have embezzled her money. Despite her own troubles, Georgia's heart went out to her. "Of course."

Chapter
Twenty-Four

Washington, DC

Vic opened the side door to the Kalorama house and headed across the pantry. He tried to keep his tread light. He wished he was invisible. Bad news was never easy to deliver to Carl, and this was bad. He was only halfway across the main hall when Carl's voice boomed.

"I got your text. What the fuck happened?" He appeared in the doorway to his office in rolled-up shirtsleeves, khaki pants, and a face crimson with rage.

"I'm not entirely sure, but bottom line, we got screwed."

"Who did it?"

"I don't know if it was intentional, but we were two votes shy." Vic slid out of his coat.

"Did you talk to Frances?" Frances Rosenblatt was chief of staff for the House Foreign Affairs Committee and, until today, their ally, they thought.

"Not yet. She said she'd call."

Carl fumed, cursed, and stomped around the hall. His cell buzzed. He dug it out of his pants pocket. "What the fuck happened?" he snapped.

A pause. "Yeah, well, what happened to all the campaign dollars we funneled to your guy?" Another pause. "This is bullshit, Frances. You know that. It was supposed to be an end run around sanctions. Everyone on the committee was on the same page. They wanted the deal. So what the fuck happened?"

A long pause. Frances was clearly trying to explain.

"The Uyghurs?" Carl said. "Are you shitting me? The Uyghurs aren't a threat. There are only a couple thousand of them and the Uzbeks are killing them off right and left." He snorted. "In between persecuting them. What the hell would they do with the weapons anyway? None of them know how to drive a goddamn truck, much less operate a surface-to-air missile. They'd shoot themselves before they'd be dangerous to others."

Carl listened to Frances but stared directly at Vic. Vic's skin prickled with goose bumps. These were the worst moments. When they were skirting the law on behalf of a client. In this case, they'd promised an insurgent guerrilla group in Uzbekistan some armored vehicles, dozens of assault rifles, light machine guns, and a handful of shoulder-launched surface-to-air missiles. It was wrong, he knew, but it was the way the world worked. Carl had taught him that. "I scratch their back. They scratch ours."

But Vic felt a keen sense of betrayal. His own, this time. The fringe group wanted independence and were prepared to die for it. Without weapons they were doomed. The Uzbek government, their well-armed militias stocked with shiny new toys of destruction thanks to Russia, would crush the insurgents faster than ink drying on the bill of lading.

Carl started to prowl around the hall. "FARA? Of course we did. Everyone has to, since Manafort. It just hasn't come through yet." He sucked in a long breath. "This is a farce, Frances. Something else is going on. No. Don't tell me over the phone. Come over here. We'll have cocktails in front of the fire."

One last pause. "No. I won't throw you in. See you later." He went into his office and tossed the cell on his desk. Vic followed. Carl spun around to face Vic. "She's worthless, you know."

"She's the chairman's consigliere."

"She's got no balls. If only McCain were still around—I'll bet they got a warning from the NSC. Or the IC. Someone is playing us," he muttered. "It's a NatSec matter . . . how can something fly through the committee three months ago, then suddenly become such a serious matter that they bail on the arms deal?"

"It's a different world." Vic winced as he said it. It was weak.

But Carl didn't pick up on it. "I don't believe it. I think it's personal. Someone is trying to screw me. The question is who. I wonder if it's that prick over at—"

Vic cleared his throat and summoned up whatever courage he could. "Actually, I've been meaning to talk to you about something, Carl."

Carl squinted. Suspicion filled his face.

"I don't know if I'm cut out for this—this anymore."

"NatSec? You've danced with them before."

"That's not what I mean."

Carl studied his assistant. "A little late to reclaim your soul, don't you think?"

Vic shoved his hands in his pockets. "I'm thinking I should go back home and practice law."

"To that little shithole in South Dakota?"

"North River is not a shithole. My father has a solid family law practice, and he's itching to retire."

"Why?" Carl canted his head. Then recognition lit his face. "I get it. You want a place to wash your hands and clean up. Park yourself for ten years. Then run for Congress." He folded his arms and begrudged Vic a weak grin. "Not a bad strategy."

Vic shook his head. "That's not the plan."

"Since when? I thought you liked knowing how the sausage gets made. You suddenly develop a case of ulcers?"

"Maybe." He drew in a breath. "We— You have to face facts, Carl. Someone was—is—squeezing you. They fucking threatened the life of your daughter. And then . . ."

"I told you never to bring that up." Carl started to pace. "That had nothing to do with this deal."

But Vic wasn't finished. He wasn't sure where his nerve was coming from. "But it set a precedent. You couldn't deliver then—and now look what's happened."

"Shut the fuck up." Carl continued to pace. "The Uzbeks are still in the hopper. It's gonna go through."

"Okay. Sure. If you say so. The thing is, you know how word gets around in this town. People are talking. Your reputation is on the edge."

"Christ. You're supposed to be working *for* me. Not against me."

"I am, Carl. But you've got to face facts. You're down to a Hail Mary with the arms deal. The same thing happened to sanctions relief. People are beginning to realize you're not invincible. And fracking? Who knows what's going to go down?"

Carl's anger spiked. "What makes you think you're exempt, buddy boy? If what you're saying is right, we've both got targets on our backs," he blustered. He opened a cabinet in the kitchen, pulled out a bottle of Bookers. He poured it into a glass—neat—and tossed it back. "There's something else."

Vic squeezed his eyes shut. With Carl, there was always something else.

"I've heard Dena's case is active again. Some damn PI; a woman in Chicago. You need to keep tabs on her. And report back to me." He poured more whiskey.

"I'm already on it."

"And you're still checking the group?"

"Yup."

"You sure?"

"Carl . . ."

"Okay, okay. It's probably just my ex-wife. She clearly didn't believe the sniper theory." He gulped down the whiskey. "But you're right about one thing. Any unnecessary attention is a threat. We need to be prepared."

"For what?"

But Carl just shook his head. "You know? I think it's time for you to go home now. I don't want you around when Frances gets here. Let's concentrate on the fracking bill."

Vic nodded and picked up his coat, glad to escape his boss's maelstrom. For now.

· · ·

Carl had a third drink, but the typical numbness that alcohol brought didn't work. He stalked into his office, a chic arrangement of Euro desk, chairs, and abstract art on the walls that never failed to impress his shitty little clients from third world countries. That was the point, wasn't it? Look like you had the world by the balls. No problems. Nothing that couldn't be resolved with a few hundred thousand.

His cell chirped. "Baldwin here..." He listened. "Good evening, Congressman Hyde. I was just talking about you with Vic. We're ready to draft your legislation on fracking."

He listened again. "Why not? I thought that was something you wanted to roll out as soon as possible."

Carl stared at the glass of whiskey in his hand. "Really? You have a shot at replacing the attorney general? No shit. That's terrific! What can we do to help?" He wet his lips with his tongue. "I see. Well, sure. We'll wait to see what the subcommittee decides. When do you see that happening?" He paused. "Well, good luck, sir. I know you'll be a fine addition to the cabinet."

When the conversation was over Carl threw his cell on his desk and gulped the rest of the whiskey.

Chapter
Twenty-Five

"I didn't want my mother to hire you," Jeff Baldwin said to Georgia the next morning. They were seated across his desk at the foundation.

"And that's because..." Georgia thought she knew what he was going to say and wished he'd get on with it. She'd done a background check on him last night and found out about the heroin, the dealing, the prison in California.

Jeffrey was wearing a black turtleneck and denims, the Jobsian uniform of the successful modern executive, but his dark eyes spoke worry. He didn't look as confident as he had the first time she met him. He also had a habit of dipping his head and pulling on his earlobe. Did he pick that up in prison? An effort to literally keep his head down?

"I thought we could handle everything. There wasn't much to handle, actually. Just grieve and get over it."

Harsh words for his only sister, Georgia thought as she glanced out the window. Freezing rain had washed away some of the snow, exposing the weary dregs of winter in Chicago.

"What about the beef jerky email? Don't you want to know who's behind it?"

"Of course. But it seemed far-fetched to me that a PI could

discover what the police and FBI couldn't." The undercurrent in his tone implied Georgia wasn't up to his standards.

He went on. "We did upgrade our security systems. That's why I needed to make the flash drive for you, as it happens."

"Okay," she said. "So, you didn't want me around. What changed?"

"The thirty grand that's missing."

"Tell me about it."

"We had a bookkeeper at the foundation. Iris. She'd been with us since the beginning. Dena hired her. Then about six months ago she told us the books weren't adding up."

"What was her explanation?"

"At first she said she didn't know and put it down to petty cash. It was only a couple hundred. Someone forgot to submit an invoice or something. Then I took a closer look. Of course, I suspected her."

"Why?"

"Because accountants and bookkeepers know all the tricks to hide embezzlement."

"And you would know."

Jeff's face turned crimson, and his lips parted. He dipped his head and tugged on his ear. "When did you find out?"

"It doesn't matter." She was stretching the truth a bit, but he didn't have to know.

He looked up at her. "I didn't take the money."

"And I should believe you because . . ."

"Think about it. Under the circumstances, I would be the first suspect, right?"

"Yep."

He sat up. "My mother was the person who pulled me through prison. She never gave up. She sacrificed her time and money—and love—to get me straightened out. Visiting every few weeks; bringing me books; urging me to take online courses. I owe her everything. And with Dena gone, there's no way I would do this to her."

Georgia almost believed him. If he was innocent, he'd bend over backward to prove it.

"That's why I've been scrupulous in going over the books."

"And?"

Jeff settled back in his chair, swiveled toward the window, then back toward her. "Apparently Iris and Dena had an argument about six months ago. I was on vacation that week. Actually I was in Vallejo seeing my parole officer. When I got back, Iris was gone."

Georgia tilted her head. "Did she quit or was she fired?"

"Dena said she fired her because of the financial discrepancies. At the time I'd just come on board and had no reason to doubt her. Dena knew I'd been doing inventory for the warden and asked me to take over. I said sure." He gave Georgia a one-sided smile. "Yeah. *Shawshank Redemption*. That was me."

"Anyway, it seemed like the perfect solution, and a good way for me to learn the foundation's business.

"That's when the discrepancies became more obvious. We're not a big organization. Only about four or five on staff. Except for the scholarships and stipends we award, our budget is fairly consistent. But gradually our expenses went up. A thousand here, two grand there." He shifted. "When I started reviewing the actual invoices, I found it."

"Found what?"

"Dena was cooking the books. She submitted invoices from fake consultants and service providers, then pocketed the money." He rolled back his chair, opened a drawer, and pulled out a manila folder. "It's all in here."

"Did you confront her?"

Again he nodded.

"And?"

"At first she denied it, but when I showed her the invoices, she said she needed the money for her activist group. She said bringing down a president was more important than balancing a P&L."

Georgia had been wondering where Dena got the money to plan demonstrations, buy signage and supplies, promote the event, and all the other tasks that an emerging political movement required. "So it wasn't for her personal use."

Jeff shot her a glance that was just short of indignant. "My sister was nothing if not committed. She didn't need any money for herself. She had access to her trust fund. Our grandfather set them up for us both. I'm sure she dipped into hers, too."

"May I see the files?"

Jeff handed them over. Georgia scanned through them. About two dozen invoices, some from Curtis Dixon, the boyfriend Georgia had interviewed yesterday, for political consultation. There were also two in the name of Ruth Marriotti, for services provided. Georgia's eyebrows rose. "What happened when you showed these to your mother?"

He slacked in his chair. "I haven't. Yet."

"Why not?"

"In her eyes Dena could do no wrong. I'm the official black sheep of the family."

"You think she'd blame you? After all she did for you while you were in prison?"

"I guess I hadn't thought that far ahead."

"But you'd take the fall for your sister? And risk that you'd be blamed for embezzling money? Maybe even thrown back into prison?"

"That's why I decided we didn't need you."

"Because you thought I'd persuade your mother you were the criminal."

"My mother's been through enough."

"If you ended up back inside, your mother would be left with no one."

"I know. That's why I changed my mind. I trust my mother. And she seems to trust you."

"So you want me to tell your mother Dena stole the money?"

Jeffrey swiveled nervously in the chair, but his tormented

expression told Georgia she was right. She was flummoxed. She didn't know whether Jeffrey was a masochist, an expert manipulator, or the prodigal son. In other words, did he take after his father or his mother?

"Are you still in contact with your father?" she asked.

"No one is. Anymore."

"What about Jarvis? Did you know him?"

"Of course not. I never heard his name until Dena was killed."

Georgia sat back in her chair. "You know I'm going to check this out with Iris."

"I'll give you her number. I'd like her to come back anyway."

"You'll have to do that yourself." Georgia stood up. "But I'll report to your mom and tell her about these." She handed the files back to Jeffrey and looked around his office. "Could I have a quick tour of the place? I was in a hurry the other day, but I have a little more time today."

"Sure." It wasn't a smile, but he seemed pleased that she'd asked.

There were only four offices, each off the same hall. Two were unoccupied and empty. Georgia ducked her head into the third office, which Jeffrey said had been Iris's. She did the same with the fourth, now occupied by a researcher who checked out potential grant recipients. Then she went into Dena's office. The furnishings were what she expected. A clean black lacquer desk, executive chair, black lacquer table in the corner, and empty bookshelves, except for one photograph. It was a shot of Dena with her father. They were on a sailboat, and she was hoisting the sail up the mast. The shot managed to capture a bright sun, a blue Lake Michigan, and an even bluer sky. Her father stood in the background, hands on hips, a broad smile on his face.

Jeff, who had come in behind her, followed her gaze to the photo. "You know the story about the prodigal son, right?"

Georgia turned around. "Of course."

"You know who probably convinced the father to forgive his son?"

"Tell me."

"A grateful mother."

Chapter
Twenty-Six

Georgia fished out her key and unlocked the door to her apartment. She was greeted with deep silence. No coos or cries of an infant, or the sound of Vanna cooking, rocking, or feeding. All she heard was the occasional tick of the heating system. She stood beside the door for nearly a minute, then checked the spare room. The crib, diaper stand, and even the mobile were gone, along with Vanna and Charlie. The apartment no longer felt cramped, albeit in a cozy sort of way. Now it had never looked larger. Or lonelier. She blinked away something wet and forced her thoughts back to the Baldwin case.

If Dena Baldwin had been siphoning money away from the family foundation to finance the ResistanceUSA movement, Georgia would have to press Ruth Marriotti about it. Had Dena paid her a salary? Is that why Ruth was so hardworking and loyal? And what about Curt Dixon? Was he on the payroll too? Or did Dena dummy up the invoices without their knowledge?

Georgia sat down at her tiny kitchen table, trying to rationalize Dena's behavior. Money was the best way to motivate people to do a job. And starting a political movement required a lot of people to handle a lot of tasks. But she couldn't ignore the dark side: money could persuade people to act against their better instincts. And it could be used for bribes, threats, and kickbacks, which, in some hands, was another way of saying extortion.

Whatever her reasons, Dena was clearly more of a schemer than Georgia had expected. Like her father. Maybe she was more like him than *she* would have wanted to admit. By the same token, Jeff was looking more like the true prodigal son. She grabbed some cheese from the fridge, topped it on a cracker, and wolfed it down. She hadn't eaten since last night at Mickey's.

She was reaching for her laptop when she realized it wasn't where it was supposed to be. She'd left it on her kitchen table. Now it was on the counter. She froze. Slowly she turned to gaze at her living room. The cushions on the sofa had been tampered with as well. She'd left them in disarray; now they were evenly plumped. She went into her bedroom. Her closet door was open. She knew she'd closed it. She always did. Someone had been inside her home.

She backtracked to her computer. It was on, but that wasn't unusual. She opened the folder she'd created for the Baldwin case and scanned the dates and times the files had last been accessed. Sure enough, someone had been through most of her documents in the past half hour. Who? What did they want? How did they get into her apartment? She shivered. A sense of violation was worse when you didn't know who was behind it. She called Jimmy and left him a voice mail to call ASAP.

As creepy and disturbing as the break-in was, Georgia had to admit that whoever was behind it would be disappointed. Her results so far were insignificant. As soon as she untangled one knot, a twist of the rope revealed another. Money, family feuds, and politics had coalesced into a sticky wad of uncertainty. Unless her skill as an investigator was slipping. Maybe she wasn't up to the job. All she had done was retrace the FBI's work. Break-in or not, she needed a new approach.

She went to the window in her kitchen and looked out. The single mother across the street, whose kids always left their trikes and toys strewn across the lawn, was dragging two garbage cans to the curb. Half a block away, the sanitation truck announced its arrival with its shrill belches of brakes and hoots. The mailman in his boxy truck would soon pass by. Everyone had their routines. A man came out of the house across the street to help the woman with the recycling bins. Did she have a new boyfriend? Or was he a relative, maybe a brother? Georgia straightened. She had an idea.

. . .

She met Erica Baldwin that afternoon at her Glencoe home and told her what she'd learned from Jeff. Erica was silent. Georgia wondered if Erica had always known—or suspected—in a dark corner of her mind, that Dena was as flawed as the rest of the family. She was about to ask Erica whether she was okay, when Erica said, "So Jeff had nothing to do with it?"

"I need to talk to Iris, but it doesn't look like it."

Georgia saw Erica's relief, the loosening of tension. "And, Erica, I need a different approach to the case. I want to find out more about Jarvis."

"Why?" Erica asked. "What do you hope to get?"

"Maybe a connection to Dena. Maybe not."

"The FBI didn't think there was one."

"I know." She took a breath. "He has a sister."

"Right. I saw her on the news."

"I'm sure the FBI has already talked to her, but I think it's worth a shot."

"But what about the forty thousand members of Dena's group? Wouldn't they be more important?"

"I have a team of computer geeks working on that. They're doing criminal background checks. But it's going to take a while to get the results."

"Just background checks?" Erica fingered her necklace, a gold chain with a pear-shaped diamond at her throat. "What if it's someone—I don't know—crazy as a loon, but hasn't got a record."

"There's always a chance that someone could slip through the cracks. But remember, we've been looking for a needle in a haystack since we started. In the meantime, maybe I'll discover Jarvis was clearly acting alone. At this point we just don't know."

"Well, if you think it's important . . ." Erica let her voice trail off, clearly indicating she wasn't convinced.

"I do." Georgia felt like a kid who crosses her fingers, hoping she's telling the truth.

"By the way, I have to tell you something else." She filled Erica in on the break-in at her apartment. And the guy on the motorcycle who'd tailed her.

"Do you think it's connected to the case?"

Georgia shook her head. "I don't know. But you can bet I plan to find out. In the meantime, be careful. If they're breaking into my place, they're likely stalking you too. Your husband and Jeffrey as well."

Erica swallowed. "We've beefed up our security so much I don't know what more we can do. Do you think we need bodyguards?"

"I can't answer that. Ask Paul Kelly what he thinks."

Erica squeezed her eyes shut. "Oh God. I wish this was over. I want my life back."

"I get it." Georgia gave her a sympathetic smile. Now was not the time to tell Erica that her life, even when she got it back, would never be the same.

Chapter
Twenty-Seven

Five Months Before the Demonstration

"We have to take a stand," Dena said. "Fracking is the most destructive way to find new energy." It was late afternoon on a late summer day in September. She, Ruth, Curt, and DJ squeezed into a booth at The Barracks, a Rogers Park tavern. The Barracks, and the ex-military crowd who frequented it, had seen better days. The tavern was known for its cheap pitchers of beer and buffalo wings between four and six, which was how it managed to keep its doors open. The customers were known for downing prodigious amounts of alcohol, raucous talk, and the occasional brawl. Dena had dared them to meet here to "fraternize with the enemy," she joked.

"Who knows? Maybe we'll convert one or two of them." She'd laughed.

"You're right about fracking, of course." Ruth looked around uneasily. "But if we take on other issues that aren't Resistance-related, we dilute our message. We're here to get the asshole out of office and restore our democracy. That's our voice. Our strength."

"Our unique selling proposition, as the ad guys say." DJ

nodded. "People know what they're gonna get when they join ResistanceUSA."

The waitress arrived with a pitcher and glasses, and Curt poured everyone beer. "They've got a point, Dena."

Dena's lips tightened into a stubborn line. "We're not one-dimensional dummies. Just because we're dedicated to one issue doesn't mean we can't speak out on another. What was that Tom Hanks movie? The one about the band with only one hit record?"

"*That Thing You Do?*" Curt jumped in.

"Right. The Wonders." Dena glanced at the others. "We're not them. We're in it for the long haul. Think about it. We're only at the first step. If . . . no"—she shook her head—"*when* we succeed, and he's gone, there's going to be a shitload of cleanup to do. He gutted the State Department, the EPA, the diplomatic corps. He's allowed cabinet members to cash in big-time just because they can. In fact, whether they're pocketing thousands from lobbyists or sucking the government's tit, it's the most corrupt cabinet in history."

"Including people who get a cut of the action? Like your father?" Ruth said.

Dena shot Ruth a fierce glare. "Yeah, okay. Like my father." She shifted her tone. "But bottom line, you can't argue about how dangerous fracking is. It's caused earthquakes all over Oklahoma. It poisons the water. Kills animals and wildlife. Gives everyone cancer. And the producers are lying about it. They completely deny it's happening! It's incredible. Why not expand solar? Wind power? Even that algae crap they're exploring? The Resistance can handle this. It's part of our agenda."

"*Your* agenda," Ruth said. "I'm sorry, Dena, but I can't support you on this one. It seems a little outside our box."

"I thought our box was supposed to be open and flexible," Dena said acidly.

DJ raised his hands. "Okay. Hold on." He was a natural peacemaker. "Why don't we put it to the group? You could do a post and see how people react."

Dena bit her lip. "We could do that."

"And if people want to adopt it, we go ahead. You find venues to speak. You start enlisting environmental allies and all that."

Ruth cut in. "But if we take on fracking, what's next? Someone will want to talk about the Middle East. And then someone else will want to talk Me Too. Then gun control. Before you know it, we won't be the Resistance anymore. We'll just be another progressive Bernie Sanders group." She paused for what Dena thought was effect. "And you know how that turned out."

Adrenaline pounded Dena's heart. Ruth was becoming a little too assertive these days. Insinuating her opinion into just about everything. Then again, she was smart and thoughtful, she got things done, and she listened to Dena. Most of the time. Dena managed to keep her mouth shut.

"I don't know, Deanie," Curt said, using his nickname for her. His affectionate manner calmed her, even though she realized it was deliberate. "Ruth's got a point. Our mission is to impeach or see him resign. We're getting closer. The special counsel is making inroads."

"Impeachment is never gonna happen," Dena said. "Most of the Republicans are complicit, for fuck's sake. They took Russian money."

Curt ignored Dena's comment. "But I think DJ's got the right idea. If we're truly a democracy, we should test the waters."

This time Dena didn't hold back. "If I didn't know better, I'd think all three of you are a bunch of pussies."

The others exchanged glances. Ruth cleared her throat. "Dena, we're just trying to protect the integrity of ResistanceUSA."

"I get that." Dena took a swig of beer from her mug. She sat back. "Okay. You're right. All of you. I'm sorry. It just seems the bigger we get, the less nerve we have. We spend hours discussing process, not politics. Who's going to schedule the moderators, how best to get the word out. We fricking sound like corporate executives. What happened to our passion, our courage to speak out against the injustices?" She gazed at the row of bottles stacked up along the mirror behind the bar. Dusk was settling, and beams from car headlights passing outside shot light through the front window, making the bottles glow with amber, blue, and yellow sparkles. Dena slipped out of her chair and headed to the bar. "I need something stronger."

The others didn't stop her.

Chapter Twenty-Eight

Five Months Before the Demonstration

An hour and four shots of Jim Beam later, Curt and DJ had left, and Ruth joined Dena at the bar. It was after five, and the place was filling up. A group of four men came in and commandeered a table in the front. The bartender, a woman, served them pitchers of beer and plates of wings, mozzarella sticks, and meatballs.

"That crap will rot your gut." Dena watched the bartender carry a tray of baby sausages to their table.

"I doubt they care," Ruth said.

"On the house." The bartender placed the sausages in the center of the table.

Dena polished off her shot of whiskey. "So how come they get special treatment?"

Ruth shook her head.

"Let's find out." She swung the barstool around.

"Dena, you've had a few. Give it a rest."

"See?" Dena grabbed the edge of the bar to steady herself. "That's exactly what I was talking about. You guys are losing your rage. I'll give it a rest when those mobsters are out of the White House."

Her eyes were not entirely focused, Ruth noticed.

"You know I'm right."

Ruth blew out a breath. "Philosophically, of course you are. But realistically, we can't add fracking to our list. We don't have environmental experts. Christ, we don't even have an energy platform. People won't take us seriously. They'll call us a bunch of whiny kids."

"They don't say that about the Parkland kids. And they're standing up to the NRA, for God's sake."

"They're a decade younger than us. And they're fighting for gun control. More people care about guns than fracking. Most people probably don't even know what fracking is." Ruth hesitated. "Just because you hate your father is no reason for political action."

Dena belched loudly, not even trying to suppress the sound. "Where did you get that idea?"

Ruth sighed. "The night when we were applying for the permits? Remember? You told me the whole story."

"Nope. Can't say that I do."

"You were drinking then, too." Ruth eyed her.

"You just don't want to spread your wings, Ruth. You're all cowards."

A chortle made Dena twirl her barstool and check out the men at the table. One of the men looked big and solid and wore a handlebar mustache that was perfectly groomed. He wore something on his head that resembled one of those Arab scarves. A keffiyeh, she thought. A second man, leaner and lankier, wore an army fatigue jacket over jeans. The remaining two, jackets off, showed off arms covered with tats. Loud guffaws interspersed with murmurs punctuated their conversation.

"You gotta have guts," Dena said, her words sloppy. "How much you wanna bet I can convince those guys to rally to our side?"

Ruth looked them over. "Dena, stop playing games. Let's go home."

Dena shook her head. "Told you I was gonna convert one or two. Watch."

"Come on, Dena." Ruth took Dena's arm.

Dena shrugged it off. "Fuck off, Ruth."

The bartender came over. She had a heart-shaped face, prominent chin, brown hair tied back in a ponytail, and a muscular build that said she was strong enough to manage rowdy customers. Now she smiled. "You've been going at it pretty good for a while. How 'bout a cup of coffee?"

"No fucking way. I'm on a mission to save our country."

The bartender stared at her for a long moment, then turned away. "Can't blame a gal for trying."

Dena slid off the barstool and stood up.

"Where are you going?"

Dena tottered. Ruth squeezed her eyes shut, thinking, *Here we go.*

Dena approached the table. "Hey, guys, how y'all doing this evening?"

The men stared at her as if she was an alien who'd just parked her spaceship on the street.

"It's okay. I won't bother you." She giggled. "Too much." She glanced at the guy in the fatigue jacket. "You in the service?"

"Not anymore." He gave her the once-over. His expression softened into approval, Ruth noticed. She couldn't disagree. Dena *was* pretty. And sexy. At the same time, though, the guy with the Arab headgear shook his head at Fatigue Jacket.

Dena didn't notice. "Where'd you serve?"

"Iraq. Two tours."

"Best shot in the platoon," one of the guys with tattoos said.

She nodded. "You all serve together?"

Arab Scarf shot Dena a cool look. "I don't want to be impolite, miss, but we're in the middle of something here."

"Oh. You want me to get the hell away from you." Dena swayed.

He plastered on a fake smile. "You said it, not me."

Dena slipped a hank of hair behind her ear. It was a Veronica Lake move Ruth knew meant she was flirting, trying to seduce, make herself irresistible.

"I'll go. But I want to tell you something. I'm involved with—um—a political group. We're gonna kick the president out of office. I mean, he's fucking destroying our country day by day with his corruption, lies. Yeah, and treason. Playing fast and loose with the facts." She looked at each man in turn. "He fucking decimated the State Department. And the EPA. And ya know what? If Mattis wasn't there, we'd all be dead from World War Three. You're military guys. We need you. The country needs you. Will you join us?"

A disconcerting silence was her answer.

Dena glanced at each man in turn. The only ones who made eye contact were Fatigue Jacket and Arab Scarf.

"You got the wrong crowd here," Arab Scarf said.

"Are you kidding me?" Dena said. "You voted for him?"

"That ain't none of your business, lady. Now, get the fuck away from us."

Ruth suddenly appeared at Dena's side. She grabbed her arm. "Let's go, Dena."

Dena yanked her arm away. "I'm not finished."

"Hold on, man." Fatigue Jacket cut in and flashed, of all things, a smile at Dena. He yanked a thumb at Arab Scarf and said in an apologetic tone, "He's got a short fuse." He looked eager to hear more.

Dena picked up on it. "Is that right?" She gave him one of her hundred-watt smiles. "And who are you?"

"I—I'm Scott."

Dena looked him over.

He wasn't bad-looking, Ruth thought. A heart-shaped face, long shaggy hair, bushy eyebrows, but his brown eyes were soft. Not really Dena's type. Then again, who was?

"And what do *you* say, Scott?" Dena purred.

"I don't give a shit who's president. They're all crooks." He cocked his head. "I just want to get away. I did two tours, saw my buddies get blown up. Didn't make fuck-all difference. We get what we deserve." He took a swig of beer. "First a nigger president, now a crook. Me? I just want off the grid." He glanced over at Arab Scarf, whose arms were now folded across his chest.

Dena gasped. "Scott! Did you just say the N-word?"

Oh crap. Ruth braced for all hell to let loose.

But Scott didn't cede any territory. "What else you gonna call him?"

Dena drew herself up. Cleared her throat. "How about President Obama, for starters?"

The group broke into laughter.

"You are the worst kind of coward, you know that, Scott?" She pointed her finger at him. "Oh sure, you complain, call people names, but when push comes to shove, you want out. Run the other way. You're just another garden-variety racist."

Scott's face turned crimson.

Arab Scarf cut in. "Okay, lady. It's *really* time for you to leave us alone."

But Dena kept her finger pointed at Scott. "Right-wing zealot ... what the hell am I saying? You probably don't know what the word means. Get off the grid. Jesus Christ. You might have fought for our country in Iraq, but the stakes are way higher now. And you're quitting. He's a dictator. Do you know what that means? And all you want to do is escape? I don't know about the rest of your buddies, but you, Mr. Scott, are an asshole."

Ruth grabbed her again. "We're leaving now, Dena." She turned to Arab Scarf. "I want to apologize for my friend. She—"

He waved her off and turned toward the bartender. "Kitty?"

The bartender, who was watching it all, tipped her head to the side.

"Get her out of here."

"You got it, Jerky."

"Jerky?" Dena scoffed. "Figures. He's a fucking jerk."

The woman came over and grabbed Dena's arm. Dena finally

sagged and let herself be walked out. At the curb, the bartender leaned over to Ruth. "It's probably better if she never comes back here, you know what I mean? The boys hang out here all the time."

"I'm really sorry. She's plastered."

"You don't say." Kitty looked at Ruth. "Get her home and let her sleep it off. The corner's not bad for cabs. Have a good night." She headed back to the door.

Dena was muttering. "Soldiers . . . what pussies . . . Get off the grid. Holy crap."

"Wait," Ruth called out to Kitty. "We didn't pay you for the shots." She fished in her bag.

A pained, weary look came across Kitty's face, as if she wanted to wipe her hands of the entire matter. "Don't worry about it."

Chapter
Twenty-Nine

The Present

Sheridan Road is home to both the priciest and the shabbiest buildings in Chicagoland. Mansions line streets from Evanston to the Wisconsin state line, and expensive apartment buildings form canyons from Lake Shore Drive south to the Field Museum. In between, though, are modest neighborhoods and even pockets of blight. Rogers Park, just south of Evanston, is on the modest end, and that's where Georgia was headed the next morning.

When she turned onto Morse Avenue from Sheridan, she recognized Katherine Jarvis's building right away. She'd seen it on the news. Tucked away a block west of Sheridan, a pair of three-flats were flanked by taller apartment buildings. One of the three-flats had been renovated and sported a bright red door and tidy lawn. But Katherine Jarvis's building was marked by peeling paint, uneven porch steps, and windows lined with a sludge of filth that looked baked in.

She parked, trudged up the rickety steps, and entered the vestibule, a tiny room with mailboxes on one side. "Jarvis, K" lived in 1B. She hit the buzzer and waited a full minute. Nothing. She buzzed again. Still nothing. Jarvis wasn't there. Georgia was disappointed but not surprised. She probably had a job. Georgia went back to the Corolla and settled in to wait.

Clouds scudded across the sky, creating two distinct climates that vied with each other. When the sun hid behind the overcast, it was a dreary late winter day in Chicago. But when the clouds parted, the sun was a cheerful harbinger of daffodils and warm weather. The dichotomy reflected Georgia's mood.

While she waited, she called Katherine Jarvis's cell, which she'd found online. It was disconnected. Her Facebook page had disappeared too. She couldn't blame her. After all the press coverage and tumult and invasion of her privacy, her life had to be a mess. She probably hadn't had time to mourn her brother. Still, she might have switched to an unlisted number. Georgia would continue to stake out her home.

She checked her messages. Two voice mails. One was a telemarketer. How did they get her number? Did they buy lists from phone providers? Had to be a scam. She should look into it. Someday. She deleted the call.

The second call came from a number she didn't recognize. She clicked on the replay.

"Georgia, this is JoBeth. Vanna and I have been trying to find you. We want to talk. I'm thinking of staying here in Chicago. I could take care of Charlie while Vanna finishes school. Peaches, you've done a wonderful job with Vanna. She's matured. Thoughtful, thinking ahead. That's all because of you. Please call us. I know you miss Charlie. He's something, isn't he?" Her chuckle sounded nervous. "Anyway, think about it. I love you."

Georgia stared at her cell's screen. She hadn't been JoBeth's "peach" for twenty-five years. Then, like the mottled sky that intermittently blotted out the sun, Georgia's mood swung. Her mother was bouncing her on her knee. She couldn't remember when or where she was, but a recording of Ray Charles warbling "Georgia on My Mind" in his gravelly voice played in the background. JoBeth sang along. Georgia felt safe and protected. And loved. But the song's mournful lyrics sparked a twinge of regret too. An omen of things to come? Georgia deleted the number. She was on the outside. Even if it was her own choice.

By ten that night Georgia decided Jarvis's sister wasn't coming home. She drove back to Evanston. She was back the next morning before eight with a steaming latte. Still no answer when she buzzed. She bundled up in her car to wait.

Twenty minutes later, a young man burst out of the vestibule and down the steps to the sidewalk. Checking his cell, he hurried toward Sheridan Road. He waved to hail a passing bus, but the vehicle didn't stop. Georgia climbed out of the Toyota.

He dug out his cell and tapped a few keys. Calling an Uber? If so, she had about five minutes before it arrived. She jogged to the corner. His back was to her.

"Hey, sorry to bother you. I know you're late."

"How did—" Jarvis's neighbor whirled around. A quilted North Face jacket, khaki pants. Wavy brown hair, a cleft chin, round, suspicious eyes.

"I saw you come out of the three-flat down there." Georgia gestured toward the building.

Those round eyes narrowed. "Are you stalking me?"

Everyone thought the world revolved around them. "I'm looking for Katherine Jarvis."

"Oh." Comprehension dawned. He studied her. "You don't look like a reporter."

"That might be because I'm not." She hesitated. "We were friends in grade school. I wanted to see how she was doing."

His eyebrows arched, as if he didn't believe her. She didn't blame him. It was a lame pretext.

"Do you know where she is?" she asked.

"You really don't know her, do you?"

"Why do you say that?"

"Because if you did, you'd know everyone calls her Kitty." He drew himself up. "And you won't find her."

"Why not?"

"She's gone."

"When?"

"A few weeks . . . maybe a month ago. Not long after her brother shot that woman."

"Where'd she go?"

"I don't know."

Georgia frowned. "Did you know her brother?"

He shook his head. "I only . . ." Then he stopped. "Who the hell are you? What do you want?"

Georgia sighed and pulled out her license. "I'm an investigator. Private. The family hired me to look into a couple of things."

The neighbor scanned the license. A white sedan pulled up, the Uber decal festooned on the windshield. He handed her license back. "Well, whoever you are, I gotta go."

"Can you at least tell me where she worked?"

The neighbor shifted, conflicted. The Uber driver, who was holding up traffic on one of the busiest streets in Chicago, gestured impatiently. The neighbor ran his tongue around his lips. "Before she left, she tended bar at the Barracks. You know, off Sheridan." He opened the back door of the Uber and climbed in.

"Thanks. Appreciate it."

He nodded. The car was about to pull away, when Georgia grabbed the handle of the door and pulled. The brakes squealed, and the driver shouted, "Lady, watch it! You almost lost an arm."

Georgia held up her hand, dug in her bag, and pulled out a card, which she handed to the neighbor. She tried to smile. "Please call me if you find out where she went. Or anything else, for that matter."

Chapter Thirty

The Barracks had to be one of the only bars on the North Side that opened at nine in the morning. Then again, military people typically didn't drink on a schedule when they were deployed. Georgia suspected they didn't give a shit when they started or stopped. Being alive was celebration enough to toss back a few.

She paused before entering and peeked through the window. A big table in front. Long bar, metal barstools, linoleum floor. Grimier and seedier than Mickey's, it was still, like Mickey's, a dive. Georgia had misspent much of her youth at similar establishments. Dive bars were comfort food, she would say. She knew what she was getting and it was mostly drunk. She pushed through the door. But she wasn't that person anymore. Was she?

The place was empty. She walked the length of the bar and found a door she assumed led to the kitchen. "Hello?"

No response. A low-pitched machine noise whined on the other side. She raised her voice. "Hello? Anyone here?"

She turned to leave.

"One minute," a reedy male voice replied.

The man who came through the door had significant scarring on the left side of his face, which puckered and raised his skin in random lines, some shot through with red.

Georgia must have gawked, because he said, "IED. Afghanistan. Kandahar. Ten years ago. What can I get you?"

"I'm sorry. I didn't mean to stare."

"Hard not to." He paused. "So, what'll it be?"

"Coffee?"

"I'll get it." He motioned to the empty barstools. "Try to avoid the crowd."

She grinned and took a seat. Tall and skinny, with thinning hair, he wore a small white towel draped over his shoulder. Just like Owen.

A minute later, he came back with coffee, sugar, and creamer. "I'm actually an investigator," Georgia said.

"I knew you weren't a real customer."

"How?"

"Most people who drink in the morning don't have anywhere to go. You're dressed for work."

"What's your name?" she asked.

"Charlie Stokes."

"That's my nephew's name. Charlie."

He shot her a wry expression. "So, what do you want?"

"I'm looking for Kitty Jarvis."

"Her?" He grimaced.

"You know her?"

He shook his head. "Lady had a rough time, I hear. But I started after she left."

"She quit for good?"

"As far as I know."

"You know where I can find her?"

He shook his head. "She didn't leave an address or cell."

"How long have you been here?"

"A couple of weeks."

"Since the end of February?"

He nodded.

"Would the owner know how to get in touch with her?"

"Maybe." He grabbed a scrap of paper and scrawled down a number.

"Thanks."

"A couple of guys who knew her brother drop in from time to time. Maybe they know something."

"Who are they?"

"No idea. Military, I guess. Tats up and down their arms."

She pulled out a card. "Next time they come in, could you give me a call?"

"Sure." He read the card. "Well, Ms. Davis, I hope you find what you're looking for."

. . .

Georgia spent the rest of the day wearing out shoe leather, as the gumshoes would put it. She didn't mind. Pounding the pavement was basic PI work, or it was before everything migrated online. Now investigators worried about carpal tunnel rather than blisters.

She tracked down the Barracks' owner, who, it turned out, owned several dive bars in addition to the Barracks. He had no contact information for Kitty. Sure, he'd call her if Kitty got in touch but warned Georgia the chances were slim. Yes, he'd been interviewed by the FBI. Georgia sighed. Would she ever break new ground on this case?

She dropped in on Ruth Marriotti, who looked a lot healthier than she had the first time they'd talked. She had dispensed with the walker, there was color in her face, and her hair was styled. Even her apartment looked clean. Georgia noticed a couple of bright paintings on the wall, a collection of china figurines on an end table, and coasters that looked like tiny vinyl records. She had to admit the place had an eclectic charm. She sat on the sofa.

"Dena gave us whatever money we needed, but it wasn't that much," Ruth said.

"Money for what?"

"Oh... let's see. There was signage for the demonstration—that was probably most of it. A huge banner on the stage, and posters in and around Grant Park. We had to pay for private security, too. That was a big chunk. Lot of good it did." She snorted. "Let's see. We had flyers to copy and post all over the city. We emailed them all over the country, too." Her brow furrowed. "Oh yeah. Permit fees. They weren't cheap. And DJ did some Facebook ads, mostly boosted posts. We also did some Google ads. Not cheap. Then there was office stuff, like printer ribbons and paper, you know. Oh, and Dena usually picked up the tab when we went out."

"Where'd she get the money?"

"I assumed it was family money."

"She told you that?"

"She didn't have to. I mean, her grandfather was one of the richest men in Chicago," Ruth replied with a trace of smugness. "Franklin Porter. He cornered the silver market forty years ago. Partnered with the Hunt brothers. He sold just in time and made a fortune. The Hunt brothers, not so much."

Georgia changed the subject. "So other than what you just said, did Dena pay you a salary?"

Ruth pursed her lips into an annoyed expression, as if the question was beneath her. "ResistanceUSA is strictly volunteer," she said. "Curt brought up the idea of starting an online store, you know, with T-shirts, mugs, and that kind of crap, but we had other priorities."

Georgia picked up on Ruth's patronizing tone. "You weren't in favor of it."

Ruth looked directly at Georgia. "We had a mission. The last thing we needed was a distraction. I wasn't convinced it would generate enough to make it worthwhile."

Was she was flexing her leadership muscles? "What did the other admins think?"

"DJ agreed with me. He wasn't big on the idea."

"And Dena?"

"She said she was okay with it, but someone else would have to manage it." Ruth sniffed. "Probably because Curt came up with it."

"Her boyfriend."

She nodded. "But now DJ's gone. And I haven't heard from Curt since it happened. So, well, it's still—um—unsettled."

"The store?"

"Everything."

"How are you doing?"

"Not bad. I go to the doctor later this week. If he gives me the okay, I'll start back to work next Monday."

"That's great."

Ruth managed a smile.

"What about the Facebook group? Who's going to take it over?"

"Good question." She hesitated. "Probably me."

Georgia found it curious that Ruth sounded so blasé about a job to which she'd devoted more than a year.

Chapter
Thirty-One

On her way home Georgia tried to reach Curt Dixon, but there was no answer on his cell, and he didn't return a text. She wondered if he'd gone back to Tennessee. He'd said he might. Maybe he wanted to forget all about Dena and the Resistance and move on with his life.

Back home she fixed a Diet Coke with lemon and called Paul Kelly.

"So what's this I hear about Franklin Porter cornering the silver market?"

Kelly cackled. "Old news. That was forty years ago."

"What happened?"

Kelly launched into an explanation of how the Hunt brothers hoarded silver in the 1970s and drove up the price more than seven hundred percent. "At the time Porter was more of a wannabe tycoon, but he'd bought a bunch of silver, too. Turned out he wasn't as greedy as the Hunts." Once the commodities exchange levied heavy restrictions on borrowing to buy silver, the Hunt brothers defaulted on their loans, and the market panicked. "Porter was careful not to overleverage himself, so when prices dropped he made out like a bandit," Kelly said.

Georgia wasn't sure how people made money when prices fell, but she was willing to take Kelly's word for it.

"Who told you about Porter?" he asked.

"Ruth Marriotti."

Kelly harrumphed. "The woman knows her history."

They talked more about the case. Georgia told Kelly she was looking for Jarvis's sister but so far had been unsuccessful.

"You sure that's where you should be spending your time?" he asked.

First Erica. Now Paul. It was enough to make her second-guess herself. But she didn't tell him that. "Actually, I am. At least for the time being."

. . .

Dusk was settling in when she heard the scratch of a key in the lock. The door opened. Jimmy.

She greeted him with a smile. "Howdy, stranger. This is a surprise."

He came over and took her in his arms. "I missed you." He kissed her.

When she came up for air, she said, "Me too. I'm sorry for being a bitch the other night. The night I left."

"You okay now?" He searched her face.

She ran her hands over his hair, pulled him to her, and kissed him again. He tightened his hold. When they parted, she said, "Much better now." She released her hold. "Hey, did you come down here the other day when I was out?"

"When?"

She told him.

He shook his head. "That was the day we busted a meth dealer in Kenosha. Why?"

"I think someone might have broken in, but I can't figure out how."

Jimmy stiffened.

"They didn't take anything. But things were, well, moved around. Like my laptop."

"Do you think someone was copying your hard drive?"

"There's nothing much to copy."

"Except your history. All the background checks you did. Other info you downloaded."

"That's what I was thinking. But why?"

"You'd know better than me." He went to her laptop and raised the cover. "I suppose we could have someone take a look at it at the crime lab."

"I appreciate the thought, but what do I use in the meantime?"

"I don't like the idea that someone is surveilling you."

"You think I do?"

"On the other hand, maybe it was Vanna or JoBeth. Maybe Vanna forgot something of Charlie's. Or needed to know where to pick it up."

Georgia considered it. "I hadn't thought about that. You're probably right."

"But if it wasn't, I don't think you should be alone right now. Why don't you come to the apartment?" He grinned. "We can do a test run."

"A test run?"

"Of living together."

She sucked in a breath. "Wow."

"Wow, what? You don't like the idea?"

"I don't know. I hadn't thought about it." She smiled. "It's tempting."

"That's the second time you haven't 'thought about it.' Think about this. If we lived together, imagine all the things I could help you think about."

She laughed. "That's got to be the most convoluted thing that's ever come out of your mouth."

"And I thought it was pretty clever."

"So tell me. What kinds of things can you help me think about?" She brushed her fingers down his cheek.

"I'll show you." He took her hand and led her into the bedroom.

Chapter Thirty-Two

They slept in the next morning, and when Georgia woke up, she wanted to make love again. She'd missed Jimmy's body and the way it fit so perfectly with hers. She made coffee for them, which she carried into the bedroom, but after two sips, she set her mug down on the bedside stand and took his away too. Then she leaned over and lowered her face to his chest, using her mouth to make sure he knew what she wanted. He closed his eyes, sighed, and took her head in his hands. They were ready to go to the next step when her cell trilled.

"Crap," she said.

"Let it go." His voice sank to a whisper.

She considered it, but she'd put out several feelers yesterday. It could be someone with new information. "I'm sorry, love."

Jimmy groaned and rolled over. "You owe me. Big-time."

She brushed her fingertips across his chest and picked up her cell. An unfamiliar Chicago number. "Davis here."

"Joel Siegenthaler. We met, uh—on the corner of Sheridan and Morse yesterday."

"Of course. Thanks for calling, Joel. What's up?"

"So this weird package was delivered the other day. For Kitty. Well, it was actually for her brother."

Georgia rocked forward, alert and focused.

"It's a yurt."

"A yurt? You mean one of those tents shaped in a circle?"

"I guess. Not my thing. First I heard of 'em."

Georgia slid out of bed and went to her laptop. "Hold on." She googled "yurt" and clicked on "Images." A page of photos popped up. Yurts were round portable tents with wooden frames. Nomads in Central Asia had used them for centuries, covering the tents with animal skins. But modern yurts, made from stronger materials, could function as vacation cabins as well as extra guest rooms, home offices, or just a place to relax. Most yurts today weren't portable, and many were custom-made.

"It didn't come assembled, did it?"

"No. It came in a big box with a bunch of smaller packages inside."

"And this yurt had Jarvis's—I mean Scott's—name on it?"

"That's what the super said."

"When did it arrive?"

"About two weeks ago. I told the super about meeting you, and she told me about the thing. It's been sitting in the basement. She wants the company to pick it up since Jarvis is gone."

"What's her name and number? The super?"

"Elizabeth Start." Siegenthaler gave her the number. "I told her you might call. She and her husband probably know more about Kitty than anyone else in the building."

"You rock, Joel. Thanks for following up."

"Well, you never know when I might need a PI."

"Damn straight."

· · ·

Georgia threw on some clothes, kissed Jimmy good-bye, and headed out. While she waited for the Toyota to warm up, she called Elizabeth Start.

"The quicker you can get rid of this thing, the better," she told Georgia. "It's taking up all the space in our basement."

"On my way."

Chapter Thirty-Three

The woman who opened the door at Kitty Jarvis's building wore a paisley granny dress that had to be a relic from the sixties. A pair of round Benjamin Franklin glasses perched on her head. Long frizzy brown hair threaded with gray was held back with a clip. Georgia extended her hand. "Georgia Davis."

"Elizabeth Start." She shook Georgia's hand. Georgia immediately thought of Elizabeth Smart, the woman who'd been abducted at fourteen and held captive nearly a year. As if she knew what Georgia was thinking, Start said, "I'm not Elizabeth Smart."

Georgia grinned.

"Most people call me Betsy. Come on. We need to go through the back." She threw on a coat and led Georgia around to a few steps that led down to a back door framed by latticework on both sides. She fished out a key, unlocked the door, and flipped a light switch as she went inside.

It was an unfinished basement, with a cracked concrete floor and a strong musty odor. The exterior walls, also concrete, were fortified with several green strips of hardened foam that indicated the foundation was cracked and had leaked water. It reminded

Georgia of the basement in the house on the West Side where she'd grown up.

"So." Betsy pointed to the center of the room. "Can you take these boxes of whatever out of here?"

Half a dozen boxes of assorted sizes and shapes occupied most of the basement floor. Georgia tried to pick up one, but it was too heavy. "How did they get here?"

"A delivery service. Not UPS, but I don't know the name. My husband keeps telling me he's called several times, but it's been two weeks and nothing's happened." She shook her head and folded her arms. "It's getting impossible to get anything done these days. No accountability. People don't care about anything except themselves."

"You have the shipping info?"

Betsy dug into the pocket of her dress and pulled out a folded paper. She handed it to Georgia. The paper was addressed to Scott Jarvis, 1280 West Morse Avenue, Chicago. The sender was International Yurt Limited, with an address in Washington State. Georgia frowned. "You wouldn't know who their Chicago distributor is, would you?"

"Are you kidding? I've never heard of a yurt."

Georgia pulled out her cell and took a picture of the label, which included a series of numbers, which she hoped was the order number.

She bent down to inspect the various boxes. When did Jarvis buy a yurt? And why? Georgia was surprised he had the money. Yurts weren't cheap. If it was custom-made, the price could run five thousand dollars. Unless it was a gift. But then why would he blow himself up afterward? If he was given a shelter that could be assembled almost anywhere, didn't that indicate a healthy desire to stay alive? Could it have been compensation for killing Dena? Or did his sister buy it for him? Maybe she wanted him out of her hair. He'd been living with her since he was discharged from the military.

Georgia straightened, took a step back, and bumped into

something she hadn't noticed. When she turned around, she realized it was a case for a huge musical instrument. "Sorry . . ."

"Oh, don't worry. That's just my cello. It's here temporarily."

Georgia raised an eyebrow.

"I used to play. In the Northwest Symphony Orchestra."

"Really?"

Her cheeks reddened. "We played at Maine West in Des Plaines. They still do."

"But you don't?"

"I broke my leg a few years ago. Had to miss the season. There were only four concerts anyway. Then Ken needed me, and we got busy here. I just let it go."

"Forever?"

"I suppose nothing is forever."

"Sure. Maybe you'll get back to it."

She didn't reply. Georgia took that as a "no." Too bad. The world needed people who could add beauty, however big or small their contributions.

"I really should have Ken take it upstairs. It's too damp down here," she mused as if she was talking to herself.

Georgia cleared her throat. "Do you have any idea where Kitty went? Or when she'll be back?"

"She said she had to get away for a while." Betsy's expression softened. "Can't blame her."

"She must have left an emergency contact. Or a phone number? An address?"

Betsy shook her head. "She didn't want to be bothered. But she said she'd send the rent in if she stayed away longer than a few weeks."

"So she's planning to come back . . ."

"I assume so."

"Would anyone else here know anything? A neighbor? Someone on her floor, maybe?"

"People here keep to themselves. My Kenny and I probably know more than anyone else."

"That's what Joel said."

"So, what do you think? Can you get rid of this for us?"

"I'll do my best to track it down and have it returned."

Betsy gave Georgia a nod. "You're an investigator, Joel says?"

"That's right."

"Is something wrong? I mean aside from that girl being shot by Kitty's brother? And then him committing suicide?"

Isn't that enough? Georgia bit back her reply. "There are—well—some loose ends I've been asked to look into."

Betsy nodded again. The muscles around her mouth loosened. "Well, I'll ask around. You know, the building."

Georgia smiled. "Thanks."

Chapter
Thirty-Four

Georgia spent the next twenty minutes in her car researching stores that distributed International Yurt products, but the clumsiness of finding the right websites on her phone drove her crazy. Besides, Jarvis, or whoever bought the yurt, might have ordered online from the company itself. She called International Yurt.

"Hi. I'm in Chicago. Could you tell me who distributes your products here?"

A woman's voice said, "Hold on. I'll connect you to sales."

A moment later, "This is Jerry. How can I help you?"

Georgia explained.

"So you're interested in becoming a Chicago distributor? Hold on. I'll transfer you."

Before she could say no, she heard a click and tinny music, which was interrupted with an ad for, of course, International Yurt Limited. She hung up and redialed.

"Hello, this is Jerry. How can I help you?"

"Hello, Jerry. You transferred me before I had the chance to say I'm not interested in becoming a distributor. I'm an investigator working on a case, and I'm hoping you can give me a list of your recent customers in Chicago. I'm happy to send you a fax of my license."

"Are you with the police?"

"I'm private."

"In that case, I can't do that without a subpoena or court order."

Georgia squeezed her eyes shut. "Okay. Then what about your distributors in the Chicago area?"

"That's easy. There are only three. I'll transfer you to my assistant, who can—"

"Wait." This time she caught him before he disconnected.

Betsy Start was right. It was becoming way too difficult to complete what should be simple tasks. "I'm interested in just one order. It was for a yurt from your company. I have the customer order number. Can you at least tell me which store sold it?"

"Unfortunately, that's proprietary information."

Georgia felt her teeth grinding in frustration.

"But our distributors in Chicago are the Camping Unlimited chain. Actually, they're our wholly owned subsidiary. There are three in Chicago."

"Can you tell me which store ordered the one for this customer? I have his name."

"Sorry. Privacy issues."

She sighed. "Okay. Thanks anyway."

She looked up Camping Unlimited: one in Northbrook, one in Naperville, one in Bloomingdale. Naperville and Bloomingdale were more than thirty miles away, but Northbrook was close by. She drove over. Camping Unlimited occupied a corner property in a recently built mall. A parking area lay in front of the store, but few cars were parked there.

Inside was a huge sales floor filled with every piece of equipment a camper would need, as well as many they didn't. Tents, even a yurt, it looked like, in one corner. Stoves, lanterns, ropes, dried-food packages, sleeping bags. She also spotted Wi-Fi connection products, even portable air-conditioning units. With gear like that, what was the point of leaving home?

A huge customer service desk took up the middle of the sales floor. Georgia approached it. Recalling Jerry's reluctance to share with her, at least over the phone, she decided on a different strategy.

A younger version of Woody Allen stood behind the desk bent over a computer.

"Good morning."

The kid looked up. "Can I help you?" he said in the sullen, minimum-wage, "I don't really care if you live or die" voice.

"I hope so." She flashed him a cheery smile. "A friend of mine ordered a yurt here a few months ago. I'm interested in the same thing."

"Oh." He gave no sign he knew about Jarvis. In fact, his tone signaled relief. "Let me get my manager." Was a yurt too expensive or complicated for him to handle? He picked up the phone and pressed a couple of numbers. "Gail, there's a customer here who's interested in a yurt." As he replaced the phone, he offered Georgia a weak grimace, which must have been his version of a smile. "She'll be right out."

Gail, a blowsy woman in jeans, sweatshirt, and sneakers, emerged from a door across the floor. She trotted over. "So, you're interested in a yurt?"

Georgia gave her a bright smile too and nodded. "A friend of mine had one delivered to his apartment. I think he ordered it around Christmas, and I wanted to check prices and amenities and all that."

Gail stepped behind the customer service desk to another computer. "What's the customer's name?"

"Scott Jarvis." Georgia held her breath, hoping the manager didn't recognize the name of Dena Baldwin's shooter.

"Sounds familiar." Gail frowned. Georgia tried to ignore the thumping of her heart. Gail hunkered over the computer and clicked a few keys.

"Here it is. Jarvis. Rogers Park. Morse Street."

"That's it! Can you tell me about the yurt? I think he said it was a custom order."

"Lemme see." Gail read something on the computer monitor. Her eyebrows arched. Georgia fisted her hands. Had she just realized who Jarvis was?

"Yeah, it was custom all right. Lots of bells and whistles," Gail said slowly.

"Like what?"

Gail proceeded to read the order out loud. "Twenty-foot yurt. A door. One window. Outer cover. Stove and stovepipe." She stopped and looked up. "Wow. Sounds like the guy was gonna move into it permanently."

"Really?"

"These things are almost like RVs or trailers nowadays. Without wheels. Hold on." She bent down to retrieve a catalog under the desk and handed it to Georgia. "Here. You can see what all's involved. They *are* pretty cool."

"How much would one like his run?"

Gail checked the monitor and whistled softly. "Over four grand when all is said and done."

Georgia made her eyes widen. "Well, I guess that's that. I don't have that kind of money."

Gail grinned. "Who does?"

"To be honest, I didn't know Scott did either," Georgia added.

"Wait a sec." Gail looked at the monitor again, then at Georgia. Georgia mentally crossed her fingers. "You should ask him yourself."

"Why do you say that?"

Indecision came across the manager's face. "Sorry. I'm really—I'm not supposed to reveal financial information."

Georgia cocked her head. "It's just—well—I don't know Scott all that well. I'd like to know him better. You know what I mean? I just wanted to find out if there was someone—well, never mind."

A knowing look replaced Gail's indecision. "You've got a thing for him, and you want to know if he's got enough money to buy a yurt."

"Well . . ." Georgia hoped she was blushing.

"Or if someone else bought it for him."

Georgia looked up. They were conspirators now.

Gail hesitated. "Let me put it this way. I didn't sell it to him."

"You didn't?"

"Looks like it was another employee, Jackie."

"So you don't know if . . ." Georgia let her voice trail off.

"Like I said, even if I did, I couldn't tell you stuff like that."

"Not even if someone else was here with him? I heard this rumor, and I— Well, it would really help me out."

"I'm sorry." Gail's expression was full of regret. But something else, too. Resolve. What had she discovered?

"So, is Jackie here?"

"She's off until Monday." Today was Thursday. "But she might remember something." Gail kept a steady gaze on Georgia. "You should talk to her. Really."

Georgia knew what Gail was trying to tell her. "Thanks. I'll be back."

Chapter
Thirty-Five

Washington, DC

"You hear anyone talking about me recently?" Carl Baldwin loomed in front of Vic's office door.

Vic looked up from his desk. His unexpected presence unnerved Vic, as Carl must have known it would. It had something to do with the angle of the doors. Vic's office was across the hall from Carl's, but not directly. He couldn't see Carl exit his office, and Carl couldn't see Vic leave his. But Carl could sneak across the hall and surprise him. Vic suspected Carl had designed it that way.

"No more than usual, sir." Vic hoped his boss would appreciate his attempt at humor.

But Carl scowled and folded his arms. "Come into my office. We need to talk."

Vic glanced around his own office, wondering why it wouldn't do. As if he knew what Vic was thinking, Carl said, "I just ran a sweep. I know it's secure."

Vic slipped his cell in his pocket, took a legal pad and pen, and followed Carl across the hall. Despite the Euro-modern furniture, Carl's office wore a spartan air. Plain vanilla blinds, empty bookshelves, one framed photo on his desk, and a signed baseball from former Cubs right fielder Sammy Sosa. The photo was of Dena in a bikini, hoisting the mainsail of a sloop on Lake Michigan. Carl stood behind, grinning at his daughter. Vic deposited himself in an Eames chair.

Carl watched Vic gaze at the photo. "You still monitoring the group?"

Vic nodded.

"Anything new?"

He shook his head. "It hasn't been dormant, but traffic is nothing compared to the way it used to be."

"What about that PI in Chicago?"

"I'm putting some background together. You'll have it tomorrow."

Carl rubbed his hand across the stubble on his cheeks. He hadn't shaved today and his button-down shirt was rumpled. "Something's going on. And I don't like it."

Vic angled his head.

"Three fails in a row are two fails too many."

Puzzled, Vic flipped up his palms.

"The Russians, the Uzbek arms deal, and fracking," Carl said.

"Fracking hasn't come up for a vote yet."

"Hell, they haven't brought it out of the goddammed committee. They're sitting on it."

"It happens."

"Not like this. Someone's jamming the bill. Chipping off members one by one."

Vic sighed inwardly. Everything was a battle with Carl. Lobbying used to be access and persuasion. Today it was pay-to-play. Which meant that when Carl was flush and could outbid the opposition, no one was a more stalwart, fearless gladiator for his clients. But when he was outplayed or outspent, he cried victim.

"Do you have proof?" Vic asked. "Left-wingers? Environmentalists? Anti–fossil fuel group?"

Carl shook his head. "That's the thing. I can't figure it out.

And meanwhile, you were right. The word is out that I've lost my touch."

There was something different about Carl today. His customary narcissism was on display, but an undercurrent of worry ran through it.

"Let me do some investigating. Could be fracking just isn't a priority anymore. The Middle East is blowing up, and whenever that happens, oil is more valuable than gas. Plus, the earthquakes—"

Carl cut him off. "You remember when I had you track Dena's fracking activism?"

"Sure."

"I'm beginning to wonder if she pissed off the wrong people."

"What do you mean?"

Now Carl looked at Dena's photo. "What if her murder was a warning shot? To me?"

"Whoa, Carl. Slow down. DC doesn't work like that."

"And you would know because . . ."

Vic shifted in his chair. "Five minutes ago you're railing against a left-wing conspiracy. Now it's the oil industry. You don't think you—that's a little paranoid?"

"Sometimes they *are* out to get you. Look at the past couple of months."

"You think someone is deliberately sabotaging your career?"

"Like I keep saying, it's your career too, buddy boy."

"But how would they do it? And why?" Vic templed his fingers. "It would require at least half a dozen congressmen to intentionally change their vote just to hurt you. I think it's unlikely. It's just a streak of bad luck."

Carl picked up the Sammy Sosa baseball from his desk and lobbed it from one hand to the other. "I don't know."

You're not that important. The world doesn't revolve around you, Vic thought. Carl had always been aggressive. Full of bluster, sure. Yet focused like a laser when he needed to be. But he hadn't been the same since Dena died. He gazed at his boss. His face was puffy and fleshier these days. The lines on his forehead dug deeper. Judging from his rumpled shirt and day-old stubble, his grooming, usually the pinnacle of precision, was slipping. Was he hitting the bottle? For the first time since he'd been working for Baldwin, he realized his boss was afraid. And he was sharing that fear with Vic.

"Look, Vic. We have access, right? That's what we offer our clients. Access and persuasion. But our clients aren't satisfied with that. They expect us to perform miracles. Lift sanctions. Broker arms deals. Invest in their real estate. The United States may be up for sale, but there are strings attached to that sale. They want results, not just 'access.' And if they don't get it, we're vulnerable."

"Vulnerable? To what? You make it sound like we're living in a third world country. A place where the rule of law doesn't count."

Carl leveled a look at Vic but kept his mouth shut.

That was the moment Vic decided to pack up and leave the shithole that was Washington. If this town could chew up a man like Baldwin, what would it do to him?

Chapter
Thirty-Six

A mild breeze, the first of the season, greeted Georgia as she left her apartment the following Monday. Grimy piles of snow on both sides of the road oozed water into gutters, and kids splashed in the puddles that formed. Sadly, the thaw wouldn't last. Chicago weather was as fickle as that wind-borne feather in the *Forrest Gump* movie.

She drove back to Northbrook and parked in the lot of Camping Unlimited. She pushed through the door and went to the customer service desk where she'd had the conversation with Gail. The young Woody Allen guy was nowhere to be seen, and the desk was unmanned. One of those steel call bells you see in hotels sat on the counter, and when Georgia pressed down, it chimed cheerfully.

A young woman with blue and green hair, black nails, and a nose ring emerged from a back room and hurried over. She appeared to be younger than Gail but older than Woody.

"Sorry. I was in the back."

"Love the hair." Georgia smiled.

"Oh, thanks." The woman fluffed her hair on one side. "I did it over the weekend."

"It makes a statement," Georgia said. "Are you Jackie?"

"How did you know?"

"Gail told me I should talk to you."

"She did?" Jackie's tone made Georgia think the two women weren't best friends.

Georgia nodded. "You sold a yurt to a man, I think around Christmas. His name was Scott Allen Jarvis. Do you remember him?"

She worried a hand through her hair. "The name sounds familiar."

Georgia didn't say anything.

"Jarvis, Jarvis . . . Hey. Isn't that the man who shot the woman a few weeks ago?"

"You keep up with the news."

"It was horrible. Never in a million years did I think I'd see something like that in Chicago. In Grant Park." Her eyes went wide. "Wait a minute. Is that the guy I sold the yurt to?"

"I'm pretty sure it is. I have some questions about him."

Jackie went rigid. Then she hugged her arms. "Oh my God. Oh my God." Her voice rose. "Am I in trouble?"

"Don't worry. You didn't do anything wrong."

"Are you a cop?"

Georgia tried out her most reassuring smile. "No. I'm an investigator. Private."

Jackie's eyes were still as round as plates. "Holy shit."

"I'm working for the family of Dena Baldwin. The woman who was killed."

Jackie bit her lip. "Of course, I remember that sale. Happened right after I started. I got a huge commission. Biggest one I've gotten."

"Can you pull up the bill of sale on your computer so we can check the details?"

"Sure." She clicked a few keys and waited. Then: "Okay. Here it is."

"When did he buy it?"

"December twenty-first." Jackie said. The pitch of her voice went down, and she seemed calmer.

"How much did he pay for it?"

Jackie's gaze went to the bottom of the monitor. "Hold on. There's a second page." She pressed a key. Then she blew out a breath. "Wow. Over four thousand."

"Nice Christmas present for himself."

"It was really high-end. All kind of extras. But—wait a sec. I don't think he paid for it."

"Is that so?" Georgia leaned over and propped her elbows on the counter.

Jackie fingered one of several earrings in her left ear. "He was with a woman."

Georgia dug out a photo of Kitty she'd found on Google when she did a background check. "Is this the woman?"

Jackie took the photo and studied it. "I can't swear to it, but I don't think so."

Georgia was taken aback. She had been confident that Kitty had bought Jarvis the yurt. "Are you sure?"

"The woman with him was . . . different."

"Can you describe her?"

"Lemme see. She seemed average. You know, height and weight. No makeup."

"What color hair?"

Jackie looked out, trying to concentrate. "I don't know. She was wearing a hat. You know, one of those wool caps."

"Eye color?"

"I couldn't tell."

"Clothes?"

"Sorry. She was wearing a coat."

"Brand? Color?"

"It wasn't a North Face. But it was gray." She cocked her head. "Maybe his girlfriend. Did he have one?"

"I'm not sure. Were they—was she affectionate? Holding hands, that kind of thing?"

"I don't—wait. Now I remember. No. He went off to look at sleeping bags." She waved vaguely toward another part of the store. "And she paid." Jackie shot Georgia a triumphant look, as if she'd solved a particularly knotty problem.

Georgia's pulse raced. "Did she use a credit card?" A bill of sale could be subpoenaed. The credit card number would be on the paperwork.

Jackie frowned. "No. Says here it was cash. Oh, right. She paid with a check."

A check could be subpoenaed, too. "You're sure?"

Jackie nodded.

"Who ordered all the add-ons? I mean it cost four thousand dollars, right?"

"Right. Like I said, it was my best commission. Lemme think. I think they had a list when they came in. Oh wait, I remember. They kind of argued about a couple of things. She thought they weren't necessary. But he wanted them."

"What were they . . . those couple of things?"

"Hold on." She went back to the computer monitor and scrolled down. "Um . . . extras, mostly. Looks like he got a yurt cover. For the outside. And a stove inside. Oh, and an extra window."

"So he got everything he wanted?"

"Pretty much."

Georgia pulled out Kitty's photo again. "And you're sure it wasn't this woman?"

She grimaced. "I just don't know. I only saw them for a few minutes."

"Did you hear them call each other by name?"

Jackie shook her head. "Not that I remember." Her cheeks flushed. "I'm not helping you, am I?"

"You're doing great. Really." Georgia smiled. "Okay, aside from the address on record, did they talk about where the yurt was actually going to be set up?"

Jackie shook her head. She looked like she might cry. "I'm so sorry."

"Does the expression 'beef jerky' mean anything to you?"

"Huh?"

Georgia repeated it.

"The stuff you eat? Um, no."

"Neither of them mentioned it when they were here?"

"I don't remember. Then again, why would I?"

Georgia smiled her thanks, gave her a card, asked her to call if anything else came to her. On her way out Jackie exclaimed, "Hey, I just remembered. He said he would be taking it up north. A lake, he said. Near the family cabin."

Georgia backtracked, instantly focused. "Did he say where 'up north'? What lake?"

A distraught expression came over Jackie. "I'm sorry." She rubbed one hand up and down the other arm.

"It's okay." Georgia cracked a joke. "There are only about a thousand lakes up north."

But Jackie's face collapsed. She looked as if she'd missed the last train out of Dodge and had to face the bad guys alone.

Chapter
Thirty-Seven

Georgia, buoyed by enthusiasm, couldn't wait to get home. Finally, she was making progress. She'd ferreted out information she was sure the FBI didn't have. Now she had to figure out how it related—if it did—to her case.

A woman bought Jarvis a yurt that he intended to live in "up north." Probably either Wisconsin or Minnesota. Again, she thought, that didn't sound like a man on the verge of killing himself. It sounded like a man with a plan to escape and survive—albeit off the grid—once he killed Dena Baldwin. So who was the woman who bought and paid more than four grand for his yurt? A girlfriend? A partner? Was she planning to share the yurt with him? Moreover, what woman has four thousand bucks to shower on a boyfriend? Where was she now and why didn't the police or FBI know about her? There hadn't been even the whiff of a rumor about a girlfriend. Just Jarvis's sister. Who might turn out to be the buyer after all.

But whoever it was wrote a check. And once Georgia had a copy of the check, a lot of those questions would be answered. Georgia pulled to the side of the road and called Paul Kelly.

His secretary answered. What was her name? Joan. That was it.

"Oh, hi, honey," Joan said after Georgia asked for him. "He's not here. He's in court."

Georgia was surprised. Paul had always seemed more of a transactional lawyer than a trial attorney. Still, even the best business lawyer had to show up in court occasionally. She asked Joan to have Paul call her.

"Is it an emergency?"

"Well, no. But it's important that we talk today."

"Sure, honey."

. . .

Georgia invited Jimmy over that evening, and when he arrived, she filled him in on her day. "I'll tell you all the details later."

"Later?"

She went to her laptop and clicked to her favorite pizza delivery place. "I feel like celebrating. How are mushrooms and bacon?"

"Bacon is your favorite way to celebrate?" Jimmy asked.

She finished ordering and paying for it online. "Second favorite."

"Oh? What's the first?"

"I seem to remember an IOU you have on me."

A smile came across his face. His eyes sparkled. "I remember."

"Well, this woman pays her debts." She checked the time. "We have forty-five minutes."

. . .

When the delivery boy buzzed her apartment, Georgia threw on some sweats and a T-shirt and answered the door. She tipped the guy and inhaled deeply as he handed it over. There was nothing better than the aroma of cheese, fresh piecrust, and bacon, all mixed together. She got out a beer for Jimmy, Diet Coke for her, and carried everything into the bedroom. The sight of Jimmy, just coming out of her bathroom, almost made her drop the box. He was wearing her red satin bathrobe. It barely covered his chest and stopped at mid-thigh. Her reaction made him dive under the covers.

She giggled. "Nice try. But the color is all wrong on you."

"In that case"—he sat up and slipped off the robe—"this is a clothing-optional pizza party."

"I'll go for that." Georgia set the pizza box on the bed, stripped off her clothes, and got under the covers beside him. She opened the box, pulled off two slices, and handed one over. "Try not to spill, okay?"

"What . . . you don't like to roll around in bed with crumbs and bacon bits?"

She leaned over and kissed him. "You're more fun. To roll around with."

He took a swig of beer.

She bit into her slice. Few foods were as unhealthy as pizza, but the rich, savory combination of cheese, tomato, and piecrust was addictive.

"So, here's what I think," Georgia said after wolfing down two pieces. "If Paul can subpoena the check that paid for the yurt, we'll finally get some answers."

"It shouldn't be a problem to get a subpoena."

"I know," she said happily.

Jimmy reached for another slice. "You know, I've been thinking about something."

Georgia slid the empty pizza box to the floor and snuggled closer. She started to lightly caress the hair on his chest, making little circles with her thumb and forefinger.

"Hey. I'm still eating," he said.

"I know," she murmured.

"What if 'beef jerky' isn't the snack that comes in those packages?"

Georgia stopped stroking his chest hair. "What do you mean?"

"It's always been a weird clue. Like a puzzle we're supposed to figure out. What if 'beef jerky' is code for something like a weapon? Or even a person?"

Georgia sat up, all business now. "Well, Jarvis *was* military. He did two tours in Iraq." She pulled the sheet up to her neck. "Is there a brand of military grenade called Beef Jerky? Or maybe a piece of equipment?"

"Never heard of anything, but that doesn't mean it doesn't exist."

"You think his girlfriend might know? Maybe it has something to do with the yurt."

"It's possible."

She looked over. "You know, something else has been bugging me about the yurt. Why would Jarvis want to kill himself? I mean, the guy had a brand-new yurt to look forward to. He was taking it to a remote lake up north. He doesn't sound like a man who wanted to kill himself."

He gulped down the rest of his beer. "So you're thinking someone set him up? Someone by the name of 'Beef Jerky'?"

"It's worth pursuing. Great work, Sac. I'm on it."

He set the empty beer bottle on the nightstand. "You don't have to do it right away. I have other good ideas. Ones that we can do. Together."

But Georgia climbed out of bed and headed into the living room to retrieve her laptop.

Jimmy sighed.

Chapter Thirty-Eight

Georgia googled "IEDs and beef jerky." There were no connections. She tried "Bushmasters and beef jerky." Nothing. Dogged determination kept her at it. She had no idea what time it was when Jimmy's light snoring told her he was out. She checked the clock. After nine. She'd been working for more than an hour. And she hadn't heard from Paul Kelly. She leaned over Jimmy and picked up her phone, which woke Jimmy up.

"Everything okay?" he asked.

"Sorry. I didn't mean to wake you. I just need to call Paul Kelly." She took the phone to her side of the bed and punched in Kelly's number.

Jimmy grunted and started to roll away from her, presumably to go back to sleep. Then he stopped. "Hey. Did you ever talk to JoBeth?"

"JoBeth? Where did that come from?" Georgia looked over.

"She called me a few days ago."

"You? Why?"

"She's been leaving messages for you but says you never call her back. She really wants to connect with you."

"Right."

"But you don't want to connect with her."

Georgia put the phone down. "Look, Jimmy. I know you're trying to help. And I know you have a close relationship with your mother. And your aunt. And everyone else in your very big, fat Greek family. The very idea that family members might be estranged from each other is inconceivable to you." She pulled the sheet and blanket up to her chin. "And to be honest, I miss Vanna and Charlie. I keep telling myself I shouldn't be upset by a girl half my age. But then I realize this isn't any girl. Vanna's been through hell and back." She hesitated. "And we're sisters."

"With a mother."

"See, that's the thing. *She* has a mother. I don't."

"But you do."

"I can't go there, Jimmy. She walked out on me."

"And you survived." He sat up and cupped her face in his hands. "You're a wonderful human being. Kind and considerate. You don't have a mean bone in your body."

"My backbone."

He inclined his head.

"It's become very strong. And cruel." She thought she was making a joke, but it fell flat.

"Not cruel. Maybe stubborn . . ."

"Listen to me. I've lived all my adult life without a family. Then Vanna showed up. I thought it would be the two of us. And then there was Charlie. And you."

"Us against the world."

"I don't know if I'd—"

The trill of her phone cut her off. She glanced at the screen. "I've got to get this. It's Paul."

Jimmy let her go and fell back against the pillows.

"Hey, Paul. I was just calling you." She told him about the yurt and how it was paid for. "Can you get a subpoena for the check? It would move things forward in a big way."

She listened to his response. "That long?" A pause. "Fucking bureaucracy. But yeah. Go ahead. And thanks."

"Now I need to tell you something," Kelly said. "Dena's father, Carl Baldwin, is AWOL."

"What are you talking about?"

"He disappeared. And no one knows where he is."

"How do you know?"

"Erica was trying to get some finances settled, but he never returned her messages. His assistant called today—the guy has no idea where he went. Erica and I agree that you need to get yourself to DC and find him."

"But I'm just getting somewhere here."

"Look, Georgia, whatever is going on with Carl Baldwin could be more important than a subpoena. And Erica wants you to go. I just got off the phone with her." He paused. "Wasn't there a man associated with Dena you needed to interview in DC?"

"Yes. Willie Remson. He lives outside DC."

"Well?"

Kelly was right, Georgia realized. She planned to go to DC at some point. And now wasn't a bad time. Zach Dolan and his team of hackers were still doing background checks on ResistanceUSA group members. And Kelly had just told her a subpoena could take as long as a month to process and deliver. She started to warm to the idea. She could kill three birds with one stone: she could look into Carl Baldwin's disappearance; interview Remson; and put some distance between JoBeth and herself.

"By the way, Georgia . . ."

"Yes, Paul?"

"Be careful when you're nosing around DC. It could be dangerous."

"I'll take precautions."

Chapter
Thirty-Nine

The next day Georgia pulled out of the rental car lot at Reagan National Airport equipped with her GPS, a map, and her Baby Glock, which she'd checked during the flight. She'd only been to Washington once before, on the obligatory high school trip, and she didn't remember much about it. She'd been well into drinking and sex at the time, both of which she'd managed to do even though they'd been supervised. Apart from a trip to both New York and Boston for training when she was a cop, she hadn't spent any time on the East Coast.

As she headed down the George Washington Memorial Parkway, she marveled at how warm the winter temperatures were compared to Chicago's. She was reminded that they called DC a swamp not only for its politics. She passed the Washington Monument and crossed a bridge into the city, where the Lincoln Memorial greeted her. Spotless and glistening white from a distance, the monuments gave "good face," she thought. Appropriate for the capital of the country.

She'd booked a hotel room not far from Baldwin's Kalorama office, or so Google Maps told her. But as she navigated from Georgetown to Connecticut Avenue, an oppressive, claustrophobic feeling pressed down on her. It was the density.

Homes and buildings were sandwiched together without enough space between them. The Midwest, with its flat prairies that provided unlimited views to the horizon, as well as the expanse of Lake Michigan, gave Chicago a sense of vastness. Even the spaces between houses were ample. But here in DC a person could easily spy on their neighbor just by peering out a bedroom window. She wondered how people here functioned with such an unrelenting violation of their personal space.

After driving around the same one-way streets three times, Georgia wanted to drive her rental car into the Potomac River. As the city's population exploded over the years, the clogged streets created a permanent rush hour. City officials had tried to accommodate the traffic by making many of the narrow DC streets one-way, which meant visitors like Georgia who didn't know the ins and outs of DC geography could circle forever without knowing how to untangle themselves.

That wasn't the way it was supposed to be, she thought. L'Enfant, the French architect who'd laid out the nation's capital—she was surprised his name popped into her head; it must have been buried there since her high school trip—had designed a sense of order into the plan. Downtown streets were either numbers or letters and ran perpendicular to each other in a grid, while avenues, named for each state, cut across the grid diagonally. All three came together at circles in an impossible snarl of cars, buses, and pedestrians.

Finally she arrived at a small boutique hotel on Connecticut that Erica Baldwin had recommended. Naturally, there was no parking available, so she was forced to hunt down a parking lot, which took another twenty minutes. Exhausted, she collapsed in her room, grateful she would only be in DC two days.

· · ·

Around six that evening Georgia reached the affluent suburb of Chevy Chase, Maryland, where she parked across the street from a modest two-story colonial. Like the other homes on the block, Willie Remson's home was too close to his neighbors', but it perched at the top of a tiny hill, and the setting sun shot beams of rosy light into the windows. A two-car garage on a lower level was occupied by a minivan. Georgia was prepared to stake out as long as it took, but luck was with her, and barely ten minutes later, a young boy and girl skipped out a side door, followed by a woman in jeans and an all-weather jacket. She recognized his family from Remson's Facebook photos. The girl, who Georgia estimated was nine or ten, shouted to her brother. "Mommy won't let you eat anchovies. It gives you a tummy ache." Georgia rolled down the window.

The boy, who couldn't be more than six or seven, stuck out his tongue at his sister, which provoked an immediate response. "Mommy . . . Wills stuck out his tongue at me."

"Wills, cut it out. Janet, get in the car and stop tattling on your brother." The harried, monotone voice said their mother was having a bad day.

They piled into the car, backed out the driveway, and took off. Despite the fatigue and frustration of travel, a surge of energy pulsed through Georgia. She was on the move.

She made sure to stay half a block behind the minivan, which as far as Georgia could tell, doubled back to the street, Connecticut Avenue, that she'd driven out on. But when the minivan reached East-West Highway, it turned and headed west to Wisconsin Avenue, where it turned several times, eventually pulling up to a pizza parlor. The kids spilled out and skipped to the door in high spirits. Georgia let a few minutes go by, then followed them in, pulling a ball cap down on her face.

The place was exceptionally clean and modern, with a honey-toned hardwood floor that looked spotless. The warm honey tone carried through to the chairs, and marbled slabs of Formica topped the tables. The booths were upholstered in navy, and photos of pizzas sprawled across the walls. A chalkboard with the daily specials hung above the counter. The familiar aroma infused Georgia with pleasure, and she was almost as excited as the kids.

The family commandeered a booth on one side. Happily, in the center of the room was a pizza bar with stools for singles, and a couple of people were already there. She took a stool with her back to the Remsons but within earshot.

The wife settled the kids, then made a call. "Hi. We're here. Where are you?" A pause. "Should I go ahead and order?" Another pause. "Mushrooms, bacon, onions on half. Okay. See you soon."

The Remsons' tastes were similar to hers. She smiled to herself. She got up, pulled the ball cap farther down, and sauntered up to the counter. Mrs. Remson was there also, ordering a large pizza and four Cokes. Then she added mozzarella sticks. Remson's wife was petite, with short dark hair cut in a pixie style. She wore no makeup, and her denim suit and sneakers said she was in "working mom" mode. Unlike Dena Baldwin, Georgia thought.

Georgia ordered two slices and a Diet Coke. She was just polishing off the first slice when the glass door opened, and a small, compact man with a mustache compensating for a bald spot on his crown walked in.

A chorus of "Daddys" greeted him, and the two kids ran over to hug him. He blushed but gamely returned the hugs. As they returned to the booth, he leaned over to kiss his wife. "How are you, sweetheart?"

"Great. But don't move." For an instant, Georgia froze, thinking she'd been exposed. But when she turned around, she breathed a sigh of relief. A waiter had come over with the pizza and cheese sticks and was only inches from Remson, who backed up despite his wife's warning. The waiter flailed, and the tray of pizza slipped from his grasp. Georgia dove for the pizza and managed to grab it before it wound up on the floor. The mozzarella sticks didn't make it, though, and spilled onto the floor.

"Oh my God, I'm sorry," Remson said loudly. "Are you okay?" He turned to survey the mess.

"It's okay." The waiter looked over at Georgia, who was still crouched on the floor hanging on to the pizza. "*¡Eres un ángel!*"

He held out his hands and Georgia handed him up the pizza. "*Tuve suerte,*" she said.

The waiter shook his head. "*¡No! ¡Es un milagro!*"

Georgia felt her cheeks get hot. Remson and his family were watching them. From their confused expressions, it was clear they didn't speak Spanish. The waiter placed the tray on the table and left, returning with a broom and the manager in tow.

"We are so sorry," the manager said. "Thank you, miss." He gestured to Georgia. "Both your meals are on the house. And we'll bring you a fresh plate of mozzarella sticks," he said to the Remsons.

"No need," Remson's wife said. "It was our fault." She angled a glance at her husband, indicating it was *his* fault, not theirs.

But the manager fussed and brought them a fresh order of cheese sticks. Remson's wife called to Georgia, who had returned to her stool at the bar. "Miss, how can we thank you?"

"Not necessary," she said. "Glad I could help."

"That was some catch. Are you sure you don't play for the Nationals?"

Georgia shook her head politely. She wasn't happy her cover had been blown. But it had been her own damn fault. Then again, things happened for a reason. Didn't they?

Chapter Forty

Georgia was back in Chevy Chase the next morning before seven. A cold rain that had begun overnight drummed on the roof of the Toyota. But she'd slept well. Her hotel room turned out to be a delight: a king bed, flat-screen TV, audio system, whirlpool bath, and refrigerator stocked with everything she could imagine, all in a renovated but dignified older building.

She was prepared to stake out Remson's home as long as it took, but he exited his house thirty minutes later, opened his garage door, and, a moment later, backed a white Volvo down the driveway. She followed at a discreet distance as he crisscrossed streets and ended up on Wisconsin Avenue heading northwest. Wisconsin eventually became Rockville Pike, and he kept driving past a huge shopping mall. Outside the dense urban area, rain mixed with ground-level fog, which made Georgia think of Chicago's Forest Preserve on a cold, rainy day. Finally Remson pulled into a parking lot about the size of a football stadium. Behind it a five-story building with a neon sign said they'd arrived at DataMaster.

She waited for Remson to stop, then parked a few rows away. She noted video cameras attached to poles every few rows. She should have parked elsewhere. Too late. Using her umbrella to shield her face, she followed him into a businesslike lobby. It was still early, and she watched as he got on the elevator alone and punched a button. The elevator stopped at the fifth floor. It was too risky to follow him up, but she spotted a coffee shop in the lobby and went in to plan her next move. After ordering a latte, she headed to an area with a view of the elevators. She sat in a roomy upholstered chair beside a fake fireplace with soft lighting, which some coffee shops were now adopting so that their atmosphere oozed "cozy and comfortable" rather than the ultrasleek of Starbucks.

She sipped her drink and looked up DataMaster on her phone. Its website proclaimed it was a total Internet security firm that offered ironclad protection of corporate systems and provided a host of cybersecurity solutions and services. What services? And what solutions? Based on what had emerged about companies like Cambridge Analytica and the Israeli-owned Black Cube, companies like DataMaster might be offering much more.

From talking to Zach Dolan, Georgia had learned that some data-protection companies had one mission for some clients, but another for others. Companies that sold data-protection systems might also offer data-mining services and, in some cases, actual intel gathering for political and corporate clients. Was DataMaster one of those? Were they harvesting data while masquerading as a data-protection company? Was Willie Remson a geek who stole Facebook data? Is that why he hung out on Dena's ResistanceUSA page? Maybe he'd maintained the flirtation with Dena only as long as it took him to get all the group members' information, and then disappeared. The timing worked.

Or was Georgia just paranoid?

Judging from the fact that the entire building was leased to DataMaster, whatever the company was doing was working. She sipped her drink, glad for the umpteenth time she'd never joined Facebook. She and Sam had discussed it. Sam's graphics business depended on a robust online presence—Sam called it "branding." Her social media accounts, including her company's Facebook page, showcased examples of her work. But Georgia didn't want to be found. She was the "finder."

The issue was how much information data miners had on the individuals they targeted. But finding out what company had what data was, according to Zach, "pissing in the wind." This was a new industry, and there was no oversight. On the other hand, Sam argued that organizations like Facebook made Georgia's work easier. As a hunter, Georgia profited by the accumulation of data in one place. Why complain?

Sam had a point. In the past, only law enforcement or the alphabet intelligence organizations had the resources to pry into people's lives. Now the same information could end up in the hands of anyone who paid for it. Including Georgia. In fact, Zach complained that the price for data, especially on the dark web, had shot up ever since the EU enacted stricter privacy laws. Whether that was good or bad was a question Georgia ducked. She didn't have the answer.

She caught up on emails while she waited. Nothing from Jackie, the woman who'd sold Jarvis the yurt, but she hadn't expected much. She checked in with Jimmy, then Paul Kelly. Carl Baldwin was still AWOL.

"Anything on Kitty, Jarvis's sister? Do we know if she's back in town?"

Kelly hadn't heard anything. Georgia called Betsy Start, the manager of Kitty's building. She hadn't seen or heard anything, and Kitty's mail was piling up. But the store had called, and they would be picking up the yurt in a few days. She thanked Georgia for her help.

By the time she finished her calls, the lunch hour was approaching, but a steady rain persisted, and she hoped the lousy weather would keep people inside. A deli-style sandwich place stood next to the coffee shop, and by half past eleven, people were lined up out the door. Thirty minutes later, Willie Remson appeared alone. He went to the back of the line. While waiting, he took off his glasses and polished them with a handkerchief. What guy carries a hankie these days? Georgia waited until he'd paid for his sandwich and a pop.

She intercepted him at the elevators. "Willie Remson?"

He spun around. "Yes?"

She wasn't wearing her ball cap, and it took him a moment to recognize her. Surprise flooded across his face. "You!"

He tipped his head to the side. "Do you work—" He cut himself off as comprehension dawned. His eyes narrowed, and he looked around in every direction, as if he wanted to cut and run. "You've been following me."

"My name is Georgia Davis and I'm an investigator for an attorney in Chicago. Could I have a few minutes of your time?"

"I—I don't really have a minute. I'm on a deadline."

She ignored him. "The coffee shop will work. There's a private alcove in the back."

Chapter
Forty-One

She gestured for him to lead the way. A small table near the restrooms was available, and they sat. "Please"—she pointed to his lunch—"feel free to start. This won't take long."

Remson pushed the bag a few inches away. An act of rebellion? She smiled again. "So tell me about your relationship with Dena Baldwin."

Remson froze for an instant, then massaged his mustache with his fingers. He folded his hands together on the table. "I didn't have a relationship with Dena Baldwin."

"No?"

"I signed up for the group she started. I don't even remember the name of it." He refused to make eye contact with Georgia.

"Does ResistanceUSA ring a bell?"

He fidgeted in his seat, then looked at Georgia. "What do you want from me?"

"What did you want from Dena and her group?"

He hesitated. "Look. My wife doesn't know anything about this. I scrubbed my Facebook account. I don't want any trouble."

"So you do know what this is about."

He straightened his spine and raised his chin defiantly, and for a moment, Georgia thought he might show some mettle. Then he slumped. "She knew what she was getting into. I never hid the fact I was married."

"Yes. All those pictures of your family on Facebook were a good cover."

"I'm not a sexual predator, you know. I love my wife and kids."

"Right. You just dabble."

Remson folded his arms. "I assume you've read through the correspondence. If you have, you'll know that she started it."

Georgia nodded.

"Well?"

"You jumped right in. Hardly took you a minute to reply."

A spit of irritation flashed in his eyes. "Then you know nothing happened. She was a real piece of work. As soon as I figured that out, I got out."

"I see. So *she* was the predator."

He kept his mouth shut.

"You volunteered to do some work on the site. IT stuff, right?"

If his eyes could have narrowed any more, they would have been slits. "What of it? I hate the president and what he's done to this country. I was happy to do my part."

"And what exactly did you do?"

"Actually, not much. I didn't get the chance."

"Why not?"

"Dena was always picking fights with people. Especially her admins. She liked to play victim. When she wasn't having fantasies about us," he added.

"How do you know she picked fights with the admins?"

He shrugged.

"Because you hacked into her private messages?"

Remson reddened from the neck up. He'd stepped into his own shit.

"What else did you hack into?"

"Nothing." He squirmed. "Really. That's the truth."

"But you were planning to."

He left the question unanswered. Then: "Dena was a player.

I guess she got bored . . . I mean, she was already sleeping with Dixon. Or maybe it was a habit. Our—our conversations only lasted a week or two."

"Three weeks actually. Plenty of time to harvest data from members of the Facebook group."

Remson opened his mouth, then shut it.

"I mean, here you are working for a highly successful data-protection company, which just might have a data-mining business on the side." She leaned forward. "You and your company could be in a lot of trouble."

"What are you going to do?"

"What are you going to tell me about who killed Dena Baldwin?"

"You already know. It was that ex-military creep. Jarvis."

"And he blew himself up so there wouldn't be much of a crime scene afterwards. Pretty convenient, wouldn't you say?"

"I don't know anything about that. I swear." Beads of sweat popped out on his forehead. Was Remson telling the truth?

"Ah, I see. You were just trying to steal data for a client. And coming on to Dena was the easiest way to get what you needed." She paused. "Who was—or is—that client?"

He bit his lip. "I'll get fired if I tell you."

She sat back, trying to suppress her triumph. She was right. DataMaster *was* hacking for a client, mining data for a probably nefarious purpose. She reacted with what she hoped was a casual wave of her hand. "You're going to get fired anyway, once I call the FBI."

"Wait. Wait a minute. You can't! I mean, please don't."

"But you and DataMaster are breaking the law. Bigly."

He sucked in a breath and looked down. Then he met her eyes. "If I tell you who it is, will you keep me out of it?"

"I might be persuaded to call you a confidential informant, but eventually it will come out. And whether your company figures out you were the informant is entirely out of my hands."

"I was just doing my job," he said miserably.

"If I had a quarter for every person who told me that, I'd be a millionaire."

Remson looked down at his hands again. He spoke quietly.

"It's a congressman. From Pennsylvania. Jackson Hyde."

"And why would he want the Facebook data of the ResistanceUSA members?"

"His district is into fracking in a big way. The state of Pennsylvania supplies almost twenty percent of the dry natural gas in the country."

Georgia was puzzled. She didn't understand why a politician in a fracking state would want data about an anti-president Facebook group. Luckily, though, she didn't have to. That was an issue for Paul Kelly to figure out. She was just the investigator. She asked her last question.

"Do the words 'beef jerky' mean anything to you?"

Remson looked confused. "Wha—what?"

"Beef jerky."

"Not a thing. That shit is terrible. Full of nitrates. It's really bad for you."

Talk about "really bad for you." Georgia didn't know much about fracking, except that it caused earthquakes and poisoned water with the chemicals used to pump out the gas. But she didn't say anything and slid back her chair.

"Wait. Where are you going? What's going to happen next?"

"Just live your life normally." She got up. "Pay attention to your wife and kids."

"But you can't just ruin my life like this and then walk out!"

She knew she was going to say it. Knew she shouldn't. It wasn't polite. Or professional. But she couldn't help it. "Watch me." She turned and walked out of the coffee shop without looking back.

Chapter
Forty-Two

Georgia called Kelly with what she'd learned from Remson. Over the phone, she heard him call out to Joan.

"Hey, Joanie, text me a link to the bio of Jackson Hyde, Republican from Pennsylvania." The text alert dinged less than thirty seconds later.

"She's efficient," Georgia said.

"Don't I know it." Then he was quiet, apparently skimming the bio. "Well, it is interesting. But I don't know what it means."

"I don't either."

"Lemme think about it. So what was Remson like?"

"The guy folded like a paper airplane."

"Must have been your superior interrogating skills." He cackled. "But data mining isn't something to ignore. I'm sure the FBI would be interested in what the company is up to."

"Maybe they already know."

"Could be. But I'm thinking a voluntary info dump from us might loosen their tongues about Jarvis. Maybe even 'beef jerky.'" He cleared his throat. "You know the Bureau has more than they're letting on."

Georgia squirmed and stared out the rental car's windshield. "Yeah. But give me another day. I'm about to pay Carl Baldwin's assistant a visit. You never know. Maybe we can hand the Bureau a nicely wrapped package tied up with a bow."

There was a pause. Then Kelly said, "Your job isn't to solve the crime, you know. Just to investigate."

"I know."

"Sure you do. Okay. Call me tonight."

"I will. Oh. Tell Erica the hotel is lovely. But traffic is horrible in this city. It takes forever to get anywhere."

"Yeah, everyone's looking for their fifteen minutes, but in DC the traffic makes them stretch it to an hour."

. . .

Georgia followed her GPS to the Kalorama neighborhood. She was surprised at the affluence on some streets, the third world look of others. Obama lived nearby, she knew. She wondered if she might bump into him. She was admiring the buds on the trees and the tentative sprouts that would be daffodils and tulips in a few days, when she checked her side-view mirror. She'd picked up a tail. She tried to pin down the car and model, but she couldn't. All she knew was that it was American-made, a sedan, and dark gray, maybe blue.

She turned the corner and drove around the neighborhood. The tail stayed with her. She should exit the area, ditch the tail, and come back later. But that would mean driving through unbearable DC traffic. She gritted her teeth and drove to Connecticut Avenue, heading back in the direction she'd come. Damn the tail. It was still there. She checked her rearview. Two people in front, the passenger smaller than the driver. A woman?

Were they from DataMaster? It was possible. Video cameras surveilled the entire parking lot. A decent corporate security force would have homed in on her license plate, discovered it was a rental, perhaps even that a woman named Georgia Davis had rented it. Then again, that was a lot of work to do just because a PI talked to an employee at lunch. She kept driving. She had no idea where she was, but a sign said she'd reached Woodley Road. She turned left, and eventually emerged into a lovely residential area with what looked like a mansion on one side. As she drove past, she saw it was a school. With a French name.

Only in Washington.

She checked for the tail again. Still there. Damn it. She reached Cleveland Avenue. It was the first avenue she'd seen that wasn't named for a state. But it was a city. Or was it a president? History had never been one of her strengths.

She drove down the avenue, which was on an incline. At the bottom of the hill it merged into Calvert Street, a corner of which was occupied by a school that actually looked like a school. It was time to ditch the tail. Luckily, providence intervened. Just ahead on the right was a hotel, the Omni Shoreham. She accelerated, turned sharply into the hotel driveway, and pulled up at the entrance. She climbed out as if she was in a hurry, tossed the valet her key, and told him she'd be staying for a couple of days.

She raced inside, took out her cell, and arranged for a new rental car, told them where this one was, and waited forty-five minutes. When she was ready to take a cab to the new rental place, the tail was gone.

Chapter Forty-Three

A rosy late afternoon sun slanted through the windshield when Georgia pulled up for the second time to Carl Baldwin's Kalorama home. She'd checked several times, but this time no one was following her. To be safe, though, she parked a block away and walked around the corner. She passed through a wrought-iron fence with one of those fancy curlicue gates. A tightly inlaid marble path led to a huge red door with an ornate brass knocker. The door was flanked by white columns.

Despite the elegance, all the shades were drawn, and the house looked deserted. She rang the bell. It reverberated with a hollow, tinny sound. No one came to the door. She rang again. Nothing.

She made her way around the side of the house, removing her jacket as she did. No wonder the cherry blossoms bloomed in March. It was positively balmy here. She reached a side door, not as elaborate as the front, but solid, with thick rectangular windowpane inserts on the upper half. They wouldn't be as easy to shatter as an intruder might think. Even if they were, they were undoubtedly tied to an alarm.

She knocked. Nothing. She'd started to work her way to the back of the property when a pale face appeared in the glass inserts. The inserts broke up his face into pieces, and he might have looked clownish, except for his expression, which was troubled. Georgia smiled and waved with what she hoped was a friendly greeting.

He cautiously opened the door. "Who are you and what do you want?"

She introduced herself. Erica Baldwin had already told him she was on the way, because her name registered. His worry lines smoothed out, and he opened the door wider. "Thank God you're here."

This had to be the first time anyone involved with the case was glad to see her. "I hope I can help," she said. "You're Vic Summerfield, right?"

"The one and only." He led her through a spotless kitchen equipped with every appliance, gadget, and amenity known to humankind. A manufacturer's sticker on the oven door told her no one had yet cooked in it. "Did Carl Baldwin just move in?"

Summerfield spun around. "Hell no. Carl's lived here three years."

"Oh."

He followed her gaze to the oven. "He's not much of a cook."

"I see." What a waste. But she wasn't here to discuss the absence of culinary skills. "So you want to fill me in on what happened?"

"Well, you already know I'm Carl's assistant. I help him in his lobbying work."

The way he emphasized "lobbying" made Georgia wonder if there was other work Vic *didn't* help him with. They emerged from the kitchen into a huge hall with two offices, one on each side. To the left were columns that separated the offices from an opulent living room, dining room, and foyer.

"Nice digs," Georgia said.

Vic didn't reply. Georgia studied him. He had sandy hair, close-cropped military style, unless he shaved his head to hide a receding hairline. He looked too young for that, though; she pegged him in his thirties. Unremarkable brown eyes, same with his nose. But he was well put together. Strong, broad shoulders, slim waist. "You a swimmer?"

"How did you know?"

That's my job, she thought. But aloud, she said, "Just a guess."

"Do you swim?" he asked. She heard eagerness in his voice.

She shook her head. "I work out. And I box."

He shot her an approving look. "Let's go into my office."

"Which is Carl's?"

He pointed across the hall.

"May I take a peek?"

"Of course."

She crossed the hall and looked in. A spacious room, decorated in Euro-Scandinavian style. An oriental rug on the floor; silver pen set on the desk, inbox and outbox. Beyond that the room was spartan. Three bookshelves were empty except for a photo. Two people on a sailboat, one a young woman in a bikini hoisting a sail, a man smiling benevolently behind her. It was the same photo Dena Baldwin had in her office at the foundation.

"Okay," Georgia said after they were settled in Vic's office, a paler imitation of Baldwin's. "What's been going on the past seventy-two hours?"

"Well," he began, "like I said, I came to work two days ago like normal. Sometimes Carl's at his desk. Sometimes he's still upstairs."

"What time do you usually start?"

"Generally about eight. Unless I swim. Then it's nine."

"Go on."

"Occasionally he's still asleep. If he had a late night."

"How often does that happen?"

"He often meets with clients at night."

"Why?"

"It's the way DC works. If you want to keep your business private, you're careful." He hesitated. "No big, splashy lunches or dinners. Usually you meet in small, dark bars. Hotel bars are good."

"Go on."

"When he didn't come down by ten, I called his cell, but it went to voice mail. Then I went upstairs to make sure he was"—he gulped—"okay. He wasn't there."

Fear splashed over him. But something was slightly off about it. It seemed as if he'd slipped into character.

She shook it off. "What did you do?"

"I freaked out."

"You didn't think he might be shacking up someplace? Or at his gym?"

"Carl has never worked out a day in his life. And if he was seeing a woman, they would stay here. By noon, when there was no call or text, I called Erica."

"Why her? They've been divorced for years."

He thought about it. "You know, I'm not exactly sure. We were still finalizing a few financial things and, well, because of Dena's death so recently, I guess I felt she should know."

"What financial things?"

"Mostly how the estate was going to be handled now that Dena was gone."

"Got it."

Underneath his desk Vic crossed his legs, and his foot juddered.

Georgia asked, "Is there a place he goes to get away from it all? Somewhere on the Chesapeake Bay? Annapolis or the Tidewater area? He likes to sail, right?"

"He doesn't sail anymore. At least not that I know of."

"What does he do to relax?"

"He doesn't. He's here all the time."

Georgia scratched a phantom itch on her cheek. "How long have you worked for him?"

"A year and a half, and in all that time, he never took more than a day off. And then only when he was hammered."

"Does he have a drinking problem?"

Vic was quiet for a moment. "Not compared to some in this city."

"Maybe his disappearance has something to do with reallocating the estate." She mused. "Maybe he disappeared so Erica couldn't change it."

"That doesn't—well, it doesn't feel right. To be honest . . . actually . . ." He hesitated again. "Work wasn't going well for us."

"Oh?"

"We lost on some important legislation. It was getting so bad he was afraid he might have to close up shop."

Chapter Forty-Four

"Tell me." Georgia crossed and recrossed her legs.

Vic explained what had happened with the Russians, the Uzbekistan situation, and the fracking bill. "Some of it was bad timing . . . or corrupt politics . . . or competing against dark money."

"What do you mean?"

"Succeeding in DC is a game, a race, actually. You need to pick winners—both the issues and the folks behind them—before anyone else. Then you get on the pay-to-play merry-go-round. See, the only important thing for a congressman is to get reelected. They need money to do that. Carl can help get them that money. In return for considering *his* interests, of course."

"Where does this money he gets them come from?"

"Different places. Depending, again, on the issues."

"Are you talking bribes?"

"We call them 'quid pro quos.'"

"An Illinois governor went to jail because of that."

"And the president almost pardoned him."

"It's against the law."

"Sure it is." He splayed his hands. "So what? It's pretty much mandatory here."

Georgia thought about it. "And I thought Chicago was a swamp."

"Welcome to Washington," Vic said. "I'll tell you what my father told me when I told him I wanted to move here. He used to watch *Huntley-Brinkley* religiously."

"The news program."

"Right. He said David Brinkley nailed it."

"Nailed what?"

"In the old days politicians left DC on Memorial Day and didn't come back until after Labor Day. Summers here are almost unbearable. Temperature ninety-five degrees; humidity the same. So . . . a swamp."

"And?"

"Then they air-conditioned the Capitol buildings. Congress could work year-round. So they started all sorts of overreaching government programs and spent like sailors on a spree. That's how Big Government and deficits were born, Brinkley said. Sixty years later, we're still at it."

"You sound like you don't like how it turned out."

He shook his head. "You're right. I'm leaving. Going back to South Dakota to practice law with my dad."

"Sounds like a plan." She smiled. "But that doesn't help figure out where your boss is now."

"I don't know. Like I said, he was acting weird. Almost paranoid."

"I think this city does that to people."

"True, but this was more. After the fracking legislation fell apart, he kind of lost it."

"How?"

"For starters, he thought he was being followed."

Georgia arched her eyebrows, thinking of the car that had tailed her. "By whom?"

"He didn't know."

Georgia leaned forward. "Hold on. Your boss got money to bribe some congressmen to pass fracking legislation. But it doesn't work. Wouldn't the people who gave him the money in the first place be ticked off?"

"Of course they would."

"Would Baldwin give them their money back?"

"It was gone by the time the legislation got to a vote."

"Well then?"

"They gambled, they lost. That's the way it works here."

"There wouldn't be any repercussions?"

"Oh, they could smear Baldwin. You know, attack his reputation. In fact, that's probably what's happening. Why we're on the ropes."

"But they wouldn't actually hurt him . . ."

Vic rubbed his temples. "You wouldn't think so." He looked up. "Except, you know, right before he bolted, he said something weird."

Georgia cocked her head.

"He said he thought the fracking people might have been involved in his daughter's murder."

Georgia went rigid. "How? Why?"

"I don't think he knew. At one point, he said it might have been a warning. But then he thought they were punishing him."

"That's crazy. If they were upset about the vote, they'd take it out on *him*, not his family. He was the one they were pissed at. Right?"

"Well, you see, the thing is, Carl has close connections to the current administration."

"So?"

"They wouldn't like it if something happened to him. So his enemies might have targeted his daughter instead." Vic looked around as if those connections might appear out of thin air to bolster his theory. "Look. I don't know. Carl could have been making stuff up. Like I said, he was acting crazy." He hesitated. "But Dena was pretty vocal about fracking. She got her group to take a stand against it."

Georgia was surprised he knew anything about Dena's activities. "How do you know that?"

Vic reddened. He pushed back his chair and stood up. "Carl made me join the group. To keep tabs on her. It was part of my job."

"I thought they were estranged."

"They were." He stood up. "Listen. You want something to drink?"

Georgia was still processing what Vic had said. She replied absently. "You have Diet Coke?"

"That's what Carl drinks. There's a case in the pantry. I'll be back." He headed toward the kitchen.

Georgia tried to sum up. At least two people in DC were monitoring Dena's Facebook page for different reasons. Her father made promises he couldn't keep to people with clout. Lots of money changed hands. So who or what was Beef Jerky? Was Jimmy right that Beef Jerky was a person? Did he exist? Given Baldwin's troubles in DC, did it matter? Maybe someone from DC had set up Jarvis. But then, where did the yurt fit in? And why did the Bureau close the case so fast? Had someone applied pressure on them? The current administration was known to do that. Maybe the Bureau just didn't want the scrutiny. They had their killer, no matter if his body was blown to bits. With blowback from both the Left and the Right, it was a no-win situation for the FBI. And for Georgia?

She heard Vic moving around the kitchen. She got up, crossed the hall, and went back into Baldwin's office. She started going through his inbox. It was overflowing with legal documents, copies of the *Congressional Record*, proposed legislation, and letters, all of them official-looking and written in language that people never used. But there was nothing to indicate where he'd gone or why. Or anything about Dena, for that matter. His outbox was empty.

She frowned and checked her watch. Vic had been gone nearly ten minutes. Much longer than it took to open a pop. He was a member of Dena's Facebook group. Was that just an estranged father's way of keeping tabs on his daughter? Or was it something nefarious? She headed into the kitchen.

Chapter
Forty-Five

Georgia pushed through the kitchen door. "Vic, how long did you stalk Dena on the Facebook group?"

No sooner were the words out of her mouth than a man shot out of the shadows behind the door. He grabbed Georgia around her chest with both arms, one arm high enough to press against her throat. She struggled to pull his arms away, but he had at least fifty pounds on her and much more strength. She'd learned a couple of karate moves at her gym, but she wasn't in the right position, and his grip was so tight he lifted her off her feet. Her body arced backward, and her feet dangled uselessly in the air. He reeked of stale body odor and bad breath.

Georgia was barely able to focus, but she did spot Vic at the island in the middle of the room. He was holding the Diet Coke in one hand and an empty glass in the other. She couldn't tell if he was part of the attack or had been blindsided himself, but his face was frozen in terror. She remembered her Glock; it was in her khaki bag in Vic's office. She should have had it with her. Jimmy had cautioned her to always carry it in unfamiliar places. But who would have predicted a takedown in an affluent mansion in the nation's capital?

It was getting tough to breathe. She twisted and squirmed,

trying to free herself from her attacker's hold, but his grip was too powerful. She tried to bite his arm, but his forearm pressed against her throat, too low for her to open her mouth. That forearm was suffocating her slowly. She tried and failed to open her mouth for air. Red and purple spots formed in her eyes. She felt herself slipping away. She gasped. She needed air.

As if he knew, her attacker eased off the pressure. She didn't know why, but instinct told her this was her final chance to rally. Using all her lung power, she sucked in a deep breath, tensed every muscle, and tried a final shove to break his stranglehold. Her pulse was so loud she heard it pumping in her ears.

Suddenly she felt a sharp sting on her neck near her carotid artery. She had only a few seconds to realize it was a needle. The spots in her eyes became a spread of purple edged in red, filling her entire field of vision. Over the next ten seconds she felt herself go rag-doll limp. Then it all went to black.

Chapter Forty-Six

After it was over, Georgia realized what an efficient op it had been. Her attacker had been quiet and well organized. He knew exactly where to apply pressure and when to inject the knockout drug. Propofol or ketamine laced with something, followed by a secondary anesthetic, she guessed. In other words, the goon was a professional.

At the time, however, she knew nothing, except that she didn't want to wake up. It was comforting to float in a warm, welcoming void, suspended between mindfulness and sleep. She felt weightless and untethered, as though she could drift anywhere she could imagine. A moment later, though, a loud crash broke through her unconsciousness. A door slam? An engine coughed. She was in a moving vehicle. She tried to crack one eye open, but it was too much effort. Her body bumped and jounced with the motion of the vehicle. A van. She was on the floor of a van lying on her side. That was enough for now. She sank back into the warm, inviting darkness.

The van was still in motion when she woke again. The void was thinner and she knew she was back. The van was running fast but not at breakneck speed. She tried again to open an eye. This time she could. It was dark, but the window at the top of the sliding panel door was covered with dark material that allowed a sliver of light to slip in around the edges. Georgia had no idea how long she'd been out, but the fact that light was spilling through the flap of material indicated it wasn't that long. An hour. Maybe two.

The van must be traveling on a highway, because the ride was fairly smooth. She began to roll over, but stopped. Her hands and feet were tied, and a gag was stuffed in her mouth. If she didn't end up in the right position, she might suffocate. Or choke. She stayed motionless and tried to take stock. Her hands and feet radiated pins and needles, and there was a sharp pain at the injection site. Whatever he'd used had penetrated deep.

A male voice called out from the front. "T minus ten."

"Got it," a second male voice replied.

Someone was in the back of the van with her. He must have been there since they'd been at Baldwin's. But it wasn't Vic's voice. A team of goons. She considered moaning so they'd know she was awake—their reaction might tell her more—but decided to hold off. Any unexpected behavior by a hostage was always dangerous. There would be time later. She hoped.

The van slowed and turned left off the highway onto a road rutted with rocks and stones. Georgia was jerked to one side, then the other. Was the damn road even paved? At a particularly powerful bump, she groaned instinctively.

"Hey, man," the thug beside her said. "I just heard something. She's awake."

He didn't use his partner's name.

"Roger that. No problem," the man from the front replied.

The van turned right, and the wheels crackled on gravel, slowed, and came to a stop. Georgia's stomach lurched. She tried to inventory what she had available to make a stand, but she had no weapon, she was tied up, and she had no idea where she was or who her attackers were. She was helpless.

The engine died. The driver's door opened, then slammed shut. The side panel door slid back with a squeak. The driver peered in. Georgia craned her neck, but his face was in shadow, and she couldn't make out his features.

"Put the blindfold on," he said to his companion and withdrew. The crunch of his footsteps on gravel receded. He didn't want her to see him.

Georgia was still lying on her left side. The second man approached her from behind and tightened a rag over her eyes. It was a clumsy attempt. She didn't resist.

"Have a nice ride?"

The gag was still in her mouth. She didn't reply. The man nudged her in her ribs. "Hey. I'm talking to you. I know you're awake."

Georgia was even more convinced the first knockout drug was propofol—a fast-acting but short-lived drug used by doctors in the initial stage of anesthesia.

"So that's the way you want to play it?" Did this jerk not realize she had a gag in her mouth and couldn't speak?

He climbed out of the van. A moment later, he pulled her out of the van by her legs. She assumed he would pause once her torso was free so she could lever herself to a standing position. But he kept yanking her until her head bounced on the runner below the van's door. At that point he tightened his grip on her legs, which made the back of her head hit the ground hard. Waves of pain, vertigo, and nausea flooded through her, and for a moment she thought she might go under again. She managed to hold on.

Footsteps scraped on the gravel. The driver was returning. She felt him untie whatever had bound her arms and feet, but he left the blindfold in place. "You're gonna stand up now," he said.

Each man grabbed one of her arms and pulled her upright. She promptly vomited through the gag and went limp.

"Goddammit!" The man who'd been in the back of the van yelled.

"Back off," the driver said. "It's the drug, asshole. And the whack on her head, thanks to you."

The men tried to steady her, but she kept stumbling. She was desperately thirsty. The men slow-walked her forward.

Though the stink of her own vomit was strong, she eventually sniffed what she thought was fresh hay. She hadn't smelled that clean, sunny scent since she was a little girl with her mother spending summers in Georgia. Hay meant farms. Cows. Horses. Maybe chickens.

The men stopped. One man restrained her while the other opened what sounded like a massive door. The scent of hay sharpened and mixed with horse manure. A barn. She heard the snuffles and grunts of animals. Horses. The men led her inside and pushed her down on a bed of prickly straw. Her balance was still rocky, and she slumped over.

"Dammit, asshole, you gotta prop her up."

"Sorry, Reince."

A quick hostile intake of breath from the driver. She had a clue. Two clues, in fact. A barn. A name. Three, if you included the van.

The driver propped her against a wall. "Okay, little miss PI. I'm gonna take the gag outta your mouth. You're not gonna scream, right?" He laughed. "Actually you could, but there's no one to hear you. Not for miles."

She nodded. He removed the gag, but not the blindfold. She cleared her throat, which was raw and thick with vomit. "Why?" she croaked.

"You don't say a word and we'll keep this short and sweet. This is your only warning. Back off. Quit nosing around."

"Do you have Carl Baldwin?" Her voice was hoarse.

A sudden sharp thwack across her face stung. The asshole had slapped her. It reverberated through her head like an echo chamber. Nausea climbed up her throat. Her head was spinning.

"I told you not to say a word. You understand?"

Georgia knew she should be frightened, but she only had room for one emotion at a time. Right now that emotion was rage. How dare he humiliate her like this? If they wanted to kill her, she would have been dead already. She shook her head. "I want to know—"

He cut her off with another blow. She went slack. Pain overwhelmed her. She shouldn't have provoked them. She wanted to lie down. Go to sleep.

"Do you understand?"

This time she tried to nod. She wasn't sure her head actually moved, but it must have because there were no more blows, and the driver spoke.

"You're in way over your head, missy. You don't know what you're dealing with."

She didn't react.

"So you go on back to Chicago and tell Mrs. Baldwin you're done. Finished. Stop digging around. What's done is done. She can't bring back her daughter, and neither can you. Got that?"

She didn't reply, but apparently he thought she received the message.

"And just in case you don't believe me, we know all of you and how to find you. Erica Baldwin, Paul Kelly, Jimmy Saclarides. Oh yeah. We know about your sister and your mother, too."

Georgia's gut twisted.

He let that sink in. "Now you're gonna go back under. And when you wake up, you get yourself the fuck out of Dodge and back to Chicago."

Before she had a chance to reply, another sharp pain stabbed her arm. She fell into darkness.

Chapter
Forty-Seven

When Georgia came to again, she didn't move. Whether ten minutes or two hours went by, she didn't know. Slowly she struggled to a half-seated, half-reclining position. She opened her eyes and gazed at a row of horse stalls before realizing her blindfold was gone. She could see. The barn door was closed, but light leaked around its edges. She counted eight stalls, of which four were occupied by horses. They seemed to be used to her presence and scent, because they munched hay placidly. Her hands and feet were free also, and she leaned her arms backward for support.

But when she forced herself upright, one of the horses pawed the ground and she heard snuffling. A wave of vertigo passed through her, and she wanted to lie down. But whoever owned the animals would probably be here soon to muck out their stalls.

She debated whether to wait for whoever would be coming. Did they know the man named Reince and his buddy? Or had she been dropped at some random farm along the way? Somewhere in the back of her mind, she knew they raised horses in Virginia. Was she on a horse farm?

She used the wall of the barn for support and slowly stood up. She wobbled, and her throat was on fire; she would kill for some water. She dragged her feet to the door and used all her strength to slide it open. A rosy dawn sun touched the horizon, tinging deep purple-pink clouds with a ribbon of gold. Beyond the barn stretched a large meadow surrounded by a white fence. Grass was growing, and trees were budding.

If horses were sheltered here, water couldn't be far away. She slowly circled the barn and spotted a faucet near the door on the other side. She bent over to turn it on, but another wave of vertigo threatened to make her lose her balance. She crouched instead and twisted the handle. Thank God. She cupped her hands and drank, then splashed water on her face.

Afterward she felt halfway human. She knew she didn't look it. She was glad she didn't have a mirror. Her face had to be bruised, along with the injection site on her neck, and her ribs were sore from all the jouncing in the van. On the other hand, she hadn't broken any bones, and her legs, apart from a sore ankle, seemed to be in reasonable shape. She would make her way to the road and hitch a ride back into DC.

She limped slowly toward a blacktopped road. About half a mile in the distance a large structure loomed. Two stories, maybe three. A home? Farm building? Business? She reached for her cell in her pocket before realizing she didn't have it. Damn. Was there a connection between the building and the thugs who kidnapped her? Could someone in the building tell her who owned the barn? Did they own it?

She headed toward the structure, unsure how close to get. What if she was walking into a trap? She thought it over. The odds were that the goons who'd attacked her wouldn't show themselves in broad daylight. They were probably crashing at home, satisfied that they'd scared her shitless.

As she drew closer, the building materialized into a country home with a redbrick exterior, white columns and portico in front, and a dome in the center. It looked familiar. When she figured it out, she smiled. Ellie Foreman's boyfriend, Luke Sutton, lived in a similar-looking home on the banks of Lake Geneva,

Wisconsin. Georgia recalled Jimmy telling her that Luke's father rebuilt the family home into a replica of Thomas Jefferson's estate. She couldn't remember the name of Jefferson's home, but it was famous.

She did recall Jefferson was from Virginia, though, which added to her theory that she was in the Virginia countryside. She stopped to listen. Aside from the occasional whoosh of a passing vehicle and chirps from birds, there was silence. Nothing from the house.

To be safe she cut back to the field and approached the house from the side. While she didn't see anyone looking out, it would only take a quick glance from whoever lived in the house to spot her. She angled behind the house and closed the distance from the back.

A Dodge Ram pickup was parked at the end of a gravel driveway. Not the van in which she'd been transported. Beside the truck was a three-car garage. A gazebo with a glider, the kind that often graced southern homes, occupied most of the back. Next to it was a garden, already teeming with daffodils and tulips.

Oversized vertical windows on the first floor let sun pour in, and smaller windows ran horizontally across the second floor. Two were open. Georgia crept around to the front. An elegant portico protected an imposing front door, which was open. The temperature was mild, and a slight breeze wafted over her. Was someone airing out the place?

She gazed back at the meadow. The contrast between the evil that had confronted her last night in the barn and the tranquility of this morning was hard to process. Did the occupants of the house know what had happened in that barn?

As she gazed at the scene a powerful yearning came over her, and a long-buried memory floated up. A meadow somewhere in the South, not unlike this one. She was at a picnic. She and her mother sat on the grass. Her mother was teaching her how to make a buttercup necklace. A bright sun like today's tinged the grass and buttercups with gold; a soft breeze wafted over them. Her mom called her Peaches. Georgia was happy and safe.

Her throat tightened. It wasn't worth the risk to find out who lived in the house. She turned and followed the driveway out to the road. Her attacker was right about one thing: she needed to get the hell out of Washington, DC.

Chapter
Forty-Eight

When she finally got back to her hotel room, the first thing she did was check that the hair she'd left in the doorjamb was still intact. It was. No one had come in while she was gone. She was surprised; they'd had time to toss her room if they wanted. Then she called Paul Kelly and filled him in. She could hear the fury in his voice. She assured him she was okay and would be back that night.

After a long, hot shower she examined herself in the mirror. Her face was purple and yellow, and a shiner around her left eye was prominent. She carefully applied makeup, but the black eye was still conspicuous. She would pick up a pair of sunglasses. She didn't have her jacket – she'd left it at Carl Baldwin's house. Her Glock too. She dressed in jeans and a tank top.

She had one more thing to do in Washington. She called the number she had for Vic Summerfield. It went to voice mail. She looked up his address. A neighborhood called Glover Park. It wasn't far from the hotel. She called an Uber.

Vic Summerfield's condo was in a large apartment building at the bottom of a hill. The building was equipped with a uniformed doorman and a pair of glass doors through which Georgia could see two huge chandeliers hanging from the lobby ceiling. She told the driver to park on a semicircular driveway, which prompted the doorman to head over, his finger wagging.

"You can't park there," he said through the passenger window. "There are spaces on the street."

"I don't plan on being here long," Georgia piped up from the back seat. "Could you ring Vic Summerfield and ask him to come down?"

The doorman looked her up and down. "Mr. Summerfield isn't here."

"Did he go to work this morning?"

The doorman sniffed. "I have no idea, and even if I did, I wouldn't tell you."

Georgia climbed out of the Uber, fished out her PI license and a twenty-dollar bill, and handed both to the man. "I'm investigating a case that involves him. I would appreciate your cooperation."

The doorman pocketed the cash smoothly and returned her license. "I don't know where he is, but he left here this morning with a large suitcase."

. . .

DC's Reagan Airport, just across the Potomac River from the city, wasn't very large. But that was the point. It had originally been built for the government's convenience and no one else. With only a quick—and cheap—cab ride from Capitol Hill, politicians and bureaucrats could get out of town in ten minutes. Georgia Ubered to the terminal. She was stiff, bruised, and hungry. She wanted her own bed. She checked for flights from DC to Rapid City, South Dakota. Several airlines flew the route, but they all required changing planes in Chicago. But only one flight left within a two-hour window of the time Summerfield left his apartment. Not only was it in the same terminal as her flight, but it was boarding now.

She wasn't sanguine about intercepting him but hurried to the gate anyway. She scanned the passengers. Most were impatient to board. She never understood why. Who would want to be trapped in a metal tube that would take them vast distances? What if something went wrong in that tube? Would they regret their eagerness to rush into certain doom?

She waited while travelers boarded the flight. Vic Summerfield wasn't among them. At one point she thought she saw him, head down, interacting with his cell. But when she approached, she realized it wasn't him. She continued to wait until the airline employees closed the door to the access ramp. Vic was a no-show. An uneasy feeling climbed up her back.

· · ·

She limped outside to the taxi stand, slid into a cab, and told the driver to take her to the Kalorama house. It was mid-morning, and for some miraculous reason, traffic wasn't congested.

"Going home, are we?" The cabbie wanted to chat.

"Not exactly."

He tried to make eye contact with her in his rearview, but Georgia refused to look at him. He got the message, and they drove the rest of the twenty-minute trip in silence.

Once she was at Baldwin's home and she was sure the cabbie was gone, she dug out her lockpicks and walked around to the side door. She peered through the glass insets into the kitchen. Nothing looked out of order. She inserted the pick, but she was rusty and had to work longer than she expected to unlock the door. She quietly let herself in.

The odor was unmistakable. It had only been a few hours since Vic's doorman claimed he'd left with his suitcase, but the stench of death was already fouling the air. Georgia swallowed and covered her nose with a kitchen towel. She stayed in the kitchen, frozen in place, until she was sure there was no movement or sounds from the other downstairs rooms. Then she took a few tentative steps across the kitchen floor. When nothing happened, she took a few more. And a few more, until she was outside Vic Summerfield's office.

Despite her years as a cop, and an all-too-intimate familiarity with dead bodies, what she saw inside Vic's office made her retch. Vic was slumped at his desk. His suitcase lay on the floor. Most of the right side of his head had been blown away, leaving a mess of brain matter, shards of bone, and hair matted with blood. From the blood oozing out of his middle, it looked like he'd also been shot in the gut.

But what shocked her the most was that her khaki bag—the bag she'd brought from Chicago and into which she'd dropped her Glock when she first entered the Kalorama house—lay on the floor next to the suitcase. She went over, grabbed it, and rummaged inside. Change of clothes, toiletries, extra burner phone she kept for emergencies. Her jacket still there, too. But no Glock. Which meant she knew whose gun had been used to murder Vic Summerfield. And who the cops would be looking for once the forensics were analyzed.

She took a breath through her mouth, willing her fear away. They had been thorough. But they hadn't expected her to discover Vic's body. For once she had an edge. She debated what to do next. She didn't want to, but her cop DNA forced her. She powered on the burner, called 911, and reported Vic's body. Anonymously. Then she picked up her jacket and bag, retraced her steps through the kitchen, and hurried back outside. She had a plane to catch.

Chapter
Forty-Nine

Georgia turned the key in the lock of her Evanston apartment. She couldn't recall ever being so glad to be home. She shuffled over to the sofa and settled down to call Jimmy. They'd spoken while she was waiting to board her flight; now he said he'd be there in an hour. Georgia booted up her laptop to check in on ResistanceUSA. She'd been doing that periodically. She was curious whether anyone might have mentioned, even in clandestine fashion, her activities in DC.

The action had picked up in the group since the last time she'd logged in. Brisk threads on several different topics covered the page. Of course when you had a president with a fresh scandal every day, it wasn't difficult for people to express themselves. Immigration and the separation of immigrant children from their parents had triggered a communal rage. Georgia noticed that Ruth Marriotti was in the middle of it, comforting some, encouraging others, and soliciting ideas from still others.

Georgia checked the "About" tab on the group's menu. Ruth was now the director/administrator. With Curt Dixon gone, and DJ dead, there were several new admins as well. They'd seen a new administration take office. Georgia checked the size of the group. It had dropped with Dena's murder but was trending back up. Good for Ruth. She scanned posts from yesterday and today. Nothing obvious or even veiled about her goings-on in DC.

She'd promised Paul Kelly she would call the FBI when she was home. LeJeune called her back five minutes later. She told him about Carl Baldwin's disappearance, the thugs who ambushed her and the first name, Reince, of one. She also told him about Vic Summerfield's murder, and her missing Glock.

"I'm certain the bullets that killed Summerfield will turn out to have come from my Glock," she said.

"You'll need to come down for an interview, *cher*. The boys will want to hear this." He paused. "From the horse's mouth, so to speak."

She groaned at his attempt at humor. "Of course."

"You think Summerfield was working against Baldwin but something went wrong?"

"I don't know what I think. I don't know if the thugs are connected to the Baldwins at all. But I know you guys will find out."

"I agree. I'll connect with our DC guys. You reported the murder before you left DC, right?"

Georgia paused, then cleared her throat. "I did. Anonymously."

"Ahh. I see. So. Expect to come down here when you're back on your feet." They disconnected.

A key scratched in the lock. The door opened, and Jimmy was there. He took one look at her. "Oh my God."

She got up and limped over. "Hey, it's not as bad as it looks."

He embraced her gingerly. "You shouldn't be up and around. You're going to bed."

She inclined her head. "I will on two conditions. First, you run me a hot bath. And second, you join me in it."

. . .

Georgia allowed herself two full days to be waited on. Jimmy brought her meals from his family's Greek restaurant in Lake

Geneva, flowers, get-well cards, and plenty of advice. Her friend Sam Mosele called to make sure she was okay, and late the second afternoon, Paul Kelly paid a visit. He wanted her to take more time off, as did Jimmy, but Georgia had planned her next move, and she was ready to pick up Kitty Jarvis's trail. After listening to both Jimmy's and Paul's adamant refusals, and declaring that she'd do what she damn well wanted, they negotiated a four-hour workday.

The next morning Georgia knew she'd go stark raving mad if she was confined any longer. She did some exercises to limber up. With her bruises fading, her ankle stronger, and the pain in her ribs subsiding, she retrieved her back-up and second favorite pistol, a Sig Sauer 9 millimeter, from the closet. She made sure it was loaded, and strapped it into her shoulder holster. She drove to Rogers Park to see if Kitty Jarvis might have come home. She hadn't. Georgia debated whether to ask Betsy Start if she'd heard from Kitty—she had done the building super a favor by having the yurt picked up—but decided not to. If Kitty wanted Betsy Start to know where she was, Georgia would have known, too. She had to give Kitty credit. If she seriously wanted off the grid, it was safer not to tell anyone.

She trudged out of the building and was halfway to her car when she turned around. There were two apartments on each floor, and Kitty lived in 1B. The first floor. She walked around to the back of the building. Like many Chicago brownstones, this building had a staircase that led up to separate porches for each apartment. A window in each unit gave onto the porch, a back door, too.

She sneaked a look around. It was mid-morning. She had time. But would she be spotted? She glanced at the adjacent buildings. Most of the windows were covered with shades, but one or two weren't. She imagined a little old lady with nothing better to do spying on her through the window and calling the police. But what choice did she have? She had to find Kitty Jarvis.

She took a breath and climbed the porch steps. She guessed

that 1B, Kitty's apartment, was on the left. She crept to the window and tugged on its frame. It was locked. She moved to the back door. Locked as well. She glanced around again and, seeing no one, fished out her lockpicks from her blazer. She worked with them for about two minutes, alert not only for the click of the tumbler, but to any sounds that meant she had been observed. It was a double lock, and it took time, but she finally managed to unlock the door. She twisted the knob, praying Kitty had no alarm. It was quiet. She slipped inside and closed the door behind her.

Chapter Fifty

Inside was a musty, unused smell overlaid with a soiled cat litter box. No cat was visible, though, unless it was hiding. She didn't see any food or water dishes out, which meant Kitty must have taken the cat with her. She glanced around. She was in a surprisingly big kitchen that sported new appliances and even a table and chairs. And it was clean. No dishes in the sink or on the counter, and the surfaces looked like they'd been wiped down. A hum from the refrigerator indicated it was still running, but nothing was in it; there were only two ice trays in the freezer above. Napkins lay on the table in a brightly painted holder that must have been bought at an art festival.

Georgia methodically opened all the drawers and cupboards. She scanned plates and bowls, mugs and glasses, flatware and wineglasses. Where was Kitty's junk drawer or cabinet? Every kitchen had one; it was the place where stray papers, letters, and other notes were stashed. Maybe she'd find the address of the family cabin there. She opened a drawer that held screwdrivers, Allen wrenches, pliers, duct tape, nail polish, a Metra schedule, and an eraser.

No papers, notes, or letters. Another drawer was filled with carryout menus for pizza and Chinese.

A scraping noise in the backyard made Georgia stop short. Who was there? She ducked down below the window frame and peeked out. She heard the clang of a metal garbage can, the thud of trash being deposited, and the clash of the lid as it was refastened. She allowed herself to breathe.

She counted down two minutes, then began to explore the rest of the apartment. The largest bedroom, clearly Kitty's, contained a polished walnut bureau with a silver tray of perfumes and lipsticks on top. A queen bed was covered by a flowery duvet with matching curtains on the windows. Georgia searched through Kitty's drawers. She found underwear, sweaters, and jeans. She made sure to feel around the clothes in case any items were hidden underneath, and when her hand reached a bulky package buried under a sweatshirt, her pulse sped up.

She uncovered the package, which turned out to be a large manila envelope. She opened it and withdrew a pile of letters wrapped in a rubber band. The return address was an APO in San Francisco. Scott's letters to his sister while he was deployed abroad. She pulled out a few and stuck them in her pocket. She finished by opening Kitty's closet, but it was tiny and contained no clothes. Kitty must have taken them. Given the scarcity of clothing, Georgia wondered if Kitty planned to come back.

The other bedroom was smaller and barren. Jarvis's room. A double mattress occupied most of the space, a blanket thrown over it. A chest of drawers stood in a corner. On top of the chest was a piece of paper anchored by a snow globe of Wrigley Field. Georgia grabbed the paper. It was the receipt from Camping Unlimited, acknowledging the sale of the yurt. She checked both sides, looking for an address. Nothing. She pocketed the receipt.

After checking the closet, which was smaller than Kitty's and just as empty, she came out of the bedroom, deflated. Maybe Jimmy and Paul were right. She was exhausted, and she'd only been working an hour. It was time to wrap up. She checked the bathroom: nothing.

The living room was last. It was cozy and comfortable. Most of the furniture was modern, except for an old-fashioned rolltop desk, which took up one corner. She hurried over. The roller was closed. She opened it and let out a soft exclamation. There it was! A beige leather address book with flowers on the cover.

She picked it up and slowly flipped through it. She didn't have to go past the letter C. There, underneath the word "cabin," was an address:

9415 Lakeland Road
Sand Lake, MN 55745

Georgia couldn't believe her luck. She scribbled down the address on the back of the Camping Unlimited receipt, closed the rolltop, and started back to the kitchen. As she trudged down the hallway, a jangle of metal at the front door tore into her gut with panic. Someone was coming into Kitty's place. Georgia frantically tried to find a hiding place. Not Kitty's closet. Not Scott's either.

The front door squeaked open. Georgia ran into Scott's room, threw herself under the bed, and pulled the blanket over the side of the mattress facing the hallway. The floor was filthy with dirt, dust bunnies, mouse droppings, and who knows what else. She hoped to hell she wouldn't sneeze.

"Who's here?" a female voice called out. Betsy Start. What was she doing here? Had someone seen Georgia outside and called? Georgia held her breath. The clunk of boots thumped on the hardwood floor, growing louder with each step. Georgia lay perfectly still. She heard Start sniff, as if trying to detect an odor that didn't belong. Georgia thanked the Lord she wasn't wearing perfume.

Start went into Kitty's bedroom. Georgia heard the closet door open and then close. Same with a drawer in the bureau. The thud of her boots grew louder and she came into Scott's room, stopping no more than a foot from Georgia's head. Start opened the closet in this room too, then closed it. She stood for a moment, not moving. Georgia swallowed silently. Then Start walked out.

The thump of her boots told Georgia that Betsy Start was now in the kitchen. Had Georgia closed all the drawers and cabinets? She thought so, but there was always a chance she'd forgotten one or closed it with something sticking out. Apparently not, because after what seemed like an eternity, Start opened the back door and exited the apartment. Georgia heard her lock the door. Relief flooded through her. Even so, she forced herself to stay where she was for fifteen more excruciating minutes.

She traced her steps back to the kitchen, unlocked the door, and crept out to the porch. Less than a minute later she was in her Toyota driving back to Evanston.

Chapter
Fifty-One

For Georgia the drive from Duluth to Sand Lake was like rewatching a movie she hadn't liked the first time. About nine summers earlier, Georgia had driven up to a remote lake in Wisconsin and was met by the barrel of a shotgun. Luckily, the standoff had been resolved without violence. Georgia later helped the woman elude her pursuers and hid her in a safe house.

This time, however, northern Minnesota was still in the throes of a bitter winter. Worse, snow was forecast. Georgia hated to drive in snow. Not only did the absence of traction scare her, but the knowledge that one small twist of the wheel could force a car to careen across the highway, skid for yards on ice, or plow into an eighteen-wheeler was a nightmare scenario. Plus, snow was a silent killer. A plane crash was accompanied by loud explosions and a fireball, flames hissing and eating everything in its path. But snow often muffled sight and sound in its inexorable path to oblivion. Sometimes bodies wouldn't be found until spring.

She shook off the morbid thoughts. Jimmy had begged her not to go. Paul Kelly thought she was nuts, and Erica Baldwin was not sanguine about her success. But Georgia felt in her gut that Kitty Jarvis knew more about her brother and why he killed or was recruited to kill Dena Baldwin. She might even know about the beef jerky. Finding Kitty Jarvis was nonnegotiable. But she did compromise. She would fly to Duluth, rent a car, and drive about an hour to Sand Lake.

Jimmy was still concerned. Plenty of places in rural Minnesota still had no cell service. "What if you get into trouble? No one will know where you are."

"I'll call you every hour."

"Let me come with you."

Georgia shook her head. "If Kitty was spooked enough to flee Chicago, she's not going to be happy to see a pair of folks she doesn't know. Let me handle her." She didn't add that a woman alone could probably connect with Kitty more quickly.

Jimmy didn't have a good response, so early the next morning, she hopped on a flight to Duluth. Two hours later as she waited for a bus to the rental car area of the Duluth airport, she checked her voice mail. Three messages had come in from Vanna. All within the past hour. When Georgia replayed them, she noted how Vanna's voice sounded more stressed and higher pitched with each call.

Georgia, Charlie has a high fever, and it won't go down even with Tylenol. Mom says to wait. But I can't. What should I do?

Then:

Georgia, Charlie had a seizure. I'm taking him to the hospital. Please come, Georgia. I need you.

Then:

Georgia, it's JoBeth. Charlie's not doing well at all. They think it might be meningitis. Vanna needs you. I'll leave if that's what it takes for you to come. I know you don't want anything to do with me.

Georgia felt her stomach pitch, as if her guts had spilled out on the concrete of the airport. She hit redial on one of Vanna's calls.

"Georgia, where are you?" Her sister's voice, squeaky and tight, was halfway to hysterical. "You've got to come. Charlie is really sick. He's been vomiting, and his skin is paper white. They want to do a spinal tap. They think it might be meningitis. He's got a high fever, and he's had two seizures. I can't make him stop crying.

I can't do this, Georgia. I'm sorry for everything. Please come right away."

Georgia's heart cracked. Why had she picked today to fly to Minnesota? "Vanna, honey, the doctors know what they're doing. If they say they need to do a spinal tap, let them. They'll make it as comfortable as possible. I—I'm in Minnesota on a case."

"But this is an emergency," Vanna wailed. "Please come back. Now."

Georgia bit her lip. By the time she flew back it would be mid-afternoon. The spinal tap would be over. She told Vanna that.

"I haven't given them permission yet. Mom says they're dangerous. He could die from it."

"Vanna, Charlie isn't going to die."

"How do you know?"

"Where are you? What hospital?"

"We're at Northwest Community, but they want to transfer us downtown to Children's. I don't know. Should we go?"

"Absolutely. Children's is the best." She tried to sound calm and composed. "Tell you what. I'll call Jimmy. He'll meet you there. And I'll be back as soon as I can."

"When?"

"Late tonight. Maybe tomorrow. I'll come straight from the airport. And go ahead and ask the doctors to explain everything to you in simple language. Call me back if you still don't understand."

Vanna was sobbing now. "Okay. Georgia, I love you. I'm so sorry for everything. Can we—can we start over? Can I come home and live with you?"

Georgia's eyes welled up too. She couldn't help it. "I love you too, Vanna. Of course you can live with me. Now, listen up, sweetie. In another hour I might be in a place where there may not be cell service. So if you can't reach me, don't worry. As soon as it comes back, I'll call you." She hesitated, wondering what else she could say that would help. "You can do this. You're his mom. And a wonderful one at that. Keep telling him it's going to be okay.

And that you'll be with him every second. He may not understand the words, but he'll feel your reassurance and comfort. And your love."

Between her sobs Vanna said, "Pray for him, will you?"

This was the first time Vanna had ever expressed faith of any kind. Where had that come from? "I will," she lied.

She disconnected. The lump in her throat threatened to choke off her breath. But so did a new thought. Why wasn't JoBeth helping her daughter during this crisis? Why was Vanna turning to Georgia?

Chapter
Fifty-Two

As Georgia drove through Duluth on her way to Sand Lake, the steely overcast highlighted a band of sapphire-blue ice that hugged the shores of Lake Superior. She'd never seen ice this blue. Chicago's was dull white.

She was puzzled by Vanna's relationship with their mother. JoBeth and Vanna hadn't seen each other since Vanna ran away last year, and she'd run away largely because of JoBeth, who, according to Vanna, had been drunk most of the time and a mean drunk at that. Vanna had clearly matured over the past year, but some problems couldn't be solved by the passage of time.

Was JoBeth drinking again? How was that affecting the way she treated Vanna and, even more important, Charlie? In retrospect, it occurred to Georgia that it might have been a blessing that Georgia hadn't grown up with JoBeth in her life. She'd had to develop resiliency early on. Vanna hadn't.

After ten minutes heading south on I-35, the snow started. It wasn't an easy snow. The wind blew up, and bands of white assaulted her windshield. A few minutes later, it accelerated into a blinding snow. Daylight acquired a uniquely dystopian cast and the windshield wipers were no help. The swirl of white overwhelmed her. She gritted her teeth and slowed to thirty.

Her GPS went out, but she'd expected that and had printed out directions back in Chicago. She tried to make out the highway signs, but many were already covered by snow or hard to read in limited visibility. She kept the defroster on but she had to wipe her sleeve on the glass in order to see at all.

The most unsettling part was the silence. The storm was intense, unrelenting, and dangerous, but it didn't make a sound. The only noise was the thud of her wipers swinging back and forth. The silence added to the sense that she had crossed the border into an unfamiliar no-man's-land. The heater was on full blast, but Georgia shivered.

. . .

The sign announcing she was only a few miles from Sand Lake also pointed to an exit that led to the Fond Du Lac Band Chippewa casino. Georgia noted the irony. White people like the Jarvis family were trying to find isolation off the grid on a Minnesota lake, while Native Americans were trying to encourage people to lose their money by flocking to splashy casinos.

The snowstorm was still blustering when she reached Lakeland road twenty minutes later, but she caught glimpses of an expanse of white through the trees hugging the road. Sand Lake was still frozen. She thought she saw a couple of pickups and icehouses on the lake. Although she'd grown up in Chicago, she'd never known people camped out on the ice in winter until Matt Singer, her former lover, took her up to Wisconsin one weekend. She'd been shocked, and fascinated.

Now she pulled up to a mailbox with the number 9415. A long driveway bisected a lawn that led to a small cabin. It took effort to turn around, and her wheels kept spinning, but eventually she parked facing the direction she'd come. She holstered the Sig under her North Face jacket, tied the hood snugly, and climbed out of the car.

The wind whipped her face, threatening to freeze her nostrils as well. Except for the swish of her boots in the snow, the silence seemed more pronounced. As she drew closer, she studied the cabin. One story, wood logs. The chimney was brick, but no smoke drifted from the top. Shades covered two windows and were tightly drawn. It looked abandoned. Maybe that was the point.

When she got to the door, she hesitated, recalling the last time she'd knocked on a cabin door in the middle of nowhere. Then she took a deep breath and knocked.

Chapter
Fifty-Three

No one came to the door. Georgia waited. Then waited some more. She knocked again. No one. Crestfallen, she stepped back and reassessed the cabin. Had she come all this way for nothing? She'd been so sure Kitty Jarvis was hiding out here. But now, if she was honest, apart from unearthing an address in a remote location, the principal reason she'd come was instinct. And the memory that ten years earlier, another woman in trouble had done the same thing. The fact was that Kitty Jarvis could be anywhere. Just because a family cabin existed didn't mean she'd fled to it.

Full of self-recrimination for faulty assumptions, Georgia trudged back to her car, keyed the engine, and blasted the heat. She checked for cell service. No bars. She couldn't call Vanna or Jimmy, and she had no map to see if Lakeland Road was accessible from a different route. She recalled the road did make a circle around Sand Lake, which meant she could pick one end to stake out, but there was only a fifty-fifty chance of meeting Kitty, if she was here. She could come from the opposite or an altogether different direction.

In any case she couldn't stake out the cabin indefinitely. It was too cold and the storm was still raging. She waited thirty minutes.

And then ten more. She reflected on her life and how, despite the hard knocks, it was now full with Vanna, Charlie, and Jimmy. How she'd never imagined she would get over the heartbreak of Matt. And how, with Charlie so ill, she longed to fly back to Chicago to be with Vanna.

She was ready to start the drive back to the Duluth airport when she stopped the car, got out, and walked around the cabin to make sure no one was there. As she made her way to the rear of the property, she realized the cabin was only about a hundred feet from the lake. She could see the vague outline of a dock. She peered into a nearby boatshed, where a skiff, probably for fishing, was stored. She turned toward the lake, frozen solid, and shaded her eyes. Through the snow, she spotted a green pickup on the ice. Next to it was a shack perched on top of the frozen lake. It looked about a football field away, and snowy tire tracks led from the lawn where she stood across the ice.

Georgia had never walked on the surface of a frozen lake. The thought of doing it frightened the hell out of her. Then again, if the ice was thick enough to support a pickup, it must be okay for her Toyota. Still, she was loath to take the chance. A hundred yards wasn't far to walk. She slogged through the snow to what would have been the shoreline, but there was no demarcation between land and water. She edged onto the ice tentatively. Although it was covered by fresh snow, it felt sturdy and solid. Not so different from land. She started off.

It wasn't difficult to walk as long as she didn't hurry. Her boots gripped snow rather than ice, and she felt supported. The cold and wind were more challenging. Her leather gloves did little to keep her fingers from freezing, and her muscles, still sore from the beating in DC, stiffened in the frigid air. She shuffled forward painfully.

She knew whoever was in the icehouse would see her coming, so as she approached, she waved to signal she was friendly. A few minutes later a figure emerged from the shack holding a pair of binoculars raised to eye-level.

Georgia waved again and smiled. "Yoo-hoo... Is Kitty Jarvis with you?" No response. "I need to talk to her."

The figure, now that she was close enough to see, was a man. For an instant Georgia was surprised, then scolded herself for making another assumption. Why shouldn't Kitty have a man in her life? If it was indeed Kitty inside the shack. A moment later a woman joined the man. He passed her the binoculars. She lifted them to her eyes, then passed them back to him with a little shrug. Georgia waved again. The woman stayed where she was, but the man went inside.

When Georgia was just a few yards away, the woman retreated into the shack. The male reappeared outside with a shotgun. He raised it to his shoulders and aimed the barrel at Georgia.

Chapter
Fifty-Four

Instinct made Georgia raise her hands. She understood. Were she in their place, she might have done the same thing if an unexpected stranger journeyed across a frozen lake to "talk" to her.

The man called out. "Whoever you are, go away. We don't want to talk to you."

"I see that. But I'm not here to hurt you, and I certainly hope you won't hurt me."

"Why are you here? Who are you?"

"My name is Georgia Davis. I'm a private investigator and I've been looking for Kitty Jarvis."

"How did you find us?"

She let out a grateful breath. Kitty *was* here. "It's my job. I'm here because something isn't right about Scott's death. I don't believe he killed Dena Baldwin on his own. I think he was set up. Partly because of the yurt. I want to hear what Kitty thinks."

A woman suddenly poked her head out of the shack. "How do you know about the yurt?"

"I saw it. In the basement of your building. Your super practically forced me to remove it for her."

The woman shot Georgia a wan smile. "Betsy can be persuasive."

"May I lower my hands now?"

"Just a goddamn minute," the man cut in. "You got a weapon?"

"A Sig Sauer semiautomatic." The Sig was what she'd used as a cop. As soon as she'd formally resigned from the force, she'd bought a new one. Then she'd discovered the Glock and the Sig went into the closet. Until now.

"Slide it across the ice to me."

"It's in a shoulder holster. May I reach in and get it?"

He raised the shotgun, chambered a round, dipped his head.

Georgia slowly reached into her jacket, drew out the Sig, and dropped it on the ice.

"Kick it toward me."

She complied. It landed at Kitty's feet. She picked it up.

"Anything else?" he said.

Georgia shook her head.

Kitty nodded at him. He lowered the shotgun.

• • •

The shack smelled like a combination of coffee and fish. A hole in the center of the ice, about eight inches wide and a foot deep, revealed inky-dark water. A fishing rod leaned against a bench, and Georgia saw half a dozen fish in a cooler. Two portable chairs, a hot plate, a pile of blankets, and a propane heater completed the furnishings.

The man moved his fishing rod so Georgia could sit on the bench. She was so cold she finally understood how teeth could chatter. Kitty draped a blanket over her shoulders and poured her a mug of hot tea from a thermos. Georgia sipped the tea and gazed around the shack. "I don't understand. The heater and the hot plate . . . they don't melt the ice?"

Kitty laughed. When she did, her face came alive, turning warm and friendly. A heart-shaped face pointed to a prominent chin.

Her brown hair was tied back in a ponytail. When she talked, it was with a pronounced working-class Chicago accent, with its flat As and D for Th. Georgia had grown up around it. Her father, a Chicago cop, and all his buddies spoke like that. It wasn't until she was a teenager that she realized not everyone in Chicago spoke the same way.

"Purdy'll explain, won't cha, honey?" Kitty said.

Purdy, underneath all his outerwear, looked to be about Kitty's height. He was slim and wore glasses, which, now that Georgia could see him at close range, covered gentle brown eyes. "First off, you have to outfit the icehouse correctly. We have a waterproof outer layer that's made out of thermal fabric. Aluminum siding too. We have this propane heater, as well as a lantern that provides heat and light. And when you put a metal grating on top of it, you have a really good hot seat. And of course, we have LED lights and a portable generator in the pickup—"

"That's enough, Purdy," Kitty said. "I'm sure Ms. Davis doesn't care about the specs and equipment of our little shack."

"It's Georgia, and I do care. I've never been inside an icehouse before. But I don't have a lot of time. My nephew—just four months old—is very sick, and I need to get back to Chicago as soon as I can."

"I'm sorry," Kitty said.

"Thanks." Georgia sipped her tea, still unconvinced about the merits of ice fishing. Why did people want to spend time outdoors when the temperature dropped to single digits?

"And I'm sorry about Purdy before. He's very protective."

"That's not a bad thing. I suspect you may need it."

Kitty frowned. "Why? What do you know?"

"Actually, it's what *you* know."

"Me?"

"I have a theory you may have information—maybe things you don't know you know about your brother and what he was up to."

Purdy picked up the fishing rod, pulled one of the chairs up to the hole, and lowered the line into the water. "You came a long way to test a theory?"

"I did."

"How did you come to have this theory?" Georgia couldn't tell if he was sincere or mocking her.

"Like I said, I've been working for the family. They got an email a few weeks after Dena was killed. It was cryptic, but it implied that something or someone besides Scott was mixed up in the murder. But the email turned out to be untraceable. The Baldwins hired me to follow up on it. They want to know the truth."

Kitty and Purdy exchanged glances. Georgia caught it. Then Kitty said, "I don't know anything about the woman he killed."

"But you knew Scott."

"Yes," Kitty said. "And I'm kind of glad you're here. I've been hoping to get the word out. I'll never forgive the people who destroyed his dreams. I hope they rot in hell."

"Why?"

"So . . ." She settled herself in the other chair. "When Scott was discharged, he didn't know which end was up. He enlisted when he was eighteen. He spent nearly seven years in the army, most of it in Iraq or 'Stan. In effect, he grew up over there. Afterwards, when he came to live with me, it wasn't easy. Like every other vet, he had PTSD. He fell into a deep depression. He was such a sweet boy when he left. When he came home, though, he was different. I hardly knew him."

Georgia nodded.

"I had this job bartending at the Barracks. He would meet me there every day, and we'd talk. I wanted to help, but I felt helpless. I did talk to a therapist, who said to give it time." She paused. "Well, time passed. Months. He wasn't sure if he wanted to live or die. He used to say it would be easier all round if he just ate his gun.

"It broke my heart. I tried to suggest things to him. College, for example. He wasn't interested. Jobs, like being a mechanic. He said he didn't have the skills. What about learning them? Nope. I told him this was a second chance at life. That he'd survived for a reason. That whether it was God or whatever, he had a new path. Nothing worked."

Kitty looked like she wanted to cry. Georgia felt her helplessness.

Purdy jiggled his line. "Hey, I think I got something." He started to reel in the line. A moment later, a fish appeared, flopping and twisting.

"Another walleye!" Purdy cried happily. "Looks like we have a feast for dinner."

Georgia watched as he landed the fish and, after it stopped thrashing, put it into the cooler with the others. She turned back to Kitty. "You were saying?"

"I didn't know what to do. That's what I told the cops, by the way. And the FBI. I wanted them to know that in his heart, he was a good guy." She bit her lip. "But then it all changed."

"How come?"

"Beef Jerky started coming around."

Chapter
Fifty-Five

Five Months Before the Demonstration

Kitty was wiping down the bar on a hot September day, wondering what more she could do to help her brother. He was suffering from a severe case of PTSD. Every morning she was afraid he might not wake up, fearing he might have swallowed all his Ambien along with the booze. As it was, he slept most of the day, but that wasn't all bad. Kitty went to work around four, and he was usually up, morose and depressed, but awake. He would show up at the Barracks at some point.

The Barracks was both a godsend and a curse. It was a refuge of sorts, almost a halfway house where vets could commiserate, talk out their anxieties—all of them had anxieties—and, of course, drink themselves into oblivion. Kitty couldn't blame them after what they'd seen and done. But it was also a curse—precisely *because* it was a refuge. Vets could hide at the bar indefinitely. Forget they'd once had a life. Avoid making plans. Kitty had to tread carefully. She wasn't a therapist, just a bartender. Still she tried in a subtle way to hold out hope like a beacon. Not unlike that motel commercial that promised, "We'll leave the light on for you."

Around five in the afternoon three men came in wearing fatigues and army jackets. They commandeered the round table in the front of the tavern. Two were slim, pale, and covered with tats up and down their arms. The third was a beefy, stocky guy with a shaved head, intense eyes, and a horseshoe mustache so perfectly manicured he had to be vain about it.

Scott was nursing a beer at the bar, Kitty watching over him, when Horseshoe Man called out, "Hey, pretty lady, you got any beef jerky?"

Kitty looked over. "I might. Can't vouch for how fresh it is."

"You got it, I'll take it. Any way I can." He grinned.

The men with the tats snickered.

Kitty nodded, walked the length of the bar, and disappeared into a back room. She emerged a moment later with three packs of the stuff and brought them over to the men.

"Well, I'll be damned. You just made yourself a huge tip, little lady," Horseshoe said.

"He can't get enough of that shit," one of the Tats said with a laugh. "Always had a pack in-country."

"Damn right, Hairy," Horseshoe said. "What's your name, sweetheart?"

"Kitty."

"Well, Miss Kitty, I'm Beef Jerky." His grin widened but it didn't reach his eyes. "At least that's what they call me."

She had to smile. The name fit. "I'll make sure to order some fresh jerk," she said. "Any particular flavor?"

"Now, aren't you the sweetheart? They told me this place rocks. Any'll do." Beef Jerky gazed around the tavern, which, now that it was happy hour, was filling up. His knowing expression said he could size up a situation right away. He didn't miss a thing.

Kitty went back behind the bar. Scott was hunched over, staring into his beer, a plate of buffalo wings beside him.

Beef Jerky eyed him. "Hey, soldier."

Scott didn't make any sign that he knew someone was talking to him.

"You at the bar . . . what's your name?"

Kitty glanced at her brother, then at Beef Jerky. Up until now Scott had stayed clear of other vets in the bar, to the point that Kitty worried he was withdrawing into a shell that no one could ever crack, so she nudged him. "Hey, Scotty. That guy's talking to you."

Scott looked up with no expression in his eyes, then slowly turned around. She wasn't sure to this day what made him answer. She would always carry a shred of guilt that it had been her prodding, but after a long pause, he said, "Jarvis."

Beef Jerky nodded. "Where were you deployed?"

"Iraq. Two tours. Then one in 'Stan, Helmand Province."

"Gus was in Helmand, weren't you, buddy?"

Gus, the other guy with the tats, was deep into a mug of beer. He nodded.

"Come on over, son. Buy you another beer."

Jarvis glanced back at Kitty. "She's my sister. Don't need it."

"Well, in that case, Kitty," Beef Jerky said, "bring us a pitcher."

Kitty, eager for Jarvis to actually socialize with other vets, replied, "Coming right up."

That's how it started.

. . .

A month later, Scott was a regular at the table with Beef Jerky, Hairy, and Gus. Beef Jerky would hold court, occasionally inviting other vets to join them. Kitty began serving them extra wings, little pizzas, and other bar food. She knew this was probably their main meal, maybe their only meal of the day.

Their conversation was wide-ranging. Sometimes it was what happened to them in-country; sometimes it was what they wanted to do now; sometimes it was furtive whispered exchanges that made Kitty think they were hatching some kind of plan. Running through it, all the time, was politics. Beef Jerky was all in for the president. "He's exactly what this chickenshit country needs," he'd proclaim. "The day he said, 'grab 'em by their pussy,' I knew he was the right man for the job." He laughed.

Kitty was apolitical. So was Scott, at least when he'd been discharged, but as he got friendlier with the boys, he started to repeat some of Beef Jerky's aphorisms. There were chortles about lily-livered liberals, sticking it to blacks, wetbacks, and Arabs, and more. Kitty didn't like it, but Scott seemed more engaged than he'd been in the nine months since he'd come home. Occasionally, he even smiled. A godsend and a curse.

One day when talk turned to the future, which wasn't often, because, as Kitty suspected, most of the GIs weren't ready for it, Beef Jerky, as always, took the lead.

"What about you, Jarvis? What are you gonna do?"

Scott looked up blankly.

"Well, what did you do before you went in?"

"Not much."

Kitty cut in. "That's not true, Scotty. Remember when you were talking about creating a video game?" She looked over at Beef Jerky. "He was incredible with all those computer games. He'd play with people all over the country. He could rack up points just by breathing. He'd win free games all the time."

"Is that right?" Beef Jerky said.

"He was an expert marksman, weren't you, babe?" she said with a touch of pride.

Scott smiled, Kitty observed. That was good.

"Good to know," Beef Jerky said and ordered another pitcher. When it came, he poured beer for all of them. "So ... I got this idea for a game, Jarvis. I call it the Perfect Kill. I bet you could do it. Make it up, I mean."

Scott looked puzzled.

"I used to think about it when I was on patrol. What would it take to make the perfect kill?" He tossed back his beer. "See, it's like this. You pick your target, get some height on it. Like in a copter if you're in-country. But you could also do it in a city. You know, get to a building on the tenth floor or something.

Far enough away but still in range. That's one idea. I bet you could come up with a bunch of different setups, you being a sharpshooter and computer geek and all."

Jarvis canted his head. Kitty started to feel uneasy.

Beef Jerky went on. "Then you draw a bead and go for it."

Jarvis emptied his glass. Beef Jerky poured more beer. Jarvis shook his head. "It won't work."

"Why not?"

"Too easy to trace the trajectory. Anyone with any brains would know where the shot came from. Shooter wouldn't be able to get away clean."

"Ah, but you see, there's another step involved."

"What's that?"

"You ditch your rifle, your stock, your ammo. Everything. Then you pull out a grenade that you kept in your back pocket the whole time, pull the pin, and run like hell. The grenade obliterates all the evidence. Well, most of it. So even if someone figures out the trajectory, there's not a lot to see when they get there. You're home free."

Hairy interjected. "Wouldn't have to be a grenade, neither. You could use any kind of IED. Or make your own. Like an ANFO or something. Even a pipe bomb. Put a timer, sensor, or tripwire on it, and *boom*."

Scott seemed to consider it. "I guess."

"But a grenade is cleaner," Beef Jerky said with authority.

Kitty took a plate of pigs in a blanket out of the microwave and gave them to the men. "You be careful with that kind of talk, boys. Not sure I want to know any more."

Beef Jerky laughed. "Your brother does, though, don't cha, Jarvis?"

Chapter Fifty-Six

The Present

Georgia unzipped her jacket. The icehouse was actually kind of warm. Or maybe it was the heat of discovery. This was the breakthrough she'd hoped for. She leaned forward. "So Beef Jerky recruited Scott to kill Dena Baldwin."

"I didn't say that," Kitty said.

"But that's exactly how Dena's assassination went down. Where can I find Beef Jerky? What was his real name?"

"You can't, and I don't know."

"What's that mean?"

"He's dead." Kitty's voice was flat.

Georgia felt as if someone had plunged her into the icy water below Sand Lake. "How?"

"An OD. Opioids."

"Laced with fentanyl?" When Kitty nodded, Georgia asked, "When?"

"A couple of weeks after Scott died."

Georgia calculated the timing. "So about seven, eight weeks ago."

"End of January."

"I still don't get it. The way Dena Baldwin died was identical to that Perfect Kill thing."

Kitty sneaked a glance at Purdy. "Like I said, it's complicated."

"Complicated how? What are you not telling me?"

Kitty hesitated. "First of all, I still don't believe Scott had it in him. He was always a sweet guy. I could see traces of it even after he came home. But he was gullible. And Beef Jerky did a number on him, that's for sure. Actually, I had hoped Scott would meet a nice girl. I even called some friends to fix him up. I thought that might help. And it did. For a while."

"Scott had a girlfriend?"

Chapter
Fifty-Seven

Three Months Before the Demonstration

Six weeks or so after Beef Jerky and his pals showed up, just when the leaves were turning fiery red, yellow, and orange, a woman came into the Barracks before happy hour. She was tall, with brown hair, and attractive in a homespun way, Kitty thought. She asked for a pop. Scott sat at his regular spot near the end of the bar. Kitty began to chat with her, all the while scheming for a way to get the two talking to each other.

"Nice place, the Barracks," the woman said. "Do you own it?"

Kitty shook her head. "Wish we did, don't you, Scotty?"

The woman peered at Scott.

Kitty went for it. "That's Scott. My brother."

The woman smiled. "Nicole."

"Hi, Nicole." Kitty returned the smile. She turned to Jarvis. "Scott?"

He looked over and gave Nicole a brief nod.

Nicole didn't seem to mind. "How long have you been bartending?"

"Five years. I was part-time when I was at DePaul. After I graduated, I started full-time."

Nicole didn't ask why a woman with a college degree would make a career out of bartending. Kitty appreciated Nicole's discretion. She wasn't sure herself.

Nicole came back the next day around the same time. This time she sat on a barstool closer to Scott. She told Kitty she was job hunting but it wasn't going well. She was looking for an office manager job, but all the good ones were taken. Kitty was considerate as well and didn't ask many questions.

The third day Nicole came in was the beginning of happy hour. This time she sat just one barstool away from Scott. As the bar filled up, she reached across the barstool between them and struck up a conversation. The rising noise of the crowd made it difficult for Kitty to overhear them, but Scott nodded a lot, to the point where Nicole moved over and sat next to him. Kitty topped off their drinks whenever she could and brought them a plate of pizza squares with a smile.

When Beef Jerky showed up and invited Scott over to their table, which now had a "Reserved" sign on the top, Scott hesitated. Beef Jerky, who had seen him talking to Nicole, said, "Bring your friend over, too." Scott leaned over to Nicole and whispered something Kitty couldn't hear. A moment later, they were both sitting down at the round table in front.

Kitty thought Nicole would despise Beef Jerky. But she didn't. Or else she gave an impressive performance. She let the boys do the talking and smiled at all the right times. She asked a few questions and absorbed their responses without arguing back. Little by little Beef Jerky let down his guard, and Kitty could tell from his eye contact and smiles that he liked Nicole. Before long the group was listening to Beef Jerky mock the Resistance and pay tribute to the man in the White House. When Beef Jerky asked Nicole what she thought, Kitty heard her say, "Oh, I'm not political."

Beef Jerky yanked a thumb toward Kitty, who was clearing empty glasses off the table. "Neither is Kitty." He sniffed. "What's wrong with you women?" Then he grinned. "It's okay. I can think of a lot of other things you should be doing."

That prompted a snicker from the Tat boys, as Kitty called them, but a wan smile from another vet at the table. He was a slim guy in jeans and a sweater. His hair, while short, had some style to it, and he wore tortoiseshell glasses over big brown eyes.

"What's a matter, Purdy? You don't like your women quiet?"

"Sure I do," he said and looked straight at Kitty. "But I also like women who take charge." For some reason Kitty's cheeks felt hot. Purdy smiled.

"Oh man," Beef Jerky teased. "Purdy here ain't one for fighting. He just wants to tap those keys, don't you?"

Purdy shrugged. "That ain't true, Jerky. I wouldn't mind waking up by a crick where water runs over the rocks or roosters crow instead of the fucking traffic."

"Nothing wrong with that." Nicole glanced at Scott. "Right, Scott?"

Beef Jerky arched his eyebrows. "Jarvis here's a soldier, honey. He's got a mission to execute."

"A mission? What are you talking about?" Nicole asked.

"He's gonna create a video game and make us all rich." Beef Jerky laughed. At Nicole's confused look, he said, "We call it the Perfect Kill."

Chapter
Fifty-Eight

The Present

Here Kitty stopped her story. "There's something else we haven't told you."

"What's that?"

Kitty and Purdy exchanged glances. Kitty bit her lip and wouldn't look at Georgia. She motioned to Purdy.

He cleared his throat and cast his line into the ice hole. "So, you know Beef Jerky and his pals are vets, right?"

"I do."

"What you don't know is that they are members of a group called the Prairie Rats."

"The Prairie Rats?"

Purdy went on. "They're pretty much a right-wing hit squad and they do dirty work for conservative politicians. The Barracks is their watering hole, at least in Chicago. Mostly they come in to get loaded. But that's also where they do their recruiting."

"What kind of dirty work are you talking about?"

"Whatever needs doing." Purdy's steely expression told her everything.

Georgia took a minute to process it. "So that could include

beating up on anyone who might be too curious about them or the politicians they work for?"

"Sure."

"What about breaking into homes to gather intel?"

He nodded.

She spoke the next words slowly. "What about assassinating people they consider enemies?"

"It's entirely possible."

"Jesus Christ. How do you know this?"

Purdy pulled his fishing line out of the ice hole and looked straight at Georgia. The folksy accent he'd been using disappeared. "Because I did their IT for them."

"You?"

"They call me Purdy because I went to Purdue and majored in computer programming and engineering."

"Holy shit."

"I didn't know all of it when they recruited me. But I wondered why they offered me a shitload of money to do—um—well, things after graduation that I don't want to talk about. But when I found out what they were really up to, I wanted out. By that time I'd met Kitty." He gazed at his fishing rod. "I was lucky."

Georgia looked from Kitty to Purdy. "So Beef Jerky *did* recruit your brother."

Kitty didn't answer for a moment. "I'm still not sure about that."

"But—"

"Hear me out." She slipped the rubber band out of her hair, finger-combed it, then retied it into a ponytail. "I was happy when he started taking up with Nicole. They seemed to hit it off, and I was grateful he had an, well, an alternative to Beef Jerky. The P-Rats are bad news. When they're not working for whoever they report to, they sell and distribute narcotics."

"That's why we were surprised that Beef Jerky OD'd," Purdy added. "He's been dealing for years. He knew his product and what to stay away from."

Kitty took over. "Then Nicole and Scott started meeting outside the bar. I would ask him where they went and what they did, but he told me it was none of my business. Fine, I thought. He's right. But then he started talking about leaving Chicago. Just like he did when he first came home. 'Living off the grid' is what he kept saying. Maybe even up here." She waved a hand to indicate Sand Lake, the cabin, everything. "To be honest, I was relieved. Meanwhile, Purdy and I got—um—close, and we were starting to think the same thing."

Georgia jumped in. "And so you bought him the yurt as an incentive to get him—maybe all of you—out of Chicago."

"I didn't buy it."

"But Betsy Start called me about a yurt delivered after you left. I saw it. And when I checked I found out a woman bought it with him."

"Exactly. A couple of weeks after he died, I got the papers for a yurt with a note that said, 'Thanks for buying at Camping Unlimited. I know you and your wife were in a hurry, but there are lots of options you can add on to make it even more homey. Please call us if you need anything.' Except that 'wife' wasn't me."

Georgia frowned. "Nicole?"

"Had to be."

"What's her last name?"

"She told me once. I think it was Harris or something. But it wasn't on the receipt for the yurt."

Georgia raised her eyebrows. "You looked."

"Scott was my brother. The only family I have—had—left."

"Got it." Georgia stood and rubbed her hands together. The icehouse might be tolerable, but spending time in one wasn't on her bucket list. Yet the trip north had been well worth it. The case was coming together.

There was just one more thing. "You sent Erica Baldwin the email, didn't you?" She looked at Purdy. "Because you knew how to delete the account."

Kitty and Purdy exchanged another glance.

"As a warning," Georgia added.

Kitty swallowed. "I was freaked-out after Scott died. Because of what you said. It played out exactly the way Beef Jerky described the Perfect Kill. Except that Scott wasn't supposed to die."

"And you think Beef Jerky had nothing to do with it?" Georgia said in her skeptical voice.

"I didn't know for sure. And I didn't much care. I took time off. It was when I was ready to go back to work that I heard about Jerky's OD. Something didn't add up. The fact that he was selling dope for years, and all of a sudden he ODs? It was . . . what do you say . . . quite a coincidence."

"Too much of one."

"Right. Plus the FBI was putting heat on me even though I didn't have any answers. I freaked out."

"So you ran. And then sent Erica the email."

She nodded. "It was the only thing I could think of that might help. I didn't know if it would change anything, but I just wanted people to know Scott wouldn't have killed himself like that. He had a plan. He was looking forward to it. And . . . " She swallowed. "I know he shot that girl, but he wasn't the villain they made him out to be."

"You think he was on a mission. Carrying out someone else's orders."

"Exactly."

"I understand." She stuck out her hand. "Hey, thanks for talking to me. You've been a tremendous help." She paused. "Even though you were damn hard to find."

"But you did." Kitty smiled. "Which means you must be damn good at your job."

"I need to get back to Chicago. I have a lot of work to do."

Kitty pulled her jacket close around her. "Look. There's something else."

Georgia tipped her head to the side. "More?"

"Something kept nagging me after Scott met Nicole. But I

couldn't figure it out until we got up here and I was thinking straight again."

"What's that?"

"I always thought Nicole looked familiar. I couldn't place her. Then all of a sudden it came to me. About six months ago this girl came into the bar with a friend. The girl was pretty. And sexy. I could tell Scott was interested. But she was wasted, and she started throwing shade at Scott and Jerky and the rest of the boys. In fact, she was cruel. She humiliated Scott for being in the military. Said he wasted his time fighting for a fascist country."

A queasy feeling start to roil Georgia's gut.

Kitty confirmed it. "It was the girl who was killed. And the friend with her? Who came back to the bar two months later? That was Nicole."

Chapter Fifty-Nine

The Present

By the time Georgia's cell service returned, there were two calls from Vanna and one from Jimmy. They were all now at Children's, waiting for the spinal tap. She called Jimmy.

"What's the prognosis?"

"They can't be sure it's not meningitis without doing the spinal."

"Oh God. Poor Charlie. Poor Vanna."

"Where are you?" he asked.

"Heading back to the Duluth airport. The last flight out leaves tonight around nine. I'll be on it."

"How was the trip?"

"I found her."

"The sister."

"We talked. I have a lot of work to do. But it's all good. I know a lot more now."

"You are relentless, you know that?"

She smiled. "Hey, I have a question."

"Shoot."

"Have you ever been ice fishing? Like on Lake Geneva?"

"Not on your life. My family's Greek, not Nordic."

"Wonderful. Let's keep it that way."

. . .

During the flight back to Midway, Georgia pieced together what she'd learned. Ruth had met Jarvis. As Nicole, she had wormed her way into his life in a casual but persistent fashion. That was something Dena herself might have done, Georgia mused. But not as subtly as Ruth. Ruth had gone out of her way to groom him, by trying to fit in with his friends, offering him comfort and support, and above all, buying him a yurt, which likely depleted her savings, all with the promise of a life away from it all. Was she planning to join him? And if she was, why hadn't they gone off into the sunset together once the yurt was delivered? Was she waiting for him to kill Dena? If so, how did she convince him to do it?

Then there was the shooting itself. If Ruth/Nicole had persuaded him to shoot Dena, something must have gone wrong. Ruth had been wounded, and Jarvis himself killed. Why? Had Jarvis changed his mind at the last minute? Did he realize Ruth/Nicole was using him and tried to kill her too? Or was there some other possibility? She had the bones of the case, but she was still missing the flesh.

Chapter Sixty

Three Months Before the Demonstration

It wasn't a tough job, once she made up her mind. She'd always been "a smart cookie" as her father had told her. And resourceful; she'd had to be. Her family didn't have money like Dena's. They didn't parade around pretending they were royalty. Ruth's father worked for the gas company and her mother was a salesgirl at Goldblatt's. It took plenty of midnight shifts and overtime to cobble together enough for a tiny ranch house in Bolingbrook. Ruth decided to become a teacher, figuring that would take her far away from Bolingbrook.

It wasn't far enough. The cost of living kept going up. Her salary didn't. She worked harder, taking on a second job tutoring private school brats on the North Shore who didn't understand algebra and didn't give a damn. As long as they got into the Ivy League school their parents went to. Ruth was offended by their attitude—not that they didn't understand math, but that they didn't see its precision, beauty, and genius once they did. They just didn't care.

After the election she went through what she learned later were the stages of grief encountered when a loved one dies. Denial, check. Her family were Chicago blue-collar union Democrats who worked hard and expected a fair deal in return. She refused to believe the election had been stolen from under them. Then again, no one else did either.

Anger came next, and there was plenty of that. That's when she joined ResistanceUSA, vowing to kick that cretin out of the Oval Office. Forty thousand outraged people could be a powerful force.

Bargaining and depression followed. She'd had to make concessions. The leader of the group, Dena Baldwin, could have been one of the entitled North Shore brats she tutored. Except she did care, and she demonstrated it every day. Ruth had to concede that, on the whole, Dena was doing a pretty good job heading up the group. If Ruth wanted to rise through the ranks, she'd have to work harder. Do the tedious, routine tasks no one else wanted. She could do that. She was used to working hard.

Over time she became Dena's second-in-command, her aide-de-camp. But Ruth had her own ideas about how the group should be run, and it was difficult to remain second-best. She *knew* she could do a better job. But Dena had the final say.

Acceptance, the fifth stage of grief? Ruth wasn't there yet, and she wasn't sure she would be. Because now it was becoming untenable. Not politically. The Resistance was having an effect. The new administration was doing everything wrong, there were dozens of investigations, and the drumroll of opposition, of which they were a part, was growing larger and louder. Eventually—no one knew how long; that was the infuriating thing—he would be indicted or impeached and thrown out.

What was untenable was Dena. She'd started to make rash decisions. She was launching into virtual affairs with group members who weren't vetted. Like Willie Remson and who knew who else. She was stumbling into vet bars wasted and making a fool of herself. Ruth wanted to feel pity for Curt Dixon—he was in love with Dena despite her roving eye—but she couldn't. A submissive guy, he'd been seduced by her charm and charisma. Dena was using him, just like she used Ruth and everyone else with whom she came into contact.

In fact, Dena's behavior was becoming dangerous. Ruth

recalled how she'd had to drag Dena out of that military bar, the Barracks. If she hadn't acted when she did, Dena might still be recovering from a shiner, maybe a couple of broken bones. And the demonstration they were planning? Ruth was doing the work, but Dena was taking the credit.

Acceptance? No way.

Dena knew it, too. Their relationship had become fraught. Quick-tempered and judgmental, they started to snap at each other. Ruth wasn't perfect by any means; why should she care whom Dena flirted or slept with? Still, it rankled. Dena chose lovers with the carelessness of a hurried shopper choosing fruit in the supermarket. The only criterion was that they were anti-administration.

But then to have that right-wing vet go all goggle-eyed over her too? It was too much. Ruth couldn't take any more. But she was smart enough to realize that if she felt that way about Dena, Dena probably felt the same about her. Dena had the power. She could kick Ruth out of the group anytime she wanted. Like the way she made Remson disappear when she was finished with him.

That wasn't going to happen to Ruth. She started to formulate a plan, mulling it over that fall when she wasn't teaching or organizing or placating Dena. Ironically, it was Dena who sparked the idea. The incident at the vet bar turned out to be a catalyst, and Ruth decided to explore it. She bought a sexy top, changed her hair, put on makeup, and went back to the Barracks. Several times. Which was where she met Jarvis and Beef Jerky and his followers. It was a tough slog; she was still trying to perfect the plan. But then God intervened when Beef Jerky revealed his Perfect Kill video game.

It just might work. Of course, she made a few modifications. It had to look like the act of a right-wing nutcase. A domestic terrorist acting alone. The catch was that the shooter couldn't survive. That was key. Afterward, Ruth would publicly dedicate herself to avenging Dena's killer.

She'd have to be careful to cover her tracks. She needed to rig an IED to a timer or a tripwire to destroy the evidence and make it look like Jarvis took his own life. She started to research the mechanics of doing that at the library on the library's computers, rather than her own. She quickly realized the research would involve a trip down to the hotel to check out the roof, and she'd probably need to take Jarvis with her. How could she do that without being spotted or remembered for making such an unusual request? She came up with a solution.

No matter how careful she was, she knew she would be one of the suspects. She wasn't family, but she was considered to be Dena's closest friend. To deflect suspicion from herself, she came to an unpleasant conclusion. Distasteful as it was, she had to make herself a victim of the attack.

Chapter
Sixty-One

Dim lighting muted the brightly painted butterflies and clouds in the lobby of Children's Hospital in downtown Chicago. Recently relocated and entirely reconstructed, the hospital was now the Ann and Robert H. Lurie Children's Hospital of Chicago, but everyone still called it Children's. Whatever its name, it remained the best hospital, perhaps in the country, but certainly in the Midwest, for sick children. It was after eleven when Georgia raced past the entrance to the emergency care unit, where, again, a display of giant colorful sculptures of underwater corals—although one of them looked like carrots to Georgia—had been positioned.

When she arrived at the infant care center, the night shift was in high gear. The overhead corridor lights were off, but sconces on the walls gave out a muted gold light. Nurses in blue scrubs swished down the hall in hushed tones, but Georgia could still hear one or two children wailing. She hoped Charlie wasn't one of them. With her heart on her sleeve, she asked one of the nurses where Charlie's room was. The nurse pointed to the end of the hall, where, through an open door, she saw Vanna, Jimmy, and JoBeth, all with face masks, leaning over a cradle.

Georgia took a face mask from a dispenser near the door and

tiptoed in. When Vanna saw her, her relief was palpable, and she fell into Georgia's arms. Georgia put her arms around her sister and whispered, "You are such a brave mama; I know he's going to be okay."

Vanna's eyes filled. She hugged her sister back.

Jimmy's eyes softened and he went to them, spreading his arms around both women. The three of them stood for a moment, hugging one another.

"Is he asleep?" Georgia whispered.

"Off and on," Vanna said.

"The spinal tap?"

"Still waiting."

"All day?"

"They did a bunch of other tests first. They still don't know. They let me feed him, though."

Georgia peeked into the cradle. Charlie was clothed only in a diaper. His face was red, and the whole of his little body flushed. She straightened up and looked into the eyes of her mother. JoBeth met her gaze with one of the saddest expressions Georgia had ever seen. She dipped her head toward her mother. JoBeth returned it then looked back at Charlie. Georgia saw a tear in her mother's eye.

Ten minutes later a nurse came in. "We're just about ready. It won't be long."

"Can we stay with him?"

The nurse looked at them all in turn. "Only the mother."

"That's her." Georgia pointed to Vanna.

But Vanna shook her head. "Please, can my sister come too?"

The nurse hesitated, then nodded. "But you can't get closer than about six feet. And you need to wear gloves and masks. Let's move him to the procedure room, okay? The doctor is already there."

"Have you met him before?" Georgia asked Vanna.

"Her, and yes," Vanna replied.

"Well, let's go," Georgia said. "Wish us luck."

Jimmy kissed Georgia, then Vanna on the cheek. "I'll stay with JoBeth."

The nurse released a brake on Charlie's cradle and wheeled him out of the room.

Chapter
Sixty-Two

Georgia and Vanna followed the nurse and Charlie into what could have been an operating room but was nighttime dim. Georgia could just make out cartoonish animals on the walls. The animals were doing all sorts of cute things: a giraffe munched tree leaves, a cat licked her paw, and a monkey was caught in mid-jump from a branch.

Charlie stirred. Vanna leaned down to coo and brush his forehead. He seemed irritable and cranky and started to fuss. Vanna looked pleadingly at the nurse. "Can I pick him up?"

The nurse shook her head. "It's better if we handle him from here."

Vanna swallowed, stepped back, and grabbed Georgia's arm.

The doctor came in and gave them a warm smile. "Hello. Sorry for the delay. I'm Dr. Kumar. We've just been so busy today. And we had to rule out other things. But we're ready to proceed now." She glanced at both women. "Which one of you is the mother?"

"I am," Vanna said.

"This isn't going to be easy, sweetheart. He's going to cry. A lot. Do you think you can handle being here? It's understandable if you can't. A lot of mothers end up stepping out."

Georgia couldn't see past Vanna's mask, but she knew her sister was wavering. She draped her arm around Vanna's shoulders. But she also knew Vanna wanted—no, needed—to be near her baby. "I'm her sister. If she has a problem, I'll handle it."

The doctor seemed satisfied. She went to a sink in a corner of the room, washed her hands thoroughly, and slipped on her own mask and gloves. Then she nodded to the nurses in similar garb. They lifted Charlie out of the cradle and moved him to the table, all with loving murmurs and support. But Charlie didn't like it and started to cry.

Vanna stiffened. Georgia tightened her hold on her sister.

The doctor inspected a plastic tray on which a number of instruments and vials had been placed. "First I'll mark the incision point." Dr. Kumar picked up a marker and made a tiny circle on Charlie's back, about two inches from his butt crack. Charlie's cries intensified.

Vanna seemed to be in a daze. Georgia whispered. "Hold on, sweetheart."

"Now I'm swabbing him with Betadine. It's cold. That's why he's crying."

Vanna didn't move. Georgia nodded. The doctor peered at Vanna. "You sure she's going to be all right?"

Georgia nodded again, but her stomach was roiling, and she wasn't sure she was all right. She could only imagine how Vanna felt.

The doctor nodded to the nurses. Both situated Charlie so he was leaning over, to stretch his back. As they did, they pinned down his arms and legs. He couldn't move. His crying turned to screams. The doctor took a needle, filled it with a clear substance, and inserted it into the area she'd marked.

"Lidocaine," the doctor said. Charlie's screams scaled up the register to a high-pitched keening.

Vanna tried to pull away from Georgia. "No more," she cried. "I can't take it. Please stop."

Georgia restrained her sister, but Vanna was stronger than Georgia expected. Never doubt the strength of a mother protecting her child. "Vanna," she said into her sister's ear, "it will be over soon. Do you want to leave the room?"

"Oh God, Georgia. Make them stop!" Her screams mixed with Charlie's as the doctor inserted a long needle into the spot where she'd previously injected the lidocaine. Georgia had to suppress a shudder when the needle went in. She squeezed her eyes shut. Charlie was inconsolable, his screams rising to an intolerable pitch. Vanna retched and looked like she was going to vomit.

"Vanna, honey, let's go outside." Georgia tried to lead her to the door of the procedure room.

But Vanna resisted and stiffened so much, Georgia couldn't budge her. "No! I'm staying with my baby. He needs me."

Then a remarkable change came over Vanna. It was as if she suddenly steeled herself to her own feelings and decided to focus only on Charlie and the need to identify what was wrong with him. She stopped crying, and amid his screams, Vanna started to coo to her son.

"Charlie, baby, it's Mama. It will all be over soon. I promise. I'm here, and it's going to be okay. Just hold on, sweetheart. I promise to hold you and rock you and sing to you all night when this is over." A tiny smile curled her lips, and though it was impossible to silence his sobbing, Vanna looked peaceful and confident.

A swell of love and pride for Vanna washed over Georgia. It took incredible courage to control the anguish of watching her baby in excruciating pain. At that moment Vanna was a hero, and Georgia knew if Vanna could handle it, so could she. She hugged her sister. A little blood oozed from the injection site, but no more than a bruised knee would cause.

Finally it was over. The needle came out, and the doctor attached a Band-Aid to the injection site. Georgia was astonished that a simple bandage was the only tangible sign that Charlie had undergone such a critical procedure.

It was one in the morning. She sagged in relief. It was Vanna's turn to hug her.

Chapter
Sixty-Three

Charlie was asleep before the nurse wheeled him back into his room, but the rest of them catnapped. In the early morning hours Georgia and Jimmy went down to the always-open cafeteria for coffee. She told him everything she'd learned from Kitty in Minnesota about Scott, the Prairie Rats, and Ruth Marriotti.

"So now it's over, thank God," Jimmy said.

"Not quite. I need evidence."

"What do you mean? That's the Bureau's job. You cracked the case. Let them take over. You don't have to catch the bad guys."

"I didn't have to be with Vanna either."

"Oh come on. They're not the same thing."

"Aren't they? The FBI isn't going to arrest Ruth on my word alone. Or even Kitty's, although I promised not to tell them where she is. They need proof. You know that."

"Then let them look for it. That's what they do. For all you know, the Prairie Rats are already on their radar." He scowled. "They should be."

"I agree. It could explain what happened to Dena Baldwin's father." She sipped her coffee, which was surprisingly good for two in the morning. "I had time to think on the flight back from Duluth. Dena's father represented some energy companies who are into fracking in a big way. Dena was criticizing fracking in the Facebook group. What if the fracking owners sent Carl Baldwin a message—a warning, let's say—that his daughter should cut it out?"

"By killing her?"

"Not at first. But knowing Dena, she didn't stop her attacks. Who knows what happened?"

"Georgia, you're talking about a conspiracy to commit murder. In the name of corporate profits."

She nodded.

"You better be damn sure that's what it was." Jimmy sat back in his chair. "I don't like this at all. I wish you wouldn't take it any further. Didn't LeJeune say the FBI wanted to interview you?"

"Yes. And I'll tell his guys about the Prairie Rats and their relationship with Scott Jarvis."

"Good. Then you're out of it."

"Except for one thing."

"What?"

"I think there may be a connection between them and Ruth Marriotti." She told Jimmy about Beef Jerky's Perfect Kill video game. "And that's exactly how it went down."

"Georgia, you barely got out of DC alive and that wasn't even a week ago." He took her hand. "Please don't."

She kept her mouth shut.

Jimmy sighed reluctantly. "What do you have in mind?"

"I have a couple of ideas."

• • •

They were back upstairs on a couch tangled in each other's arms down the hall from Charlie's room when JoBeth appeared.

"What's going on?" Georgia asked in a worried voice.

"Everything's fine. Vanna won't sleep. She's singing to Charlie. Of course, he's out like a light. Jimmy, do you mind? I'd like a few words with Georgia."

"Sure thing. I'll go see if I can sing along with Vanna." He disentangled himself from Georgia and kissed her forehead.

It was just the two of them.

JoBeth cleared her throat. "Georgia, I've learned so much since I've been in Chicago. Most of it has been surprising, overwhelming, and beautiful. But some of it not so much."

"What are you talking about?"

"I have two strong, independent daughters who I have grown to cherish. Between you and Vanna, you make a mother proud. But"—she looked down—"here's the thing. I didn't do a damn thing to make that happen." She let out a breath. "In fact, I damaged Vanna. And you. I—I was a selfish child. I still am. I think only about myself. I make myself out . . . well . . . to be a victim. I throw temper tantrums, and when that doesn't work, I drink. And when that doesn't work, I run away. That's what I did to you. It's only now that I'm—well—beginning to understand how I destroyed both your souls."

Georgia didn't know what to say.

"There has only been one adult in this relationship. And that's you, Georgia. Not me. You saved Vanna's life. You helped her grow up. And, as I told you before, you have done a wonderful job." She swallowed. "And you have every right to be furious at me. To exclude me from your life. I failed you both." She stood up. "Come with me."

Georgia rose and followed her mother back into Charlie's hospital room. JoBeth leaned over Charlie's crib and kissed him gently. Then she faced Vanna and clasped her in a hug.

"Vanna, honey, when Charlie's ready to leave here, I hope you'll live with your sister. You belong with her. Not me." JoBeth released her daughter. "I'm so sorry." Then she smiled softly, turned on her heel, and walked out of the room.

. . .

The next morning Dr. Kumar arrived before seven. An early sun was just peeking through the window blinds. "Good news, everyone. Charlie doesn't have meningitis."

Vanna clapped her hands, hugged Georgia, then hurried over to pick up Charlie. Georgia couldn't stop smiling. The lightness spread through the room.

"So what is it?" Vanna asked. "Is he going to be okay?"

"In all likelihood, it's a virus with a high fever and stomach upset. The symptoms are virtually identical to meningitis."

"What about the seizures?"

"We call them febrile convulsions. They're a result of the fever. They're more common than you think. But . . . and this is key . . . while they look scary, they're not harmful to the baby."

"So he's going to be okay?" Vanna said.

"I'm sure of it. But you did the right thing bringing him in. We had to make sure."

"He won't have to have another spinal tap?" Georgia asked.

"That's right. Hopefully, never." She bent over and tenderly brushed her hand across Charlie's forehead. "As soon as your fever's down, you can go home, little champ."

Charlie gurgled.

Chapter
Sixty-Four

The hardest part of the plan was still ahead. Ruth had to convince him to kill Dena. Not only did she have to make him think it was his idea, but he also had to think he was a hero for doing it. This would test her skills at persuasion, and, frankly, she wasn't sure she would succeed. She knew that the most effective manipulators used a combination of the carrot and the stick, but before she could apply either, she had to get to know him, perhaps better than he knew himself.

That was why she'd made so many trips to the Barracks, ingratiating herself with Jarvis, his sister, who was an unexpected but surprisingly helpful ally, and his buddy Beef Jerky. Jerky was a cipher. His eyes were intense, always observing, measuring, judging, and Ruth wasn't sure whether he saw through her and her plan. The best strategy was always to play dumb. So she did, improvising by describing herself as apolitical. She could always tell Jarvis later she'd done so to make Jerky feel safe around her.

She realized they'd probably become lovers. That didn't bother her; in fact, she took a perverse pleasure in the fact that she would be screwing someone who had initially wanted Dena. Ruth would make sure that he wouldn't think that way for long. He would forget about Dena. Ruth would be the perfect lover and friend, supportive, nurturing, and accommodating.

A few weeks later, the plan was succeeding beyond her expectations. Jarvis was a ripe target, full of despair, depression, and fear. Caught between the horror of killing as a GI and the supposed reverence for life as a civilian, he was confused and vulnerable.

Her first step, after meeting him and studying the contours of his world, was to remind him of Dena. But it had to be done the right way. One night after a particularly rowdy political discussion where Beef Jerky vowed he would never stop fighting until the last fucking libtard was either locked up or dead and good white men were back in charge of the country, Ruth asked Jarvis to take a walk around the block.

"Hey, Scott, do you remember the first time we met?"

"At the bar. My sister introduced us."

"Before that."

"We met before that night?"

"Well, not exactly. I came in with this woman who proceeded to get really drunk and insulted you. Her name was Dena. She was part of this political group—well, I'm a member too, but I don't believe in it anymore." She smiled and squeezed his hand. "Especially since I met you."

"Now that you mention it, I remember her. She was hot." Surprise flooded his face. "You were the other chick with her?"

A stab of envy pricked Ruth. Dena was sexy, built for speed, while Ruth, no matter how attractive she made herself, was built for comfort. Compared to Dena, she was invisible. She nodded.

"She was a real bitch." Jarvis squeezed her hand back. "I wanted to belt her."

"I feel the same way."

"How come?"

But Ruth had planted the seed. Better to leave it for now to germinate. "Oh, I'll tell you later." She snuggled close. "Let's walk down to the lake and fool around. It's not that cold."

. . .

Her next opportunity came the last weekend of October, just past peak leaf-viewing season. She and Jarvis took a drive up to Wisconsin to a small lake Jarvis said reminded him of the place he wanted to live. With a mirror-still surface reflecting a big blue sky and the surrounding evergreens, it was a lovely place. Ruth saw only two boats on the water, and their occupants didn't look like tourists.

"It's beautiful," she said. "I can see why you love it."

"My family has a cabin up in Minnesota. Near Duluth. This reminds me of it. It's totally isolated. And since my parents passed, no one uses it much. Kitty's gone up a few times, but I haven't been there since I was sixteen."

"Is that where you want to live? In the cabin?"

"You ever hear of a yurt?"

"One of those round tents people have?"

"Right. I was thinking of something like that. You can get stuff that keeps it warm all year round. Heaters, stoves, insulated windows. Electricity. A bed and furniture, too. They are awesome. You're cut off from the world, but you can still have everything you need. I used to think about it when I was on patrol in 'Stan. The things I'd want in the yurt."

"Sounds like a dream come true."

He smiled. "You think?"

"Well then, we should get one," she said.

He whistled. "Are you kidding? With everything I want, it would cost thousands. Can't afford it."

"Oh. In that case, we can dream, can't we?"

On the drive home, Jarvis asked, "Could you see yourself in that situation, Nicole? Living off the land under the radar?"

"Absolutely," she said without hesitation. "It sounds perfect." She giggled. "As long as you're there to protect me from wolves and bears and things."

"Of course I would. But what about that group you were active in? And the woman who came into the bar. What would happen if you just up and left town?"

Ruth smiled inwardly. She couldn't have asked for a better segue. "Not a problem. Don't you remember how Dena humiliated you? And the boys? That was—is—the way she treats everyone. She's liberal, sure, but she's the most dishonest, untrustworthy person I've ever met. She started the group, but she's running it all wrong. I won't miss her. Or the group. I gave my all for over a year, and I tried to help, but I'm ready to quit. She's ruined it for me. And it's not just me. A lot of other people feel the same way."

"What did you do in the group?"

She gave him a quick summary, but embellished it with demeaning things Dena never said, degrading things she never did. "And talk about being loose . . . she fucked anything with pants. Just needed it, I guess." She sighed. "There's just one thing. I promised to be at this demonstration she's planning for January, and I always keep my promises," Ruth said with a solemn expression. "Even if she doesn't."

She was quiet for a moment. "I could run it so much better, Scott. I know it. I would build bridges, not burn them. I'd reach out to people who don't agree with us. People like Beef Jerky and the Tat boys. I'd try to find something we could all agree on and go from there. I was willing to give Dena a chance, hoping she'd grow in the same direction, but it didn't happen. She turned out to be an ambitious opportunist. From what I know, everyone else in her family's the same way."

Jarvis nodded. "Sounds like a real she-devil."

"You said it. But she'll never give up. She's power hungry. I just wish there was a way to kick her out. Get rid of her. That would make a huge difference. Even though I don't plan to be there anymore," she added hastily.

Chapter Sixty-Five

Two Months Before the Demonstration

By Thanksgiving, Ruth and Jarvis were a couple. Between teaching and the group, Ruth didn't have much free time, but she spent all of it with him. The only challenge was keeping him away from Dena. It would be a disaster if the two bumped into each other. Jarvis had come to hate her almost as much as Ruth, thanks to Ruth's lies and deceit. And while Kitty's smiles and attention to Ruth/Nicole at the Barracks indicated she approved of their relationship, Ruth didn't want to spend too much time with her, either. She had to stay detached. It was a delicate balance.

Meanwhile, her discussions with Jarvis had graduated from the theoretical to the possible, thanks to Beef Jerky's Perfect Kill game. Ruth made sure to bring it up after sharing passionate sex one night. One evening in early December, they were lying in his bed at the apartment. Kitty was still tending bar—Ruth had figured out that early evening, right after happy hour, was the best time for them to be intimate. It was during these times that she made sure to anticipate and fulfill every one of his fantasies.

Jarvis lay on his side, sweaty but content, facing her. He was smiling. Ruth returned it and ran her fingers through his hair, behind his neck, and across his shoulders. At the same time, she faked a coy tone. "Hey, Scotty. Do you remember when Beef Jerky laid out that Perfect Kill game at the Barracks? He said you were going to make them all rich."

"I remember," he replied.

"Well . . . what if we could prove that it works in real life?"

He squinted at her. "What do you mean?"

"What if—I mean, if you think it's a good idea—we could try it out at the demonstration in January?"

"What are you saying, Nicole?"

She let him figure it out, and when she saw the flash of comprehension in his eyes, she added, "You'd be a hero. You know that, right?"

"You think?"

"I know it." She brushed her fingers across his forehead. "Even the members of ResistanceUSA would be grateful. And afterwards, you and I could escape to Minnesota. Forever." She frowned. "After I recover, that is."

"Recover? What do you mean recover?"

She explained that he would have to wound her during the "exercise," as she'd come to call it. "It wouldn't be hard. Do you remember in *Homeland* when Quinn shot Carrie in the shoulder?"

He shook his head.

She described the scene.

"I can't do that."

"Of course you can. You're an expert shot. Just my shoulder."

"What if I miss?"

"You won't." She kissed him and proceeded to silence his doubts in a way she knew would work.

. . .

Over the next few weeks they scouted the hotel downtown. The lobby was decked out for Christmas with sparkling lights wrapped around staircases, in the lobby, and on trees. They weren't able to get to the roof, but Ruth hadn't expected to just yet. She wanted him to be familiar, perhaps assess what he'd need and how he'd do it. After the field trip Ruth took him to the skating rink in Millennium Park, where they drank hot chocolate and watched skaters gracefully twirl and spin, full of holiday cheer.

When they climbed into her car, she took out a J and they got pleasantly stoned during the drive north. But instead of turning off at Touhy on I-94, she kept driving.

"It's time for your Christmas present," she said and drove to Camping Unlimited in Northbrook, where she bought him a yurt. It completely wiped out her savings, but she didn't care. Savings were for unexpected events or emergencies. And this qualified as both.

Chapter
Sixty-Six

Two Weeks Before the Demonstration

After the holidays, in early January, Ruth was supposed to be grading a math quiz but was in fact studying printouts from the library about how to make an IED. She'd pretty much decided on a pipe bomb, which wasn't hard to assemble, and a battery-powered alarm clock to activate the detonator. She planned to pack the pipe with smokeless powder, which was available on Amazon for about fifty bucks and would make an excellent explosive. Although she'd never built a bomb before, she had specific directions and even illustrations to guide her. It wasn't rocket science, she kept reminding herself. And if all else failed, she could ask Jarvis for help.

While she was creating a fake account on Amazon, her doorbell buzzed. She wasn't expecting anyone and considered not answering. She had too much work to do. Then again, it could be Dena. Occasionally she would show up, unannounced, demanding something from Ruth, or complaining about someone, or just in need of attention.

She went to the door and called through the intercom. "Who is it?"

"It's Beef Jerky."

Ruth's stomach pitched. How had he found her? What did he want? She pressed the button to unlock the door to the street. She heard the clomp of boots on the stairs. More than one set of boots. As many as three. She sucked in a breath of trepidation. Unlatched her door.

Beef Jerky and the Tat boys walked in without saying a word. Then Beef Jerky spun around. "Who the fuck are you... Nicole"—he emphasized the name—"and what the fuck are you doing?"

Beef Jerky knew about the "exercise." She didn't know when, and she didn't know how, but the suspicion and narrowed eyes indicated there was no doubt. She sucked in a breath. She'd come so far. It was going to happen. She couldn't let him stop her. She could lie. Tell him it was all a fantasy between her and Jarvis. That she was just trying to make Jarvis feel worthy. Useful. A nanosecond later she recognized that wouldn't work. Beef Jerky was way too observant. And sophisticated. Would see through her. She had only one option. The best defense and all that.

"Who the hell are *you?*" she retorted.

"You don't want to know," he growled. Before she could say anything, he fingered his mustache. "You think I don't have intel? You think I don't know that your name is Ruth Marriotti, you're a math teacher, and you were one of the first people to join that pussy asshole Resistance group?"

Ruth panicked inside but endeavored to hide it from the men. How did he know? Who told him?

"You think I don't know that you want to kill the woman who started it and you're using Jarvis to do it?"

She tried one more time. "If you know all that, then you know what a danger people like her are to people like you. I'm helping you. Of course, if you can't see that, then you're not as smart as you think you are."

"Well, missy, you are right about helping us." He grimaced. "So if you'd like your thank-you now, you got it."

Ruth inclined her head. She had no idea where he was going.

"But you got no idea who we really are, and that's what I'm here to tell you." He waved his hand at her easy chair. "Why don't you sit down over there." It was an order, not an invitation. He took a seat on her couch. "After the boys frisk you."

"I don't have any weapons."

"I suspect not, but we'll just confirm it."

The Tat boys took their time, patting her down twice. They made sure to slow down when they ran their hands over her breasts. The sense of violation it triggered was nauseating, but Ruth knew that was exactly why they were doing it. She bit her lip. When they finished, they nodded to Jerky.

"Sit down," he ordered. Ruth did. She gripped the arms of the La-Z-Boy hard.

"So . . ." He took his time. "It seems we have—what you could call—a mutually rewarding objective." He didn't wait for her response. "I work with some people who are as unhappy with the Baldwin bitch as you."

"Who? And why?"

"It doesn't matter. All you need to know is that my job is to make sure Jarvis goes through with it. And that you go through with taking out Jarvis. No chickenshit sudden change of heart, understand?"

"What happens if I don't go through with 'my part'?"

"You think we don't have a Plan B?"

"What is it?"

Again he brushed his mustache with his finger. "You don't want to go there. Let's just say we're willing to give you a chance to show your stuff. Fact is, Jarvis does seem to like you. Might even be willing to do it."

She ran her tongue around her lips. "So, let's assume I do what you want. What's in it for me?" She realized as she said it that everything up until now, while she'd planned meticulously, was nothing but a fever dream of revenge. It wasn't real. The plan could crumble into tiny pieces and disappear without anyone getting hurt. And Jerky had a point. In those moments she wondered whether she had the cojones to go through with everything. The possibility of an out had always lurked in the back of her mind. She could come up with an excuse to abort the plan; Jarvis would believe anything she told him. Now it appeared that option was gone. An icicle of fear slid up her spine.

A twisted grin came over him. "Don't play that bullshit game with me. You were going to take him out anyway. We're just here to make sure you do." He leaned forward. "Jarvis always was off. Undependable. Head in the clouds. And his sister didn't help. We run a tight ship. He's too much of a risk."

Ruth crossed, then uncrossed her legs but didn't say anything.

Jerky went on. "So what's in it for you? How's this: you'll still be alive afterwards. You'll go back to that group and become its new leader. Just what you always wanted, right?"

When Ruth tried to object, he cut her off. "We know who you are and what you want, missy. Always have." He smiled. "And you'll get it. With one condition." He perched his feet on the coffee table and let the silence grow. "When I want a report about your group, or anyone in it, you'll give it to me pronto."

Ruth's mouth went dry. "And if I say no?"

The Tat boys each pulled out a pistol and aimed it at her.

Beef Jerky looked at the Tats and held up his hand. "Boys, put your weapons down You don't need them." He turned back to Ruth. "It's simple, babe. We've been keeping our eyes on you. If things go south, we've got all the evidence we need to put you away forever. We know what you're doing twenty-four seven." He pointed two fingers at her face. "Conspiracy to Murder. Accessory to murder. Plus a whole lot of other charges our lawyers 'll think up." He paused. "We'll get it out to the media. 'Resistance activist plans coup and fails.' He shrugged. "Your choice."

"No one will believe you. They'll say it's fake news."

"Riiight . . ." He stretched out the word. "You sure you want to take that chance?"

"How do I know you haven't persuaded Jarvis to kill *me*?"

Beef Jerky shifted. He took his time answering. "Well, missy, I guess that's just another risk you're gonna have to take."

Chapter
Sixty-Seven

The Present

Two days later Georgia salvaged the car seat from the storage locker in her basement and drove downtown to pick up Vanna and Charlie from the hospital. Charlie, who loved car rides, grinned and jiggled his arms like an octopus when Vanna belted him in. If there were any residual effects of his ordeal, Georgia couldn't see them. Vanna was in high spirits too. Her hair was combed and she looked like she might even have slept the night before.

"After we get him home, you can take the car and get your things from Arlington Heights, okay?"

"Sure." Vanna grew pensive. "Georgia, I know this is for the best, but I'm worried about Mom."

"Yeah, I know you are."

"What do you think she's going to do?"

"I don't know." Georgia was still working through her mother's words the night of the spinal tap. Their conversation had unleashed a storm of feelings: at first suspicion, then surprise at her mother's candor, gratitude for her praise, and, for the first time she could remember, no rancor. But these feelings were so new, so tentative, she wouldn't allow herself to trust them. "Did she say anything about staying in Chicago?"

Vanna shook her head.

Georgia sighed. "Well, I guess we'll know when we know."

. . .

When they got back to Evanston, Charlie went down for a nap and Vanna took the car to get their things. Georgia figured she had an hour to work

Her first call was to Zach Dolan. Two weeks had passed since he and his guys started background checks on the members of ResistanceUSA.

"Hey there, stranger." He picked up right away.

"How's tricks?"

"You'll like 'em. We're doing better than I thought, and we're ahead of schedule. One of the guys was able to program an algorithm that's helped. I'd guess we're about seventy-five percent done."

"That's terrific. What have you got?"

"First of all, a lot of fake accounts. Maybe eight thousand."

"That many?"

"It happens. Remember when Twitter started purging all those accounts a while back? Well, Facebook needs to do the same thing. Who knows? Maybe they already are."

"So, the group is more like thirty-five thousand, rather than forty-two?"

"Something like that. We're still finding stray accounts here and there. People who've abandoned them. Things like that."

"What about criminal records?"

"No surprises there. About thirty percent. What you'd expect. Facebook criminals match the national average." She could hear the irony in his voice. "The good news is that most of them are minor offenses: DUIs, speeding tickets, drug busts, petty larceny, domestic disturbances." He paused. "But a small percentage did commit felonies and a few did some serious time. I was going to wait until we're finished to send you the report, but I can email you what I have. How are things going on your end?"

"I've had a major break. If I can prove it, we might be home free."

"Well done. Anything you care to share?"

"Not at the moment, but do send me whatever you have." She hesitated. "Any red flags?"

"I'll have to check. Probably a few."

"What about Curt Dixon? What did you find on him?"

"Let's see." She could hear him clicking the keyboard. "Here we go. A DUI and three speeding tickets."

"OK. Vic Summerfield?"

"Nothing. I guess we haven't got to him yet."

"What about Willie Remson?"

Zach clicked, then went quiet. "Oh, this is good. Guy used to be a hacker. Convicted of fraud and identity theft about eight years ago. Suspended sentence, community service. Nothing since."

"Interesting. Be sure to email me what you have."

"Sure."

"What about Ruth Marriotti?"

After a moment, Zach said, "Nothing. Clean as a whistle."

She didn't reply.

"I'll take that as a 'thank you, Zach.' Do you want us to go on? You've already paid us. I mean Erica has."

"May as well. You never know."

Chapter
Sixty-Eight

Vanna returned with a carload of belongings, which Georgia helped unload. Within minutes, the apartment regained its cluttered, lived-in look. This time Georgia didn't mind. It felt like home.

"Mom wasn't there," Vanna said. "I dropped my key off with the building manager."

"Were her things there?"

Vanna nodded.

"Well, I guess that's a good sign. If you want her to stay."

"What do you want?"

"I don't know," Georgia said. It was the truth. She'd spent most of her life without her mother, so JoBeth's sudden presence felt surreal, and the prospect of her staying filled Georgia with unease. She reminded herself that JoBeth rarely stayed in one place for long. Even if she did remain in Chicago for a while, she would undoubtedly pack up and flee when the downward spiral began again. She started to share her thoughts with Vanna, then thought better of it.

"So, listen," she said. "I'm going out for an hour or two. You'll be okay here?"

"Sure." Vanna looked into the empty refrigerator and turned to Georgia with a smile. "Some things never—"

Georgia preempted her. "I'll stop on the way home for groceries."

. . .

Armed with a couple of pictures of Ruth she'd printed out from Facebook, Georgia drove back to Camping Unlimited. She wasn't sure whether Jackie was still there. The salesgirl had been hired as temporary holiday help; it was already the end of February.

The store was as vacant as it had been the other times Georgia had dropped in, which made her wonder how long the place would stay open. She wasn't sanguine about Jackie's prospects, either, so she was elated to see the girl, her hair bright purple this time. Georgia thanked the gods or whoever was responsible for karma and hurried to the customer counter.

"Hi, Jackie. How's it going?"

The girl looked up. She was wearing new earrings and a small nose ring. "Do I know you? Oh. Wait. You look familiar." Georgia could see her searching her memory. "Right. You're the detective on the Jarvis thing." She nervously twisted her earrings. "Is everything okay? I told my family all about you. They were really curious. How can I help?"

Georgia pulled out one of the pictures of Ruth. "Remember when I showed you a photo of a woman who might have bought the yurt for Jarvis, but you didn't think it was the right woman? Could you take a look at this photo?" She passed it over.

Jackie studied it. Georgia watched as recognition dawned. "That's her! I'm sure of it. You know how I can tell?"

Georgia shook her head.

"The widow's peak. I remember she took her hat off when she wrote the check. That's definitely her."

"Well done, Jackie. You are a miracle!"

The girl blushed with the praise. "Would you mind telling my boss that? I know they're deciding whether to keep me on, and, well, I need this job."

"Of course I will. Listen, I doubt it will come down to this, but I'm going to need a way to contact you. Email, cell, address. Could you write it down?"

"What for?"

"In case we go to trial. You would be a witness."

"Really?"

"Like I said, it probably won't happen, but just in case . . ."

"Wow." She scribbled her info on a piece of paper and handed it to Georgia.

"Thanks, Jackie. You're smart, observant, and enthusiastic. Anyone would be lucky to have you working for them."

Jackie glowed like a candle flame in a dark room.

Georgia trotted back to the car, adrenaline pumping her. She now had proof of a relationship between Jarvis and Ruth. No evidence tying either to the shooting of Dena Baldwin. Yet. That would be her final task, and she knew she had to do it fast.

There was a reason. Dena Baldwin was dead. Jarvis was dead. Beef Jerky, too. Both the Prairie Rats and Ruth Marriotti knew Kitty Jarvis. And they both knew Georgia. They also knew that both Kitty and Georgia were aware of connections between Jarvis, themselves, and Dena Baldwin's murder. The P-Rats operated on a strict need-to-know basis. They didn't want anyone on the outside knowing their business. Ruth, too, had gone to great lengths to keep her connection to Jarvis and the shooting on the down low. How much time would pass until either the P-Rats or Ruth—or both—tried to silence anyone whom they thought knew too much? Georgia could take care of herself, but Kitty was up in Minnesota without a cell phone. There was no way to warn her. And if the P-Rats could suss out that "Nicole" was, in reality, Ruth Marriotti, it would be child's play for them to track Kitty down. Georgia was running out of time.

Chapter
Sixty-Nine

The twenty-one-story White Star hotel in downtown Chicago occupied the corner of Michigan Avenue and Balboa. A five-star establishment first built in 1909, it fell into disrepair over time but was eventually restored with many of its original architectural details, including elegant sconces, chandeliers, and brass fittings. Its setting in the Loop made it a desirable location, and it boasted of being the "Hotel for Presidents" for much of its history, which Georgia thought was oddly appropriate. It had also been designated a historical landmark, but its biggest attraction, at least for Georgia, was its unrestricted view across the street to Grant Park. The roof of this hotel was where Jarvis killed Dena Baldwin.

She entered the lobby mid-afternoon. It wasn't a busy time, but enough people were milling around that she didn't think she would be remembered. Two uniformed employees managed reservations and checkouts at the front desk, but Georgia didn't approach them.

She knew enough to start with the bellhops. They knew more than folks at the front desk and were more likely to talk. But no one was manning the bellhop station, so she strolled around the lobby floor, imagining the hotel in its finer days.

A grand staircase with brass banisters took up most of the

lobby, and other rooms combined traditional with modern furniture that gave off an eclectic but sophisticated aura.

But the room that took her breath away was a giant ballroom with an enormous seafoam-and-ocean-colored carpet. Hundreds of sconces, recessed sky-blue lighting, and sculpted white moldings surrounded the room. A second-floor mezzanine wrapped around the space, with vertical windows, graceful draperies, and intricate moldings. Six huge crystal chandeliers that dominated the ceiling made her feel like Cinderella at the ball.

When she returned to the lobby, a uniformed bellhop stood behind a lectern at the station. She approached him with a smile. "Hi. I wonder if you can help me out."

The balding middle-aged man, with a belly that stuck out under his jacket, looked her up and down. Georgia could see in his expression that he knew she wasn't a guest.

"What do you need, lady?"

Georgia pulled out her picture of Ruth along with a twenty and gave both to him. "You see her in here, maybe a month, six weeks ago?"

He scrunched up his forehead, concentrating on the photo, or delivering a good performance if he wasn't. "Sorry. Can't place her."

"Is it worth asking any of your buddies?"

He rubbed the space between his nose and upper lip, as though smoothing a nonexistent mustache. "I can show it around if you want."

She pulled out another twenty and a ten and her card. "Ten more to you, and twenty to anyone who recognizes her. Here's my card."

"What did she do, this woman?"

"She got herself shot in the ass when that terrorist took out the Resistance woman on the roof of your hotel."

He nodded sagely. "A big day here, that was." He spoke with a lilt, close to an Irish brogue. Her father did too. But unlike the Irish, who were supposed to be expansive and eloquent wordsmiths, this guy was stingy with his. She knew why. At the rate he was going, she'd end up paying him five bucks a word.

"There's something else," she said.

"What's that?"

"I know you have a video surveillance system. I saw four cameras alone in the lobby, and more in the ballroom. I'm sure the FBI has the surveillance video from the day of the shooting. Who should I talk to about a backup?"

His eyebrows arched and he took a closer look at her card. "Georgia Davis, private detective." She nodded. "Well..." He paused dramatically. "Our head of security is Lee Oswald. That's who you need to see."

"Really?"

He smiled ruefully. "Yeah. You can ask him..." His voice trailed off.

She knew what he was saying and dug out another twenty.

"The guy you want to talk to is our maintenance engineer. Roy Sandhurst. Take the elevator to the second basement and follow the hall to his office."

She thanked him and headed to the elevator bank. No wonder they called it the "Hotel of Presidents."

. . .

The door to Sandhurst's office was open, and he was behind a desk poring over papers. Georgia knocked on the open door. "Excuse me."

He looked up.

"May I have a few words, please?" She introduced herself, told him what she wanted, and gave him a card.

He didn't get up but studied her card. She noted the obligatory shirt with his name emblazoned above the pocket. "You need to go to security. I can't help you."

"If I did that, I'd have to wait for a court order before I got them, and I don't have time. I think more lives are in danger."

"Who are you working for?"

She told him.

"What are you looking for?"

She hedged. "I'll know when I find it."

Sandhurst was asking all the right questions. She wondered if he'd been in law enforcement at some point. Or on the other side of the law. He tapped the edge of her card on his desk. "So you want tapes from the day of the incident, right?"

"Not quite. I need video from a week prior to the event through the day after."

"From what I understand—of course, I can't be sure—the FBI took a month's worth. From December fifteenth through January sixteenth."

She thought about it. The Bureau was exceptionally thorough. If they wanted a month's worth of surveillance video, shouldn't she get the same? The drawback was that a month of video footage would take forever to screen. She didn't have time.

On the other hand, if Sandhurst had gone from an outright refusal to a veiled hint of the footage she should request, maybe she should request the entire thirty days' worth. Even if he was simply fishing for money, it wouldn't hurt. She wouldn't need to screen it all.

"Okay. I'd like the same."

"It'll take me time to get you a backup."

"How much?"

"It's complicated. We got twenty-one floors, cameras in every hall, eight per floor, plus all the meeting rooms, entrances, stairwells, and common rooms. And you want video for thirty days. That's a lot of video. Plus I have to—um—split the money with the security guy who's gonna do the work. And he won't be able to put in for overtime. Plus I got my own job to do."

"How much to get it by tomorrow morning?"

"I'd say . . ." He paused, then looked directly at her. "Five thousand."

He was in it for the money, she determined. And the fact that he didn't appear to like the hotel security chief. Had he been considered for head of security and lost out to Oswald? Even so, five thousand dollars was out of hand.

"To save a life you'd charge me five grand? Come on."

"Okay. Three. Because I like you."

Georgia shook her head.

"Twenty-five hundred," Sandhurst said.

"Two and that's my final offer."

They shook on it.

Chapter Seventy

The next morning Georgia went to the bank for the cash and arrived at the White Star just after rush hour. She took the elevator down to Sandhurst's office. The door was open, but he wasn't there. She waited patiently for ten minutes, her foot tapping the floor in a four-four beat. Then she uncrossed her legs and tapped the other foot with the same rhythm. She had to make it all come out even.

When he hadn't arrived after half an hour, she wandered into the hall. She turned down a corridor and saw the employee entrance. She opened the door, thinking he might be outside smoking a cigarette. He wasn't. She retraced her steps and kept going past his office and came to a marked door that said "Security." Maybe that's where he was. She twisted the knob. Locked, of course. She knocked. No one came. She knocked again.

She heard shuffling on the other side. "I'm comin', I'm comin'." The door opened. A young man in his twenties, with bloodshot glassy eyes, a full twenty-four hours' growth of beard, and a uniform he clearly had been wearing for days. She took a chance. "You're the one who's been making the video surveillance copy for me."

He cocked his head. "You're the PI. Yeah. Sandhurst told me about you. I'm Ritter. What time is it?"

"He said he'd have it for me first thing. But he's not in his office and I don't know where he is."

Ritter snickered. "Roy pops in and out." He pantomimed drinking from a bottle. "You know."

"Crap. I need that footage now."

"No problem. I got it ready for you." He went back into the control room. Georgia followed him in. Dozens of monitors showed every nook and cranny of the hotel. People coming, people going, kitchen staff washing dishes, maids putting on uniforms and gathering their carts, guests checking out.

"You're really not supposed to be in this room. In fact, neither am I. I'm not on till four. Gotta go get some shut-eye."

"The footage?"

"Oh, here." He handed her a flash drive. "Since you're here, why don't you give me my cut now. I'll tell Sandhurst."

"I don't know. I told him—"

"It's only five hundred. And I told you I'd let him—"

"Five hundred? He was going to pay you five hundred for the job?"

"Something wrong with that?"

Now she knew the game Sandhurst was playing. She dug into her blazer pocket, pulled out ten hundred-dollar bills, and handed them over. "You've been selling yourself short, Ritter. Sandhurst was going to pocket fifteen hundred."

"What? And give me only five? Are you shitting me?"

"Nope. Tell him we met and I paid you fifty percent. You deserve it."

"Damn right I will."

Georgia exited the security office. She still didn't see Sandhurst, but it didn't matter. She'd saved a grand and had copies of the surveillance video. Maybe she'd do a background check on him when she had time and see what other scams he was running.

. . .

Georgia raced back to Evanston. She had a lot of video to screen, but the gnawing feeling that time was growing short stuck with her. Vanna was napping; her sister had obviously perfected the art of sleeping when the baby did, something Georgia didn't think she could do. She quietly made coffee and set her laptop up in the kitchen. She inserted the flash drive and copied everything onto her hard drive. Just in case.

Then she started screening footage. The frame rate of video surveillance footage was much improved from years ago, reflecting the need for and attention to sophisticated security systems. From the smooth images of the video she was screening, if it wasn't thirty frames per second, it was damn close, which made her job both easier and harder. Easier to detect an individual's face and behavior; harder because thirty FPS was video's normal speed, which meant there would be more footage to view. The White Star had a decent system; even the time code was stamped on the footage.

Still, it was a challenge just to get through one day's video. With eight cameras per floor, plus all the other camera locations, multiplied by twenty-one, it would take weeks to sift through. The FBI had scores of agents and assistants to assign to the task. She didn't.

She thought about asking Zach and his geek team to help but decided to make that her last resort. They hardly knew who Jarvis was and probably wouldn't recognize Ruth at all. And, just to make it more complicated, Georgia assumed Ruth and Jarvis would be wearing disguises when they were preparing for the event.

And that led her to the most important question. When would Ruth and Jarvis set the scene? Ruth wouldn't know who accessed the roof or how often. A maintenance man might sweep snow off the roof after a storm. Heating or other inspectors might check the systems and roof vents. Perhaps a few lovers might venture out for a romantic view of Grant Park. Ruth would wait as long as possible before bringing their gear up to the hotel roof. Perhaps until the day or the night before.

Georgia chose the day before the murder to begin screening tapes. They could have entered through the lobby, so she started there, searching for anyone resembling Ruth or Jarvis. She found nothing. But they may have been disguised or at least in different clothing. Jarvis could be wearing chinos and a jacket, or even a suit. Ruth might have been in a dress and heels. Georgia slowed the tape. She saw several appropriately dressed couples that seemed close in age, but when she zoomed in, they weren't Ruth or Jarvis.

Then again, they wouldn't necessarily have come in the front. Maybe they'd figured out a way to use the employee entrance. That would have been smart. In that case, they might be dressed as workers: Jarvis perhaps a kitchen employee, Ruth a maid. She screened the employee entrance, but no one matched their appearance.

What if they'd spent the night in the hotel and were already there? Of course, they would have used aliases, but they would have needed picture IDs to check in. While it was possible that Ruth managed to get fake ones, Georgia didn't think so. She started with the video from the twenty-first floor.

Vanna and Charlie woke up hungry. Vanna was weaning him onto solid food, and both women giggled when he tasted applesauce for the first time. His eyes grew as wide, and he waved his fists enthusiastically for more. Once Charlie was fed, Vanna scrambled eggs, toasted bread, and brought Georgia a plate.

"I know you're busy with your case. I'll take Charlie for a walk."

"Thanks, Vanna." Was this the new Vanna? Considerate and thoughtful? Whatever it was, Georgia was grateful; she wolfed down the food.

The sun was sinking behind the house across the street when she found it. She was surprised how brief the scene was. Had she not been carefully screening the video, she would have missed it.

The video was from a twentieth-floor hallway. A maid in a black uniform and white apron rolled a cart down the hall. The time-code stamp said about fifteen thirty, three-thirty PM the day before the shooting. The maid's back was to the camera. As she reached an exit door, she stopped and surreptitiously glanced around. The camera didn't have a great shot of her face, but the maid did look like Ruth. Still, Georgia couldn't be sure, and there was only one camera positioned down the length of this hall. Then the maid opened the exit door and rolled the cart through it, presumably to the stairwell.

Georgia paused the tape, rewound, and replayed it. There had to be a corresponding tape recorded in the stairwell. But finding it presented a challenge. The ID system for each camera in the hotel consisted of letters and numbers that, on their face, were meaningless. The numbers didn't correspond to the floors on which the cameras were mounted, nor did the letters match the various wings and halls. While that wasn't surprising in a huge hotel like the White Star, she needed to access the master log to determine where each camera was positioned. She'd have to call the guy in security—what was his name? Ritter. But he wasn't on the clock until four. It was ten to.

Georgia got up and paced. If the maid was, in fact, Ruth, what was she doing? Was she taking something up to the roof? The White Star's roof was only two stories above the twentieth floor. If Jarvis was waiting for her in the stairwell, he could carry whatever was on her cart. But what did it contain? The Bushmaster? Magazines and ammo? The IED? Everything?

The time on her cell dragged toward four o'clock. Georgia continued to pace. Finally, it was ten past. She called the White Star Hotel and asked for Security.

When she was transferred, she said, "Is Ritter there?"

"Who wants him?" a gruff voice replied. It had to be Oswald.

"Georgia Davis. He and I talked this morning."

"Ritter? There's some dame on the phone for you. You know a Georgia?"

Through the phone she heard, "I dunno. Wait. Yeah. Lemme take it."

He picked up. "You can hang up now, Chief Oswald," Ritter said.

There was an audible click. *Such privacy,* Georgia thought. Ten to one Oswald was still on the line, claiming it was necessary for security. She didn't care.

"What can I do for you?"

"You know who this is."

He chuckled. "I talked to our friend yesterday. Boy, was he pissed. It was pretty funny. I owe you."

"Well, consider this your repayment. I need some guidance on your ID system, you know, the numbers and letters you use for camera positions. You have cameras in the stairwells, right?"

"Sure."

"I need to know how to find the twentieth-floor stairwell at the end of a hall."

"That would be eight different cameras."

"I'll need all eight since I have no idea which hall it was."

"Hang on." He came back a moment later. "Ready? Here they are." He reeled off eight different ID labels. Georgia wrote them down.

"I also need the roof IDs."

"There are four cameras up there." He read them off.

"Thanks, Ritter. We're even."

With the proper identification Georgia easily found the camera recordings and fast-forwarded to the same time code on the maid's video. The fifth camera she screened showed an exit door opening and a maid rolling a cart into the stairwell. A man in a custodian's uniform was waiting. There was no sound, but the maid lifted the skirting on her cart, and the man carefully retrieved a long gun. The Bushmaster. He turned around to say something to the woman, but she shook her head and gestured for him to keep going.

Georgia had them. Except that she still couldn't be sure the maid was Ruth. Her hair was swept back and a maid's cap covered her widow's peak. She was wearing glasses, too, which hid her eyes, and her nose didn't look the same. If it was Ruth, and it had to be, she'd disguised herself well.

There was one more tape to screen. She advanced to the roof cams and added thirty seconds to the time code. Sure enough, on the second video, Jarvis and the maid appeared at the door to the roof. Jarvis looked around, headed to the east side of the roof, and pointed to Grant Park. The maid walked over and nodded. She swept her arm in a wide arc. He walked the length of the roof with the Bushmaster, lifted it to his shoulder, and sighted. When he found a location he liked, he lowered the assault rifle and placed it on the roof's surface. The maid smiled.

He returned it. She waved a hand to indicate he should leave. He looked back and beckoned to her. She raised her index finger, then shooed him away. She extracted the pipe bomb, battery, and alarm clock from under her coat, and placed them a few feet away from the rifle in an inconspicuous spot beside an HVAC unit. Again, Georgia couldn't see her in close-up but Ruth was clearly fiddling with the wires that led from the battery and timer to the detonator inside the pipe. Then she straightened up, planted her hands on her hips, and turned around.

A profound weariness rolled over Georgia. She paused the tape and rubbed the back of her neck. The case was coming to a close. She would soon be rid of Nicole/Ruth, the Prairie Rats, and the Resistance. She wouldn't miss them. She stood up. She was physically drained: her back ached, and her eyes were heavy from staring at the monitor. She poured a Diet Coke with lemon. Then she went back to the computer.

She didn't have to, but she reviewed the footage, isolated a few still shots of the maid and Jarvis, and emailed them to Zach to enhance. Just in case.

Chapter
Seventy-One

The Night Before the Demonstration

Ruth made an exception to her rule and invited Jarvis to spend the night at her condo. She didn't want him hanging out at the Barracks and possibly opening his mouth. It was risky; Dena wanted Ruth to come over and rehearse her speech, but Ruth convinced her to talk on the phone, since they both needed a good night's sleep.

She ordered pizza with bacon and onions, Jarvis's favorite, and made sure there was plenty of beer. She hoped he'd get high and pass out early so they could get an early start. But Jarvis was in an uncharacteristic talkative mood.

"When will the yurt be delivered?" he asked between beers. He was already loose and feeling no pain.

"She said about six weeks. They have to customize it, and that takes time."

He looked disappointed, and his voice sounded like a childish whine. "That means I won't be able to use it this winter."

"Probably not. But you'll be in there by spring. That should be lovely."

He thought about it. "I guess."

She went into the kitchen. "Need another beer?" She couldn't hear his reply but brought him one anyway.

"You're not drinking?"

"I'm a little nervous. You know, about tomorrow."

"Piece of cake." He grinned. "I haven't used the rifle in a few months. But it's like riding a bike. I'm looking forward to it."

She dropped a kiss on his forehead. "Well, that's the right attitude." She sat in the La-Z-Boy. "Have you seen Beef Jerky recently?"

"Yesterday."

"What's up with him?"

"Not much. Why?"

"Just wondering."

He chugged half his beer. "That's funny. He asked me about you, too."

"Really? What did he say?"

"That I should keep my eye on you. He thinks you're sneaky."

Sudden fear twisted her stomach. "What does that mean?"

Jarvis narrowed his eyes. "Dunno. He's always saying shit like that about people."

Ruth relaxed a tad. "Oh."

"So why does the buzzer say Ruth Marriotti instead of Nicole? I thought you owned this place."

"I do." Ruth had to think fast. "I bought it from someone named Ruth. Just haven't had the time to change it. I tell people I'm in 3B. Hasn't been a problem. But you're right. I should change it. I'll do it tomorrow . . . Well"—she smiled—"maybe the day after. You'll be halfway to Minnesota by then." She changed the subject. "So you gonna finish that pizza? Let me get you another slice."

She hurried into the kitchen and checked the time. Dena was supposed to have called half an hour ago. She was probably rehearsing with Curt. That was better. Ruth wasn't sure she could handle Dena tonight, knowing what was coming just twelve hours later.

Everything was in place. The Bushmaster, the detonator attached to the alarm clock, new batteries for the clock. It would be over soon. She would begin a new life.

She faked a yawn. "Well, I think it's time for bed. What do you think?"

"I'll just finish my beer . . ."

. . .

Eventually Jarvis came to bed and reached for Ruth. After sex, which lasted longer and was hotter than usual, he fell off. But Ruth tossed and turned. What had Beef Jerky *really* said to Jarvis? Had he told him about Ruth's plan? Did he order Jarvis to kill *her* in addition to Dena? The more she mulled it over, the more apprehensive she grew. Beef Jerky might have been orchestrating the entire event, playing Jarvis and Ruth off against each other. Maybe Jarvis knew she wasn't Nicole. How could she find out? It was too late. Everything was in place. There was nothing she could do. She felt paralyzed.

Chapter
Seventy-Two

The Present

That evening Georgia drove to Ruth's condo one last time. She'd called Paul Kelly and Erica Baldwin and told them what she'd seen on the video surveillance footage. Paul wanted to call the FBI right away. Georgia couldn't blame him. Erica Baldwin finally had some answers. It was time for Ruth to face the consequences and for Georgia to put the case to bed.

But there were a couple of loose ends remaining. One was what—if anything—Ruth knew about Beef Jerky's fatal OD. No one was investigating it as anything but a drug-related overdose, but given Ruth's plans to kill Dena and pin the blame on Jarvis, Georgia couldn't help wondering if Ruth had any role in ensuring that Jerky's OD was lethal. Why she'd do it, Georgia didn't know, but she wanted to find out. She strapped the Sig in her holster this time. Just in case.

At Ruth's condo downstairs, she buzzed her apartment. No response. Georgia sighed. The story of her life as a PI. She waited until one of the other residents exited, slipped inside before the vestibule door closed, and climbed up to the third floor. TV noise floated through the door. Maybe Ruth hadn't heard.

"Ruth?" She knocked. "Are you there?"

When there was still no response, Georgia pulled out her lockpicks. It was easier this time. Less than a minute later, she let herself in. The TV was tuned to MSNBC, and Rachel Maddow was opining on the president's latest shameful behavior.

"Ruth? You here? It's Georgia Davis."

No reply. She began to case the apartment. The living room and kitchen were empty. Two plates, glasses, and utensils lay in the sink. She headed toward the first bedroom, took out her Sig, and sidestepped to the closed door. She threw it open. Nothing.

She continued down the hall to the master bedroom. The door was open. An unmade bed, clothes strewn around the room, and a laptop on the bed. The screen saver bounced from one side to the other. Did Ruth see something on her computer that elicited her speedy exit? Georgia went to the computer and tapped a key. The screen came alive, and Ruth's browser popped up. It was closed. Georgia was curious about what Ruth's most recent online activity was, so she clicked on her history. What she saw made her heart pound and skin prickle with dread. Her own address in Evanston was blinking back at her.

. . .

Georgia broke every speed limit between the West Side and Evanston. What was Ruth doing at her home? Vanna and Charlie were there. She swore that if anything happened to her family, she would kill Ruth. It was personal now. She called Jimmy but reached his voice mail. She recalled he'd talked about a bigwig dinner at the old Playboy Club in Lake Geneva at which he had to make an appearance. He'd see her tomorrow. She voice-texted him that there was an emergency and he should race down to Evanston as soon as possible.

She parked a block away and sprinted to her apartment. The outside door was locked. She jammed in the key, but her hands shook so much she had to pull it out and try again. Inside she mounted the stairs two at a time. Her own door was open a crack. Not a good sign.

She took out her Sig and chambered a round. With her gun in one hand, she pushed the door open with the other.

The sight in front of her confirmed her worst fears. Vanna was sitting stiffly on the sofa holding Charlie, her eyes wide with panic. Charlie was fussing and Vanna was caressing him, trying unsuccessfully to comfort him. Ruth stood before them with something in her hands. Georgia focused on it. A pipe bomb. Probably identical to the one she'd built for Jarvis. Purple rage surged through her.

On seeing Georgia, Ruth placed the bomb on the floor a few feet from Vanna and Charlie and pulled a cell phone out of her pocket.

"Hello, PI Georgia Davis," Ruth said pleasantly. "We've been waiting for you. Now we can get this show on the road. Sit down."

Chapter
Seventy-Three

"Before we start, drop your gun and slide it over to me. I've already configured the IED to explode. The more time you waste, the less time you'll have to defuse it."

Georgia complied. Ruth hooked her cell phone onto the waistband of her jeans, picked up the gun, and aimed it at Vanna and Charlie.

"How long?" Georgia managed to rasp. She was so furious her throat had thickened and she could barely talk.

"It wouldn't be any fun if I told you that, would it?" Ruth replied with the same pleasant smile. It was then that Georgia realized Ruth was not just an evil person bent on revenge, but an insane psychopath. She had to be stopped.

Georgia cleared her throat. Her voice strengthened. "Ruth, I know what you did, and why you did it. Don't make it worse for yourself. Let Vanna and Charlie go, and I'll stay."

"No way," Ruth snarled. She glanced at Vanna. "Don't make a move, sister. By the way"—Ruth turned back to Georgia—"this one is more advanced than the one I built for the demonstration. I can set it off by remote control. Live and learn, right?" She laughed, a complete reversal of her irritation five seconds ago.

"Well, to be honest, I had a little help." Ruth was highly unstable. How had Georgia missed that?

But that was for later. Now she tried to figure out how to take her down, but without some sort of distraction, she couldn't come up with a strategy. *Keep her talking,* she thought, until something happened. *Maybe Charlie would throw up. Maybe the phone would ring. Maybe pigs would fly.*

"Why me, Ruth? I haven't done anything to hurt you."

"But you will. You know too much. It's time."

"You killed Beef Jerky, didn't you?"

"Now, that's an interesting question." Her smile widened. "I might have had something to do with it, although, to be honest, the people he worked for wanted to take care of him themselves."

"You know about the Prairie Rats?"

"The ones that run Jerky and used Scott as their triggerman? The rich conservative white men who own oil companies, fracking businesses, the entire pharmaceutical and food industries, and have their own secret political group? Yeah, I know about them."

"Are you working with them now? How can you? Their beliefs are the polar opposite of yours."

"I know. They're reprehensible. But there is something to be said about the enemy of your enemy . . . You gotta be flexible, you know?" She paused. "And I owe them."

That Ruth could maintain her composure in the face of such treachery was bewildering. "What do you mean you owe them?"

Ruth shrugged. "I was losing control with Beef Jerky. He was afraid I'd change my mind. It was important for him to get both Dena and Jarvis out of the way. He came to my place and threatened to kill me unless I went through with everything." She giggled. "He didn't know me very well, did he?"

"No, he didn't," Georgia said. She took a step forward. Maybe she could get her gun back. Or the cell phone. "But I do. Ruth, we can work this out. I can help you. Put the gun down and defuse the bomb."

"Stop right there, Davis." She swung the gun from Vanna and aimed it at Georgia. "See, that was Jerky's big mistake. I knew he was trying to convince Jarvis to kill me along with Dena at the demonstration. So I convinced Jarvis right back. And I won. He loved me," she said. "Of course, he shot me in the ass instead of the shoulder like we planned, but I'm still here and he isn't."

Love? Georgia thought. *Is that what Ruth called her relationship with Jarvis? A relationship built on deception, manipulation, and murder?* It was an effort to keep her mouth shut.

"Afterwards his employers weren't real happy with Jerky screwing it up. He'd been sloppy. Ran his mouth at the Barracks too much. I agreed. And so . . . presto! No more Jerky."

Charlie was in full meltdown now, screaming and so red in the face Georgia feared he might have another seizure. Vanna was in tears, too, and squeaked in a terrified high-pitched tone, "Baby, calm down, it's gonna be okay." Which made Charlie shriek even louder. "He needs his bottle," Vanna pleaded.

"You know, if the baby doesn't stop crying, Ruth," Georgia said, "someone will come down to see why. My neighbors are pretty concerned when they hear a baby cry too long."

Ruth swung the gun back to Charlie. "Not if I shoot the brat first."

"No!" Vanna roared. She tried to shield Charlie by settling him on the sofa and sitting in front of him. "Not my baby."

"Get back where you were, sister," Ruth scowled. "Right this minute or I'll shoot you first and then your baby."

Vanna scuttled back to her original position and picked up Charlie.

"That's better." She patted the cell phone hooked to her waistband. "So the P-Rats came to me after Jerky was gone and told me there was just one more thing I had to do for them, and then we'd be even."

"Why me?"

"You've been a problem for us. I knew that the minute you came to my apartment. Sniffing around. Waiting for me to say something incriminating. You thought you were so smart. But now...well...you just wouldn't give up."

"You don't think another explosion is going to lead them right back to you?"

"We have contingency plans."

"Sure. And their contingency will be to blame it all on you. The revolutionary who craved power. Who wanted to subvert the entire government. They may even find a way to connect you to Russia."

Ruth blinked. "You're crazy." Did a seed of doubt creep into her voice? "It's in our interests to work together. Mutually aligned objectives. For now. In fact, the Tat boys helped me with the electronics of this little baby." She gestured to the pipe bomb. "I mean, who better than a couple of vets, right?" She flashed Georgia a patronizing smile. "It's a business arrangement. We all have something on each other." She checked the time on the cell. "Time for me to get going. So. Remember, after I leave, you should start saying your farewells to each other." She grinned. "You just never know when things are gonna go boom."

"Ruth, there's something you don't know. And you should."

"Sure. What's that, Davis?" She didn't look the least bit interested.

"The Prairie Rats were hired to go after Dena's father. They've been trying to—"

The front door to the apartment swung open, cutting off Georgia's words. There in the doorway stood JoBeth with a suitcase. "I just wanted to say— Hey, what's going on?" She glanced around, spotted Ruth with the gun. "Who the hell are you and what are you doing to my girls?"

Ruth whirled around and aimed the gun at JoBeth. Georgia dived at Ruth, hoping to take her down before she could get off a shot. But before she could wrestle Ruth to the floor, the gun went off. JoBeth crumpled. Georgia belted Ruth in the gut. Ruth dropped the gun. Vanna seized it. Georgia grabbed Ruth around her chest and arms, immobilizing her. Ruth clawed at Georgia, then at herself, trying to free herself and grab the cell from her waistband. But Georgia threw her to the floor and jumped on her back, pinning Ruth with her weight.

"Vanna, get my cuffs from the top of my bureau. Then give me the gun, take Charlie, and run like hell to the end of the block. Call the police when you're safe."

Chapter
Seventy-Four

With Ruth's hands cuffed, Georgia allowed herself a short breath of relief, then rolled Ruth to one side and carefully removed the cell from her waistband. Ruth hurled a glob of spit at her face. After Georgia wiped it off with her sleeve, she did something she would never have done as a cop, although others did. She smashed her fist into Ruth's face. Ruth groaned in pain. Georgia hoped she'd broken Ruth's nose.

She examined the cell phone. She'd had rudimentary training on bomb defusal at the police academy, but that was more than a decade ago, and bombs, especially the electronics, had become much more sophisticated. She knew that a signal from the cell would complete the circuit between the battery and the detonator, but she didn't know enough to be confident about her skills and was reluctant to experiment with the device itself.

Fortunately, the cell was another matter. She took her time and slowly opened the back of the phone. She took another breath and delicately levered the battery out of its place with her fingernail. Nothing happened. The bomb was now inert.

She picked up the Sig and rammed it against Ruth's temple, holding it there—she wasn't sure for how long—until Jimmy burst in. He took in the scene at once and hurried over to Georgia.

"Help is here, Georgia," he said. "The cops are pulling up right now. You can let go."

But she couldn't. Ruth had gone silent, and her eyes were shut, but Georgia knew she was conscious. Ruth was evil. She couldn't let go. She could pull the trigger right now. No one would blame her. Ruth didn't deserve to live. In some dark corner of her mind, Georgia knew it was her rage speaking, not her rational brain. Still, she pressed the gun against Ruth's temple. When the cops did come in, it was Jimmy who pried the Sig from her hands.

Chapter
Seventy-Five

Two days later Georgia, Jimmy, Paul Kelly, and Erica and Jeffrey Baldwin gathered in Kelly's office for coffee.

"From the very beginning, Ruth was scheming, manipulating, lying," Georgia said. "The day of the demonstration, for example, everyone thought Ruth was panicked because Dena was late and Ruth might have to speak instead," Georgia said. "But what she really was upset about was the timing of the pipe bomb and whether it would explode before Jarvis took his shot." She took a sip of coffee. "The irony was she wanted nothing more than to take Dena's place. I should have known, damn it."

"Whoa, girl," Kelly said. "You had forty-two thousand potential suspects to check out, remember? Marriotti was just one."

Georgia shot him a look. "Yeah, but—"

"And don't forget about the Prairie Rats. They were manipulating Ruth."

"They came later," Georgia said. She turned to Erica. "They were hired to settle a score with Carl for failing to move fracking legislation forward. Their timing was lucky; Ruth fell into their lap. She—and your ex—were up against a force that few, including Carl, could resist. They owned Ruth. Not only did they threaten her to make sure Jarvis killed Dena, but they forced her to blow up Jarvis afterwards."

"They didn't trust Jarvis to keep his mouth shut?" Erica asked.

"That was part of it. They didn't want any evidence leading back to them or their employers."

"Employers like Congressman Jackson Hyde," Kelly said.

Georgia nodded.

"But Ruth knew everything," Jeffrey said.

"I'm sure they had plans for her, too," Georgia said. "Eventually."

The door to Kelly's office opened, and Nick LeJeune stuck his head in. "Hello, everyone. Sorry to be late to the party."

Georgia and Jimmy exchanged glances, both trying not to crack a smile. They were well acquainted with the FBI agent and his unrepentant, but occasionally charming, narcissism. Two other men, presumably agents as well, were with him.

"So glad you could join us, Agent LeJeune," Kelly said. Introductions were made and LeJeune pulled up a chair and sat on it backward. The other two men stood behind him.

"Couldn't help but overhear you talking about my favorite new organization," LeJeune said. "Last I heard, private militias based on political ideology aren't illegal. But they can be tricky. If they get too ambitious, they might be charged with fomenting a coup."

"Is that what the Prairie Rats were doing?" Erica asked, wide-eyed.

"Well, lemme put it this way. One of the biggest financiers of the Prairie Rats is a fracking producer, and he just happens to have a horse farm in northern Virginia, not too far from DC. Lots of land, good for training horses. And kidnapping pretty PIs."

"You bastard." Georgia seethed. "You knew about Jackson Hyde and the P-Rats. The Bureau knew."

"We didn't know, *cher*. We suspected. But it became a lot more credible after your boy Reince killed Vic Summerfield."

Reince. One of the thugs in DC. "So they *were* with the Rats, she said. "What about Ruth Marriotti?" Georgia asked. "Did you suspect her, too? You went through the tapes from the White Star Hotel, didn't you?"

LeJeune turned to the agents behind him. "Well?"

They both shrugged.

"You didn't see her on the tapes?"

Both men shook their heads. LeJeune turned back to Georgia. "Apparently not, *cher*. That was all your doing," LeJeune said cheerfully. Georgia knew that his cheerfulness was just a pretense. Those agents were going to be in big trouble once they left Kelly's office.

"So what you're saying is that not only did I do your work for you, but you painted a giant target on my back."

"We don't see it that way. You are a brave, courageous investigator who gave her all for her country. We're rounding up the Rats now," he added. "Thanks to you. You broke them wide-open."

"They were the ones who followed me." She paused. "And broke into my apartment," she said more to herself than to the group. "Hey, wait a minute. What about Remson, Dena's virtual lover? You had to know about his criminal background and where he works now. Why didn't you warn me? You let me walk into DataMaster."

"We've had our eye on DataMaster for a while, *cher*. And now that Remson is—uh—in a vulnerable position, we intend to probe more deeply. Again, thanks to you. We'll find out what they've sold to who, and what the damage is."

"Christ, I might as well have a badge, I've been helping you so much."

"You should consider it, *cher*. I'd love to have you on my side." He winked.

Georgia changed the subject. "You know the person I feel sorry for? Besides the grief you and Jeffrey have had to bear? Jarvis. Everyone was using him, poor guy. He enlists in the army, obeys orders without question, and then when he's out, realizes he's lost. He was ripe to be exploited. And they did. The P-Rats, Beef Jerky, and Ruth."

"Don't feel too sorry for him," Jimmy said. "He killed a woman. First-degree murder."

"I've been wondering something," Erica cut in. "Based on what you've explained, do you think he changed his mind at the end? Besides killing Dena, do you think he was persuaded to kill Ruth, too? Or Nicole?"

"Hard to say," Georgia replied. "He was an expert sharpshooter and was supposed to hit her in the shoulder. Instead he went for what could have been a kill shot. Maybe he missed. Maybe he didn't. I'm not sure we'll ever know." She went quiet for a moment. "But I'm glad Ruth Marriotti will spend the rest of her life in prison trying to figure it out."

"So, I've got another question," Jeffrey piped up. "If Kitty Jarvis's boyfriend sent the 'Beef Jerky' email, how did he get the encryption key for our system?"

"That's a good question," Kelly said.

"Well." LeJeune's brow furrowed. "The people who financed the Prairie Rats gave their people whatever intel they needed. Most of it was hacked, and I'd wager their hackers are from that Eastern European country we love to hate. We figure that's how they worked out Nicole was Ruth Marriotti. So, if Russian hackers worked for the P-Rats, it could have come from them."

"You can ask him yourself," Georgia said. "He and Kitty will be back tomorrow."

Erica nodded. "That leaves just one more question. At least for me. Who was making all those hang-up calls to Dena before she died?"

Silence caromed around the room. Then Jeffrey looked up and said quietly, "I think I know."

Chapter
Seventy-Six

A man shuffled along the Eastern Shore of Maryland near St. Michaels. Bent against the sharp March wind, he walked like a man much older than his sixty-two years. He wore a down jacket but no hat. His eyes and cheeks stung from the cold, which stubbornly refused to yield to spring. This place, so close to the sea and still part of the bay, had always called to him. He would visit whenever he needed perspective.

Yet he seemed impervious to the heavy overcast and slate water of the Chesapeake Bay. His life as he knew it was over. In a way, he understood. He wasn't at peace; he'd never be at peace. But he was resigned. For years he'd given as good as he got. Now it was reversed, and he was getting shafted left and right. The universe had its own way of self-correcting.

He hunched his shoulders against the wind and kept going, avoiding the driftwood on the beach, the shells, and the dead fish that the bay coughed up.

In the distance a figure appeared. A man. He wasn't moving, just waiting. The hunched man assumed this was the end. As soon as he was within range, the guy would whip out a semiautomatic, and it would be over. He'd always anticipated this moment, idly wondering how he'd feel. Strangely enough, now that it was upon him, he felt nothing.

The man called out. "Dad? Is that you?"

Carl Baldwin frowned and closed in on the man. At first Carl didn't recognize his son. Then as comprehension dawned, a panoply of emotions played across his face. Fear, then shame, then curiosity.

"Jeffrey? What are you doing here?"

"I've been looking for you."

"Why?"

"I've come to take you home."

Carl gazed at Jeffrey as if he thought the boy was crazy.

"I know what it's like to want redemption. Someone gave it to me." He hesitated. "It's my turn to pay it forward." He extended his hand to his father.

As the words slowly sank in, Carl understood the gift his son was offering. His eyes filled. He clasped his son's hand and allowed him to lead the way.

. . .

Georgia threaded her way through the labyrinth of Evanston Hospital, where at least eight banks of elevators and serpentine halls that all looked identical undermined her sense of direction. She found her mother's room on the third floor. Still in intensive care, JoBeth lay in one of a dozen rooms arranged clocklike around a central nurse's station. Georgia stopped at the desk and conferred with the nurse on duty, who told her JoBeth was doing well, all things considered. The bullet had ruptured a kidney, which had to be removed. But, as Georgia no doubt knew, people could function with just one kidney. Her mother was conscious for longer periods of time now, and Georgia could pay her a short visit.

Georgia tentatively went to the entrance of the room. The door was open. The TV was on, but her mother's eyes were shut tight.

Georgia put on a mask over her nose and mouth and went in. She found the remote control and muted the sound. Her mother's eyes fluttered open.

"Hi, Peaches," she said weakly.

"How are you feeling?"

"Like a few eighteen-wheelers ran over me."

"The nurse says you're doing well, all things considered."

"That's what they're telling me. A few more days and I'll be out."

"You never were one to overstay your welcome," Georgia said dryly.

Her mother cocked her head, as if trying to figure out where Georgia was coming from.

"It was supposed to be a joke."

"Ahh."

Silence ping-ponged across the room. Then Georgia said, "I have a proposition for you."

Her mother raised her eyebrows.

"Why don't you overstay your welcome some more and recuperate at Jimmy's apartment in Northfield? It's only about fifteen minutes from Evanston. We can have someone come in a few hours a day, and Vanna and I can take turns the rest of the time."

JoBeth gazed at her daughter. "Are you sure about this?"

Georgia told her the truth. "No."

Her mother smiled.

"But you saved our lives. It's our turn to save yours."

"Even after everything?" When Georgia nodded, JoBeth said, "And what happens when I'm well again?"

Georgia sighed. "I don't have a clue."

"Neither do I," JoBeth said.

"Then I guess we'll have to figure it out." Georgia paused. "One day at a time."

"One day at a time." Her mother smiled. "Sounds like a plan." She closed her eyes.

Georgia watched her mother fall asleep. Then she tiptoed out the door.

Author's Note

By ten pm November 8, 2016, along with most of the world, I had traveled through the looking glass. How could this man have become our next president? It wasn't possible.

But it was. Every day since then, we've seen him chip away at our democracy, norms, and world standing. From the nearly five thousand lies the *Washington Post* claims he's told, to flimflam meetings with the leaders of North Korea and Russia, the past two years have seen continuous assaults on the media, the FBI, and the agencies charged with protecting our health, safety, and freedom.

Personally, the effect on me was calamitous. I felt paralyzed: I couldn't write, and I couldn't talk about anything except the state of our nation. I probably drove away many people who previously thought I was a nice person. For a year I let my rage control me. My only solace was journalists and people like Louise Mensch, John Schindler, and Claude Taylor . . . and of course, my refuge, the Resistance Facebook group, Investigation of the Trump-Russia Conspiracy in the 2016 Election. Suzy Fischer (no relation, by the way), to whom this book is dedicated, started the group about three days after the election. I joined the first week.

By last November, however, I came to realize that I had given the occupant of the Oval Office all my power, especially where my writing was concerned. I'd brainstormed two different novels during the fallow period, but they didn't resonate with me. Then came the eureka moment. I was reading posts on the Investigation site one day when I realized my next novel had been staring me in the face. I needed to write about the group, its leader, and the climate in which we Americans find ourselves.

One thing to keep in mind: I write suspense fiction, so I've taken many liberties with characters, plot lines, and action. Some characters might remind you of specific people—I assure you they all came from my addled brain. But the theme of the story didn't. It is a cautionary tale, which I hope is nearly over and one that our country will not face again.

I also beg your indulgence. I was born and raised in Washington, DC. It's the only place I know that when you're at the dinner table gossiping about the neighbors, you're talking politics. It's in my blood.

Acknowledgments

I had plenty of help with *High Crimes* . . . Among the experts are Fred Bedrich, who walked me through the cybermechanics of disappearing emails and encryption systems; and UK chemist/biologist Brian Price, who helped me with things that go boom. His website, dedicated to ensuring that authors and screenwriters get the science right (crimewriterscience.co.uk), is an invaluable resource.

I also want to acknowledge authors Cara Black and Zoë Sharp. Cara got me going, and Zoë helped me finish (with a few white cows thrown in). All hail also to Kent Krueger, an early reader, as well as Eric Arnall, whose own star will soon shine. To Kevin Smith, who edited the manuscript, you made some brilliant suggestions. And to Eileen Chetti, copyeditor extraordinaire who picked up inconsistencies far and wide, I am grateful. Thank you one and all for your expert opinions, ideas, and gentle criticisms.

Teresa Russ Ellert, Miguel Ortuno, and Sue Trowbridge help keep me sane with their talent and extraordinary work. I couldn't do anything without them. Thank you.

About the Author

Libby Fischer Hellmann left a career in broadcast news in Washington, DC and moved to Chicago over thirty-five years ago, where she, naturally, began to write gritty crime fiction. Sixteen novels and twenty-five short stories later, she claims they'll take her out of the Windy City feet first. She has been nominated for many awards in the mystery and crime writing community* and has even won a few.

Her novels include the now five-volume Ellie Foreman series, which she describes as a cross between "Desperate Housewives" and "24"; the hard-boiled 4-volume Georgia Davis PI series; and four stand-alone historical thrillers. Her short stories have been published in a dozen anthologies, the *Saturday Evening Post*, and Ed Gorman's "25 Criminally Good Short Stories" collection. In 2005 Libby was the national president of Sisters In Crime, a 3,500-member organization dedicated to the advancement of female crime fiction authors. She also hosts a monthly TV show called "Solved" with the Author's Voice Network. More at libbyhellmann.com.

* She has been a finalist twice for the Anthony, three times for ForeWord Magazine's Book of the Year, the Agatha, the Shamus, the Daphne, and has won the IPPY and the Readers' Choice Award multiple times.

CPSIA information can be obtained
at www.ICGtesting.com
Printed in the USA
LVHW011523051218
599369LV00002B/280/P